My Epileptic Lurcher

Also by Des Dillon:

Fiction

Me and Ma Gal (1995)
The Big Empty: A Collection of Short Stories (1996)
Duck (1998)
Itchycooblue (1999)
Return of the Busby Babes (2000)
Six Black Candles (2002)
The Blue Hen (2004)
The Glasgow Dragon (2004)
Singin I'm No A Billy He's A Tim (2006)
They Scream When You Kill Them (2006)
Monks (2007)

Poetry

Picking Brambles (2003)

My Epileptic Lurcher

DES DILLON

Luath Press Limited

EDINBURGH

www.luath.co.uk

First published 2008

ISBN (10): 1-906307-22-9
ISBN (13): 978-1-906307-22-6

This novel is a work of fiction. All the characters in this book are fictitious. Any references to historical events; to real people, living or dead; or to real locales are intended only to give the fiction a sense of reality and authenticity. Names, places and incidents are either the product of the author's imagination or are used fictitiously, and their resemblance, if any, to real-life counterparts is entirely coincidental.

The author's right to be identified as author of this book under the Copyright, Designs and Patents Act 1988 has been asserted.

The publishers acknowledge the support of

Scottish **Arts** Council

towards the publication of this volume.

The paper used in this book is recyclable. It is made from low-chlorine pulps produced in a low-energy, low-emission manner from renewable forests.

Printed and bound by
CPI Mackays, Chatham

Typeset in 9.5pt Frutiger by 3btype.com

© Des Dillon 2008

To Joanne
Love
Has proved you to be this:
Finding you gradually
in sharp and blunt days.

Dogs love you; end of story

If reading this book inspires you to get a dog – please rescue one from one of the dog rescue centres all over the country.

A morning in the life

Anger was killing me for years but now I look at my epileptic Lurcher and remind myself it's easier to change my soul than rage against the world. If you don't know what a Lurcher is just imagine a greyhound with long hair. His name is Bailey. Black back, tan stripes here and there and cream underneath. He's tall enough to clap without bending down. The thing about Bailey is, he's ugly. I mean he's perfectly ugly. He's so perfectly ugly he's beautiful. And he's so beautiful he's perfectly beautiful. And he's so perfectly beautiful he's perfect.

When he takes an epileptic fit he's a giant fish flapping about; smashing everything in his path. Coming out, post-ictal, is worse; he starts running blindly, into things, over things and through things. If he took a fit in your living room it would be like a hurricane just went through. In the early days, we bought him a harness. We called it his handool.

—Put your handool on Bailey, we'd say when Connor told us he was about to go into a fit.

Connor the Collie tells us five minutes before the fit starts. He runs up and nudges us, goes back to Bailey, stares, comes back, nudges and repeats till we do something.

Anyway, one crazy day I had Bailey by his handool in his post-ictal running stage. He dragged me across the living room and started running up the wall. I had to press into his back to keep him from falling. That pressure allowed him to run onto the ceiling. Every time I look at them paw prints it reminds me what I was like. We kept them for people who don't believe us.

There's something about Connie and animals. I couldn't fathom it at first. But I do now. And strange things have come to pass when a selfish bastard like me ends looking after animals. Giving out love for no return and getting love because of that. I've had a sort of revolution; all cause of an epileptic Lurcher.

Here's the routine of a typical morning:

—Oof, says Bailey, at half-eight, —Oof!

I wake and get him and Connor out the padded room.

—Get the Mummy, get the Mummy, I say.

They skate and skid along that wooden floor bounding onto the bed, gowlering for attention. I go for a pee and head downstairs. I still put a plate out for Floyd.

—One for Bailey, one for the wee coosy pat Fluffy. One for the Connoroo, I say.

Kettle on. Four slices of carrot for Bailey. Four dog biscuits for Connor. Soon as he hears the coffee cup Bailey picks his nervous way down the spiral staircase. I pour milk in his bowl, Connor's and my cup.

—Drinky link, I say, —Drinky link.

He's already got his noe in there trying to finish his and move onto Connor's. Connor bumps in and they gowler about who's milk is who's. Then it's a slice of carrot and a dog biscuit. Then they want out. Want out. Want out. Want out. Oof! Want out. I try to finish my coffee but I can't relax. I get the boots Daddy.

—What are these called?

Sniff sniff. Tails up.

—The boots Daddy! I shout.

When I genuflect to tie them Bailey lays the kisses into me.

Connor stuffs his noe into my ear and sniffs. He doesn't like kissy lips. He's shy.

—Kissy lips. I say, —Kissy lips. And he'll do it reluctantly.

I sing a wee song as I tie my boots.

♫ Putting on the boots Daddy, Putting on the boots Daddy, Putting on the boots Daddy, the boots Daddy oh!

It's the four-legged dog-dance as I lace up. Their paws drumming in and out the hall. By the jacket and hat they're at the door. Dogs! No patience.

—In the tluck?

Tails slapping off the wall.

—Gardiniums Sardiniums?

Happy gowlering and nuzzling. Check no cars. Into the street. Open the tluck. It's a red Landover Defender we bought them.

—Right c'mon. In yees mcget.

Bailey leaps with the grace of a pond skater, not a sound as he lands. Connor gets in like a fat lady. I slam the door and off to the Gardiniums Sardiniums. Connor takes position on the only back seat watching the world pass. Bailey rests his head on my shoulder and I clap him best I can.

The gardens are deserted in the morning. Down through the trees we wind. First thing is a pee. Bailey can pee for Scotland.

—I pee long, I say and he likes that, —I pee long.

Connor pees in private somewhere in the deep trees. The next thing is do the ploppies.

—Right come on, do the ploppies.

Connor crashes into the dense interior of the rhododendrons, does his ploppies and accelerates out with a big Collie grin.

—Good Colin, good bnoy. Clever bnoy.

Oh – I didn't mention that, did I? We've got a whole new language for the dogs. You'll pick it up as we go along.

Bailey's a fuckin disgrace. He finds a good spot, squats and

squeezes one out. No shame. Biggest shites you ever seen.
Cause of his special diet these things are sculptures of carrot
and rice and turnip. Turner Prize Blongo. Soon as he's done he
bounds towards me perfectly out of control; jaws open,
tongue taking a beating inside his mouth. Crashing into me,
he curves his body so much he wraps round me. Having a
shite's like taking cocaine to him.

—Beachy beach!?

They likey like. Once we're ankle deep in sand they stare
at me.

—Catchy? I ask, —Who wants catchy?

I fling one stone for Connor and one for Bailey. Connor
covets it. When you try to pick it up he grabs it and runs fifty
feet. When you fling Bailey's he soars across the beach in puffs
of sand. That's when you see the greyhound in him. He stops
the stone by leaping and skidding into it with his paws
straight out. Once the cloud settles he starts digging a hole.

—Diggy dig. Bailey diggy dig.

He fires his stone out the back like an American footballer
when he's diggy dig. I pick it up and he blinks in wonder at
how I got it. I throw it and off he gallops. I pretend to go for
Connor's and he grabs it and runs.

This is how we pass the morning.

Then, —Blongo! Connoroo! Home for cooking? Cooking
Mummy? Cooky bleakfast.

They're like hairy compasses. Straight back towards the
tluck. Stopping for the last carrot and biscuit when I say,
—Nurra wan?

Connie's got their breakfast ready. She's got a pot of
chicken and vegetable on for their dinner. The dogs dive into
the breakfast bowls and when they're finished ask for a rice
cake bonio biscuit.

But no sooner are we in the living room with our breakfast than they're there begging.

—Mummy, Mummy, I say and they go to Connie.

—Daddy, Daddy, she says, —Yum yum. Daddy's got the biscuits, and back they come.

Bailey asks for food by repeatedly sticking his tongue out and in. He copied wolves on the telly one night. Swear! Connor nudges. Keeps nudging. Lick lick lick. Nudge nudge nudge.

—Ah fuck it!

And I give in. Even though Bailey's not supposed to get bread and stuff. When there's no food left Bailey lies on his cushion by the fire and Connor gets the couch. At ten past ten Connor nudges Connie.

—Tab e let drinky link, says Connie. Dogs shoot back into the kitchen.

Then it's worky work. It was only Connor who went to work till Bailey realised there's a biscuit (carrot) in it. Up in the attic they eat their biscuit, share a cushion, listen to monks chanting while I click away at the keyboard. As I write this very sentence they're cuddled up to each other on that cushion like yin and yang.

And me? I'm wondering how did I get here? To this big hou with a view out over the sea to the snowy mountinks and a measure of contentment I never thought possible.

How we got married

Thanks to my ex-cellmate Paddy I'd not long stopped drinking.
I was living on my own in the pink cloud of early sobriety.
Sending scripts away. Getting rejection after rejection.
Paddy said I'd swapped drink and drugs for an obsession with
that glitzy world.

He'd swapped his for casinos and was always trying to trick
me into going. But I get angry when I lose a fiver. He'd come
into my house and look about.

—Know what you need? he'd say.

—Sex?

—No a cat.

—A fuckin cat?

—You need something to look after. Something to nurture.
You're too wrapped up in yourself.

—Leave me alone Paddy, I'm not harming nobody!

—No, but you're not helping nobody either, he said.

I knew he was right but there was no way I was getting a
cat. Having to feed it, clap it and all that. Get a cat flap fitted.
And who's going to look after it when I'm away? I wasn't
tying myself down with a daft animal.

—What if I have to go to London to talk scripts?

—Scripts? You still at that shite?

He lifted one up and read it.

—Harry blasts his automatic weapon. Take that you son of a bitch neds. Die.

—That's not what it says Paddy.

One night he announced the most beautiful girl in the world worked in the casino.

—Aye right Paddy, I said, —I'm not going.

But he persisted. He'd call round, phone, text, or send emails.

—You'll fall in love with her right away man, she's everything you dream about in a girl. Five-four. Long brown hair. Body like that! And he traced her curves with his palms, —Almond eyes, oh and you want to see the smile man! There's something about her so there is.

—Make me another one up Paddy, her eyelashes are too short.

—I'm not making her up. She's real. Come in and see her for yourself.

—I know what you're up to – you're trying to get me in there so I'll get addicted to gambling and then you'll have a fellow ghoul to wander the night.

—She's real!

—Take a photo and bring it out.

—You're not allowed cameras.

—Do a drawing then.

But he kept at it for weeks and I got to thinking he was too persistent. Maybe there was a girl? Maybe this was *the* girl? Maybe he was telling the truth.

—Alright, I said, —I'll come but I'm not gambling more than a fiver.

I did fall in love at first sight. Long brown hair that lifted off her back when she turned. And almond shaped eyes. Amazing eyes. I thought she must be Spanish. Or foreign anyway. And there *was* something about her, something beyond attraction, but I couldn't figure out what it was.

—She must be somebody's bird Paddy, I said, —A bird like that's going to get snapped up.

—If you don't ask you'll never find out mate. Take a gamble!

But she didn't like me bombarding her with questions. All we found out was her name, Connie, and where she lived.

It was three in the morning. A pack of mangy dogs roamed the streets. I stopped and asked this woman where Teavarran Street was. She was fat and had three kids with her. None were over ten.

—Excuse me, could you tell me where Teavarran street is? I said.

She leaned in the car. Or should I say her tits leaned in. Her kids were smearing the glass.

—How? she said, —What d'you want to know for?

—I'm meeting somebody.

—Who?

This was where all the drugs in Glasgow came from. I had to think quick and I did.

—It's a bird. I'm meeting a bird up here. Know what I mean? And flicked my tongue in and out. She leaned in and shoved me.

—Dirty cunt, she said, —It's first left first right, that's Teavarran Street.

I went into the close on a roller coaster rush. Walked to the top landing and stood at her door. The lights were on and I wondered if maybe she was married or had a boyfriend. I felt danger. Paddy waved to hurry up when I came out. The buildings were wondering who we were. We drove into a dead end. There was only one way out. The fat lady and her babies were standing guard. She flagged us down. She winked.

—D'you get your bird?

—Not in.

—What about me? she said, and slid a big tit out into the orange streetlight.

—Paddy there's a bird for you, I said and we drove away to her snapping that big moon mammary back into her bra.

—You've got to get Connie out of that place, Paddy said.
—Nobody should have to live in a place like that. And from that day on it was save the princess from the dark tower.

Three or four casino nights passed with me following Connie round the tables like a puppy. Pit Bosses were starting to make comments. Smirking. After another few nights I was the laughing stock. One Pit Boss told me I was well out of my league.

—You have no chance with her mate. This Arab said, —I tried hundreds of times.

This Arab was so good looking I fancied him myself. Paddy knew him. He was oil-well rich and drove a different fancy car every week. My courage was draining away and I was getting angry at myself. I started a general conversation about eye colour.

—What colour's your eyes Connie? I said.

They were green brown. But that's not the thing. The thing is this electric shock resonated in my head and shot to my shoes. The soles of my feet were tingling. I was sure she had the same thing cause she gasped and looked to the ground. Before she started dealing again she glanced at me. Her eyes were two poems you could read forever. It was too much. I staggered back into an old Chinese woman. She called me Gwai Lo and I sat on a leather sofa behind a crowd of Chinese gangsters. Paddy sat beside me.

—What a babe eh? he said.

I decided it was now or never.

—I'm going for it Paddy. I'm going to ask her out.

—Eye of the tiger big man, he said and shoved me up.

I took a blackjack hand. The Pitt Bosses were sniggering. The Arab shook his head and patted me on the back. Twice. I tried to think up a good line but I jammed. Even when I asked for a card my mouth was dry. Then...

It just came out.

—Have you got a man?

I don't know where that stands on the list of good chat up lines but the table stopped. A wee Chinese woman winked. My face was burning. As Connie dealt another card she looked in my eyes and mouthed *no* silently. I got this delicate rush. Later when there was another set of punters at the table she asked me a question.

—Is it not about time you went home to your wife?

—I haven't got a wife.

She dealt me an ace of hearts. It was an omen. I was sitting at thirteen.

—Card.

She dealt me the ace of spades.

—Card, I said, trying to ignore that big death card. She dealt me a ten.

—Too many, she said and smiled.

I waited that early April morning outside the Casino and when she came out we were both nervous. But when I slipped my arm round her waist and she reciprocated I felt like I was breathing in snow.

On day three we lay in her bed listening to stolen cars. I had to keep the duvet wrapped under my feet cause her crazy red cat was a bit of a foot slasher.

—I think I'm falling in love with you, I said.

—That's good cause I know I am, she said and held onto me.

We lay awake and the flames from stolen cars flickering in the room was romantic. Shouts, breaking glass and sudden noises seemed another world away. We were cocooned.

We must've got some sleep cause the next thing it was bright and twelve o'clock. I got out of bed and picked Floyd up but he stuck his claws in and wouldn't let go. He was on me like a boxing glove. The more I screamed the more he hissed. Connie eventually prised him off and treated my wounds with Savlon. I was stone in love. I sang that all the way home.

♫ Cos I'm stone in love with you hoo hoo hoo hoo hoo, yes I'm stone in love with you.

It was only another two rejections when I got in. One BBC and one Channel Four. But with Connie in my life they didn't bother me. I fell asleep on the couch. In my dreams we live by the sea on the edge of nowhere with cats and dogs and things growing in the garden. And in this garden you can hear the waves. And all around the chirping of many birds. I am lying in a hammock and there's this big hairy dog on top of me with his nose tucked into my neck. Connie is planting things and she looks up and smiles. And I smile back.

That night I asked her to marry me. She looked at me before speaking.

—You serious?

—Here's how serious I am, I said and got down on one knee, —Will you marry me?

She burst out crying and said aye. That's how I got married.

Four weeks later we drove to the Isle of Skye. The drive took most of Sunday and we held hands all the way. On the Monday morning we went for a walk and I told her I'd been in jail and what for but she just squeezed my hand and said,

—We've all got pasts.

At lunchtime we got a fish supper but it was swimming in grease so we fed it to the seagulls. I sat across from her on this slipway and she stared at me.

—What? I said.

—Nothing.

—No, come on, what is it?

—Are you sure you want to go through with this?

—Of course I'm sure.

—Just that, maybe we're rushing in?

—I want to marry you more than anything ever in my life. How? Are you having doubts?

—No. No doubts whatsoever.

—You think we're moving too fast, I said.

—No – it's been four weeks, what's fast about that?

—Nothing, I said, —That's ages.

—Years.

—Eons.

We kissed. And as we walked back to the guest house to get changed this big dog followed us. That's when I first noticed Connie's way. Animals come right up like she's their mother. Even the seagulls were walking along beside her.

—What's your name? she said and I swear the dog barked back. She gave it a big kiss on the nose and it wagged its tail. I remember being disgusted by that kiss but I said nothing.

The registrar made small talk and kept looking out the windows till I asked what was wrong. He said something about time and asked if our witness had maybe a mobile phone on their person?

—Witness? Shit! We forgot to bring a witness.

—That's all fine, he said, —Not a problem. Just leave it with me, he said and left the building.

19

Connie was beautiful in this white silk dress. She looked exactly like a woman who would never marry me in a million years. I must've been staring with my jaw open cause she impersonated me and laughed. There was a beam of light coming in the window.

We were still laughing when the registrar appeared with this girl from the office next door. She was well dressed which was just as well cause she's in our wedding photos: me, Connie, this girl whose name I can't remember and the registrar. We were pronounced man and wife. I kissed Connie and was happy. She was happy too. I thought maybe she really did love me. Maybe she did want to spend the rest of her life with me. I thanked the registrar. Said to the girl with no name,

—I bet this is the last thing you expected when you left for work this morning – that you'd end up being a witness at a wedding?

—I'm in here every other day as a witness, she said, —I work in the office just next door. We take turns.

We all had a laugh at that, went back to the guest house and changed. Spent an hour sitting on the harbour talking to the big dog and the seagulls. It felt good to be married. We discussed what we wanted to do with our lives. Connie wanted out of the casino. I wanted her out too but I didn't tell her that. I was scared in case somebody stole her. Maybe that rich Arab with all his different fancy cars. Or a rich Glasgow gangster. Or some Prince from somewhere irresistible. Connie wasn't too happy when I said I wanted to be a writer. I told her I was sure I was going to make it but she didn't look too convinced. We decided I could have a year to start making money. We'd live on her savings and then I'd have to get a job.

Connor

I do metal boppums. Collies be some the times the smelly.
The stinky. Get the excited in a tluck or in the hou and coming
out my bumbers is smelly like metal and other the stinky.
Mummydaddy call it metal boppum. They make big noises like
aaargh and look at the Collie Connor Colin Mackalolly me.
Like some the times me used to chasy the Fluffy go too fast
and my claws skidz on the floor I do the metal boppums.
And when I the feart I do the metal boppums. Mummydaddy
spray the stuff on it. Smell the fowlers. I hides.

Finding Bailey

We both gave up our council flats and moved to this wee village by the sea. A cheap and nasty attic flat but to us it was a dream. We had trouble before we even moved in. This cop pulled me up for parking more than the regulation eighteen inches from the kerb.

—Have you got a ruler? I said.

—No but I've got a size ten boot.

Connie squeezed my arm and I let it go.

—Glasgow accent! he said.

—Aye. How astute.

—Where about in Glasgow would that be?

—Possil, said Connie.

This cop told us, when he joined the force, he was on Saracen Street with the four hardest gangs in Glasgow converging on the cross. He stood with his baton out fighting. There was at least a hundred in each gang. They had razors. He held the cross for an hour. Even though he was slashed to bits. Oh… and there was a woman with a baby in a pram somewhere in the story. He managed to get her to safety. All the time he was telling us this story he was looking across at Connie's legs. It wasn't the last we'd see of him.

But the village was beautiful. You could walk though this picturesque glen along a stream and cross a road onto the most amazing beach you ever seen. Us two city dudes were in our element. We loved it. Till we got a dog that was. The epileptic Lurcher. Then we had to talk to people.

Connie kept her job at the casino but it was an hour's drive. She didn't get back till six in the morning. She was falling asleep sometimes at the wheel. She slept most of the day. I had to stay quiet so I took to going long walks. I suppose I was a lonely figure wandering about the beach trying to think up movie ideas.

Time went on and me and Connie were drifting apart. The further we drifted the closer I got to Floyd. He wouldn't come near me at first that cat. If I was in one room, he'd be in the furthest away room. He was jealous of me and Connie. She'd leave instructions to feed him and let him out in the garden. But I'd forget and that would be an argument. She'd ask the cat if I fed him.

—Did Daddy feed you?

Floyd would say something and;

—He says you didn't feed him.

—I did!

—He says you didn't.

—He's a lying bastard!

But Floyd was right every time. Once Connie had nagged me into submission, feeding Floyd, giving him a drink and taking him out into the garden became part of my routine. The more I did it the more he liked me. Then, one day as I was dozing through some telly drama, I felt this weight on my chest. I thought it was a heart attack but it was Floyd purring in my face. I'd been reluctant to clap him since he was a boxing glove. And he'd slashed me a few times since, in the passing. I purred back at him and he jumped off, went to the fire.

But it wasn't long till he was waiting by the couch. When I

24

lay down he jumped onto my chest purring. It was a sin to move him he was that happy. That's when I invented chinny-chin. That wee bit between his actual nose and his eyes – I run my two day stubble along that and he purrs like mad. Loves it. That became the highlight of our day. I got a wee tape recorder to take notes for blockbusters that might rise in my imagination. But I fell into sleeps deeper than fairy tales.

One dawn Connie found me sleeping with Floyd purring like a wee engine on my chest. She sat watching for a while. The magic and fizz of our infatuation had drained. We were going through the motions hoping it would come back. But me and Floyd lying there ignited her mothering instincts. She woke us with a cup of tea and a bowl of milk.

—I think we should start a family, she said and the next day she came off the pill.

We were to have sex as much as possible the doctor said and I was happy to oblige. But by September Connie still hadn't taken. She went for tests and found out she couldn't have children. Not ever. She was broken hearted, fell into a depression and couldn't go to work. To tell the truth it was quite easy to survive on the dole. None of us drank or smoked. But Connie was getting gradually worse. We'd walk on the beach and through the glen but she wasn't able to hit the high notes of happiness she'd hit before.

Then she stopped walking, bought a paint stripper and gave herself the task of stripping every door in that flat. To this day the smell of burnt paint depresses me. And Connie. When I was out walking I'd stay out longer and longer. In the cold. Shivering even.

I phoned Paddy and asked him what to do. He said I could put some fuckin effort into this relationship and for the first time in my selfish bastard of a life I might get something back.

That wasn't what I wanted to hear. But I thanked him all the same, cause an honest friend's worth a city of sycophants. I was on the beach considering whether or not to call it a day.

There was a guy sitting in his car reading the paper, Border Collie in the back. It was smiling and breathing onto the glass. The man nodded.

The sea was moving up

                                   and down

slow and easy.

The white cries of gulls were wiped out by every wave. Seals rose and curved back like plumbers' u-bends. Out across the water; an island through mist. If you shut your eyes you could be anywhere. What to do about Connie? Breeze and salt, cycles of waves and sea birds. What to do about Connie? One dog barking. There was a dead dolphin on the sand. It stank and it was hard to look at. Something took a chunk out of its side. I said a wee prayer for its soul and walked on.

The sea melting into the beach. Like me and Connie. Flat. Gone. Dispersed. How can you draw the water back out? A school of porpoises appeared changing direction with every leap.

I sat on a bench. There was only this woman walking her dog and the guy who'd got out his car. He was talking to the woman and they both looked away from each other before she left, leaving him on his own, looking at the island.

He came up, poking at stones with a stick and the Collie chasing gulls. He nodded once at the beach.

—See that woman? he says.

—White dog?

—She came up to me and starts talking, nice day and all this, might get sun, ye know, usual. Then the dog starts tugging her back so she let it run down the beach again.

He stopped. Like he couldn't speak. I was looking at the water out of politeness.

—So she came back up to me and the dog's biting at the waves and barking. Nothing like a wee last sniff, I goes, nodding at her dog. Here, does she not just burst out greeting. Roaring.

I looked at him – blank.

—Turns out she was taking the wee thing for its final walk before it gets put down.

He looked at his watch.

—It's probably dead now, he says.

He walked away watching the porpoises. I remembered what Paddy had said. You should get a cat. You need something to look after. Something to nurture. You're too wrapped up in yourself. That's when I got my idea. The idea that was to change our lives. If we can't have a baby, let's have a dog. I was certain it would cure Connie's depression.

The vet took me into a wee back room. And in this cage was a pile of puppies climbing over each other to get to me. And that puppy smell. Like stale coffee. I put my hand in and three of them sucked my fingers. There was one I liked. It had all the Collie markings and I was sure it would grow up into a fine wee dog. I asked the vet if it was a Collie. Yes, it looked like a Collie to him. Definitely.

They'd been found in a bag in a stream in Kilwinning. I imagined them squeaking puppies sinking down and all the wee arms and legs locking, it gets colder and darker, then silence. The hiss of death coming through the water. Then getting yanked out into the light, water draining from the bag. I felt sorry for them but I felt extra sorry for this ugly wee runt. It was just a head with an excuse for a body and stubby little legs. It was half the size of the others and didn't look like it would survive. It had a black back, tan stripes here and there and cream underneath.

Connie was still in bed with Fluffy curled up beside her. I picked him up and Connie opened her eyes.

—The vet's got puppies, I said.

—What?

—Six pups they were pulled out a river. You want to see them. There's a wee black and white one. I'm sure it's a Collie.

Something woke up in Connie that second. I've watched a slow burning miracle in her. In the vet's we lifted the puppies one at a time. Looking for dicks and stuff. We wanted a boy. I kept pushing my Collie on her. It was the best puppy there but she didn't want to know. She spoke to them all one at a time eventually picking up the runt.

—Oh, you're lovely, she said and kissed this wee horror on the nose.

—Don't take that one, said the vet, —Runt. Be dead in a week.

—Do you want to come home with me? she said.

The dog squeaked. Then it squeaked again.

—Don't you listen to them. They've not got a clue, she said and she turned to the vet, —I want this one.

—But this one's a Collie, I said holding up a wee powerhouse.

The vet nodded agreement.

—Mm mm, definitely a Collie, he said.

—We're taking him, Connie said, and she held that wee puppy to her breasts wrapping her jacket round him. I shrugged to the vet and we left with Connie whispering into her jacket.

When we put him down Floyd seen a head wobbling about the wooden floor, arched his back, hissed and shot out. I shouted for the dog and Connie shouted.

—Come to Mummy.

He wobbled always to Connie. Oh Connie thought it was so funny and she laughed. Connie laughed. She fucking well laughed!

—That's the first you've laughed, Connie, for ages, I said.

She leaned over and kissed me. And hugged me. We had tears and words too truthful to come out. It was our first genuine contact for months. Connie picked the puppy up.

—Maybe big Daddy'll go in and get you a wee saucer of milky milk? she said.

Big Daddy? Milky milk? In I went cringing. But it was the start of a language that would make a whole new world from the same old things.

As he drank his milky milk Connie brought up names. She wanted to call him D'Arcy.

—You fancy that puddle swimming *Pride and Prejudice* poof what's his name...?

—It's just a nice name, she said.

I wanted Murphy so it was a stand off.

—Arsy, come on arsy, want a wee biscuit arsy? That's what I'll shout.

She gave in and cause of his tan and cream colouring, she decided on Bailey. Another name I didn't like. That night Bailey slept on Connie's shoulder. Even now when he's four feet long and three feet high, when he feels a fit coming on he heads for the refuge of her shoulder.

Connor

Mummydaddy callit me all the names. Connor. Colin. Colmenello pretty fello. Wan Long Tongue. Twinkle toes when me walking on hard floors. Reginald McGillycollie-Smythe for my posh name. Chesty Morgan. Captain Caveman when I say the whoo argh whoo argh. Clunks when I bumps the into things. Bumps sometimes. Collie. Terminator when I want the thing thing and they not give me the thing thing. OCD. Obsessive Collie disorder. Scout cause I iz first the all times. Pinkie cause my skin on the white bits. Stinky when I metal boppums. Epileptic detective when I say Blongo go into big fish.

Magic slippers

Super Cop turned up when I was at AA and told Connie he was on a serious investigation, flung his hat on the table and said,

—Three sugars and milk. Coffee. I like it hot and sweet. Just like my women.

She made him tea hoping he'd leave. He spotted a Celtic top in the washing.

—So he's a Celtic man eh?

Connie never answered she just slid the washing basket behind the unit. Then he started going on about how women love a man in a uniform. When he reached out to grab her she squirmed away and slid a big blade out the drawer.

—This blade is for cutting vegetables, she said, —I'm cutting vegetables, see.

And she chopped a few potatoes with the fury of a mad-woman then turned towards him with the blade pointing out,

—Have to cut more vegetables, she said, —Chop chop slash slash!

He up and left. Fast. Connie collapsed on the floor laughing. She was on the couch with Bailey when I came in. She made me promise on the animals' lives not to react before she told me. And for weeks after that one of us would burst into spontaneous laughter.

—Have to cut more vegetables, she'd say and come at me with a knife. We got a lot of mileage out of that one.

That incident turned Super Cop against us. He done us for no tax on the Renault. Stopped us five times in the next year. And when he realised we'd made the cars street legal he sat in his cop car on the hill, looking in the window. We bought blinds. After that we kept losing wing mirrors. I sat up a few nights but sure as fate the night I went back to bed another mirror was ripped off.

But back to Bailey. It wasn't long till this head grew a body and some legs. Me and Connie wondered what kind of dog he was. I hoped he'd be mostly Collie. Connie had a list of effeminate dogs she wanted him to be. Poodle. Afghan hound. Retriever. Then, one day when I was tormenting him with a piece of string I seen it. The rottweiler look.

—Oh no, I said, —We've got a Devil dog on our hands. Hound of Satan. Hawhooo!

She agreed. He was like a miniature rottweiler. I grabbed him by the neck. He lit up, his teeth came out and he snarled. Warning us off. We could have flattened him with a rolled up newspaper but he narrowed his eyes and opened that mouth wide and snarled. It was so funny me and Connie fell about laughing.

—Don't you gowlers at me, she said and grabbed his neck.

—Grrr he'd say. Crazy thing was, we could understand him. As he twisted his head snapping and gowlering and slobbering he was saying, —Get your hand off my neck or I'll savage you with these here big teeth.

It was so funny until he sank them sharp pins of teeth in. Drew blood. That's when I invented Black Glove. I put on a black leather glove like the ones your mother buys for Christmas. I grabbed him by the neck and said gowlers and snarled. Oh, he went off like a rocket in a microwave. The more we said gowlers the more he snarled. The more he snarled the

more Connie and me laughed. When he got hold of my
fingers he wouldn't let go. I could lift him in the air. Grrr.
And these wee teeth clamped together in the thick leather.
Black Glove was a whole night's entertainment.

It soon got to the stage I'd say, —Black Glove! Black Glove!
And he'd skid along the floor, get in position and start
gowlering.

Connie was happy and I was happy. Things were looking up.
Except; the sex life was nil with Bailey sleeping on Connie's
shoulder. I persuaded her he should sleep in the kitchen now
he was steady on his feet. By then he was practically house
trained cause Connie took him to the garden every three
hours night and day.

—Magic Slipper, she'd say and he'd go wild as she stuffed
her feet into the slippers. She'd carry him down some steps,
coax him down others.

It was a big day when Bailey did all the stairs himself.
We got in front and cheered every step he took. Even when
he tumbled we clapped and by the bottom his tail was
wagging and his head was up.

—Tlever Bailey we said, —Who's a tlever pnuppy.

Even Floyd was getting used to him. He'd pass on the stairs
with a perfunctory hiss. Time passed and Bailey learned to lift
a magic slipper and run in wagging it like a big blue velour
tongue.

—Pnuppy want magic zlippers? Connie would say, —Magic
Zlippers?

The language is always evolving. Dogs like new things.
Like new forests; they get their noe into the dirt and snuffle as
they move along, the smells changing all the time.

In the morning I'd get up, open the kitchen door and say
—Bailey, Bailey, Bailey, fast, —Bailey, Bailey, Bailey. He'd

cartoon scrape across the tiles and jump biting my noe squeaking his puppy squeak.

—Letters! I'd shout.

He'd tear along the lobby scooping up as many as he could. I was always waiting on that life transforming letter. The one from some big film company. Bailey would run into Connie, leap onto the bed and tear the letters apart with her laughing and saying,

—Aw no lippy the lettiz. No lippy the lettiz Blongo.

It worried me the lipping of the lettiz and when I got the Steven Spielberg one I told Connie it had to stop. It was an official letter from LA and Bailey was on the bed holding it down with one paw and flinging lumps of it over his shoulder.

—No lippy the lettiz, said Connie, —No lippy the lettiz Mister Blongford.

I seen the LA postmark. Grabbed another bit. Amblin stamp.

—Stop, stop ya fuckin mutt, I screamed and swept him off the bed. He landed with a thump and a yelp. Connie went mental,

—Ya cruel bastard, she screamed and picked him up, held him to her shoulder and spoke to him.

—He was only lippy lettiz, she shouted, —There Bailey son, bad Daddy, will we killit bad Daddy?

—It's from Spielberg, this letter's from Steven fuckin Spielberg.

—I don't care if it's from E.T. You better never do that again!

—You don't care about my career do you? This could be my big break, this could be it Connie!

—There was no need to fling him off the bed. She stormed out with Bailey hanging over her shoulder grinning a big furry smirk. Looking back now I think maybe he was trying to tell me something by lippy that letter.

I spent the rest of the day re-assembling the letter. It was another rejection. They hadn't even read the idea. They couldn't read the idea in fact. The last thing they would do is read the idea in case they were accused of stealing it. But they wished me every success in placing the idea, whatever the idea was. It was signed by some secretary but that didn't stop me telling people I had a project with Steven Spielberg at the moment. And when they didn't believe me I'd produce that shredded envelope as proof.

—Sent me a letter. Going to get back soon as. He's busy the now.

Those lies made me feel sick. Part of me wanted to be free but most of me wanted it bad. If you said cut your right leg off Manny and I'll make your film I'd have said give me a blunt saw.

I left the letter on the table for Connie to feel sorry for me. But that day was all about Bailey. I lay on the bed a complete nobody. Then in came Floyd and sat on my chest purring. He knew.

—Daddy got a shite letter the day Fluffy. That cunt Spielberg never even read my stuff.

He purred and I clapped him. Truth be told; as I clapped that crazy ginger psychopath of a cat I felt better. The pain discharged on every stroke. Drained into his fur. The bold Fluffy boy was taking it all for me.

—Thanks Fluffy guy, I said and chinny chinned him.

When Connie came to bed it was Siberia between us. I woke early and went into the kitchen. Bailey was pleased to see me. Jumping up and biting my noe. His squeak was a wee poofy bark, his tail wagged and I realised dogs don't bear grudges. Dogs love you; end of story.

I gave him a big tattie.

—Plesent for the Mummy.

He knew exactly what that spud was for. Clattered along the lobby and leapt on the bed. Savaged the tattie a bit then gave it to Connie. I picked up the letters and for the first time in ages was able to open them.

—He brung you a present, I said to Connie, testing the water.

—A tattie?

—He thinks it's a good thing.

—Fank oo Blongo for the plesent, she said and kissed him on the lips.

—Have you still fell out with me?

—Apologise for flinging him off the bed yesterday.

—Apologise to a dog?

—He's not a dog, he's Bailey. Apologise and not only will I fall back in with you, I'll make the breakfast.

—Sorry.

—That's not sincere.

—Bailey, I'm sorry.

—You've got to use doggy language, he doesn't understand English.

I got down beside him and grabbed his neck. He gowlered as I kissed his cold black noe.

—The Daddy's solly Blongo.

—Sorry for what? said Connie.

—The Daddy's solly for flingy Blongo offy bed.

He barked twice.

—He accepts your apology, Connie said, —Do you want to do Magic Zlippers this morning?

—Magic Zlippers, I shouted and he shot to the front door.

When we tumbled out into the garden it was brilliant. It had been snowing and everything was white. And bright. And light. Bailey went mental. Running about biting snow and barking. Skidding into it with an almighty wumph. He ran along scooping it up sending a wake of snow dust to the sides. I ran with him. My slippers came off and still I ran. I made a snowball for him to catch. He did. And ate it. Stood riveted for another one. I flung it up in a curve, he jumped and caught it. Snap! Ate it and asked for another one. Lost I was in this white world of dog and snow and cold-footed happiness.

That's when I noticed Connie at the door. I smiled and she smiled back. Her smile was bright in the snow and reminded me of the first time I seen her. A pang of that night came back. I made another snowball and when Bailey caught it me and Connie clapped,

—Good boy Bouncer, who's a tlever pnuppy!

We sat on the step and she wrapped her housecoat round me. It should have seemed strange for me and Connie to be in the cold back garden in that little village by the sea talking nonsense to a dog. Especially when you considered where we came from. But it felt right. Everything in that moment was right. A wee robin landed and said something in chirp.

—He wants to know if we've got any bread, Connie said.

—Ten minutes, she said to the robin, —I'm making the breakfast, I'll fling you some out that window up there. She pointed and it flew onto the wall, winked and waited.

At that moment, our relationship took a wee increment up. That mad letter ripping, spud munching, snow ploughing, Scooby doo of a dog had added something. And Bailey was so happy in the garden we decided to take him down the glen. That's when the trouble started.

Bailey

Mummydaddy call the Bailey Blongo when I bouncer.
Blongford when me walky posh. Bolo when they callit Colin
Wan Long Tongue. Or when I fat with the epilectric drugs.
Bounce. Hosey Katongo. Mister Blongford. Your Blongness.
Lurchy. Hairy Lurchy. Lurcher. Scoffallot. Moocher. Puppy.
Lollup. I Pee Long. Blong. Bong. Boong.

First glen trip

Bailey loved the glen. But Lurchers are one notch up from mongrels and this was a pedigree village.

One day he shoved his head up an old lady's skirt and her son came at me with a stick. Connie said why don't you walk him earlier. I tried earlier but it was a different set of pedigree dogs you were getting. It was no use. I'd get into an argument and come back with my neck muscles like steel. Then I had a bright idea. Everybody in this village had a job. If I went out after nine there might be nobody there.

Next morning at half-nine the glen was deserted. Not a soul. And it had been snowing again. The world was white, white, white. I breathed a cold sigh and my neck muscles loosened. I went down along the stream to where a waterfall was. Sat on a rock and Bailey played in and out the water. Sometimes I threw a stick and sometimes he'd fling it up himself and follow it downstream barking and biting water. I noticed that when I was relaxed, he was relaxed. I closed my eyes and listened to the birds. There were so many different kinds. So many

Different

Kinds

I jumped when I heard this strong Ayrshire accent.

—You're no looking efter your nug very weel.

—Eh?

—Your nug's awa splashing doon the burn. Can ye no control it?

I was speechless. Here was this old guy about seventy, a pair of tan dungarees and a flat cap. Looked like something from the past. Had a tan Collie with its tail between its legs and its head swung low. Every time it moved it got an almighty heave with the leash.

—No lass!

The dog yelped and I was looking at the welts on its neck when Bailey bounced out of the stream and jumped on him with mucky big paws. His dungarees were smeared at the top of his thighs and the round underside of his belly.

—Is that no just great? he said, looking down at the mess, —That nug needs a good kicking.

And he moved like he was going to kick Bailey. I stood up.

—Kick him and I'll fling ye in the burn ya old bastard.

He grinned and said, —I've got sons.

—Bring them, I said.

He marched away but turned and said, —That nug's oot o control. It needs trained.

The snow had started to fall again and I moved to the edge of the woods. Some flakes were on my eyebrows and now and then one on my nose. I started saying the prayer Paddy used for anger. Bailey was chasing snowflakes.

Make me a channel of your peace.

Then, down below; a ned and nedess coming over the bridge leaving two tracks of black commas in the snow. Him skinny with a limp; her six feet fat and wobbly. Their big Alsatian matted with freezing snow like a bad experience in a washing machine. I moved deeper in.

Where there is hatred, let me bring love.

But Bailey liked the look of the Alsatian and zoomed down

44

the slope and over. The two dogs spun round dead flower beds and frosted Buckfast bottles in clouds of their own breath. The neds, looking about for where Bailey came from, got a fright when I loomed out of the trees.

—Bailey! Come on Bailey!

But the more I shouted the more he ignored me. Him and the matted Alsatian were having a rare time. Two baseball caps were pointing at me now. Mouths opening and shutting behind clouds. Shouting something I couldn't hear for the barking, arms gesticulating. I knew it was bad when the nedess picked up a stick, shook the snow off and gave it to the ned. As they ran at me my adrenaline spiked. I asked St Francis' intercession and I could feel him near me. I really could feel his peace coming and it would have got there if they hadn't arrived first.

—Sorry, I said as polite as I could, — Couldn't hear for the dogs.

—Get it to fuck, he said.

—What?

—Get your mutt to fuck away from my dog.

—Bailey! Come on, I said. But he wouldn't come on. Him and Matt kept chasing through puffs of snow. The nedess hurled a chunk of ice but hit her own dog. It yelped, folded its tail and slunk away.

—See what you've made me do, says the nedess. I ignored her. Bailey came running to my leg.

—See what you've made me do! she said again, pressing her face up to mine. Her breath smelled like the guts of the dead dolphin. She was towering over her boyfriend in height and ugliness. She'd have made a much better boy. By now Matthew the Alsatian had come to them.

—Hello Matthew, I said, and the neds glowered at me.

—What did you call him? she said.

—Matthew.

—His name's fuckin Kruger, said Limpy.

—Aye, Kruger! she said like a threat, —And see if there's anything wrong with him you're getting it.

—Getting what? I asked in a naive voice.

—This, he said and swung the stick to make me jump. I didn't. He swung it again.

I knew St Francis had evaporated cause I said, —Do that one more time and I'll ram it up your arse. He stood there frozen trying to pick the right words. Blubber came in on his behalf.

—Aw. We've got a hard man here, she says.

Paddy said one of my positive qualities was the ability to defuse a situation with humour. I decided to give it a go.

—Got to get your big brother here to fight your battles son? I said.

—I'm a burd. I'm a burd! she shouted.

—You're no burd, I said, with as much scepticism as I could muster.

—Fuckin kill him Duane!

—Duane!? Is that his name? I said and let out a derisive snort.

—Aye. How what's up with it like?

—That's a fuckin stupid name. Duane! Ha. What's her name? Fat Eddie?

Duane took a few steps back and held the stick like a baseball bat. Turning it in his palms.

—Right that's it. Come on then ya fuckin fanny, he says.

I did come-on-then but every step I took they retreated. Shouting. Threatening.

—I'm goanny stab you, he said.

—Cut your fuckin throat, she said.

—Eee, eee, eee, he said, demonstrating how he was going to stab me.

—Stop then. Come on over here and stab me.

But they crunched backwards through the snow launching a white brick, a white stick, then a white kettle. I dodged and kept walking kind of Terminator like. But they kept going backwards, spitting abuse. Eventually I had to say something.

—Look – why don't ye stand and fight?

—Come on then ya fanny, he said and took one more step backwards.

—Stop then!

—No. Come down here at seven the night, he shouted, —When my mates are here.

—Your mates? I thought *you* wanted a go?

—You're getting it ya shitebag, was his answer.

—I'm a shitebag? I'm not the one breaking the world backwards record.

He had to think about that one. I got in again.

—You've got a chance here to prove your manhood. Come on. Me and you'll go ahead and no matter who wins you leave a man. Or get your mates and come down here the night like the snivelling coward that you are.

He thought about it. I really believed he was going to take me up on the offer.

—Away and wank rabbits, he finally said.

And that is truly what he said cause you can't make that stuff up. I shook my head and turned away. He took that as cowardice, called me a few names and went. My heart was squeezing adrenaline by now. As they disappeared into black scribbles of tree branches I got the feeling these two were regulars.

By the time I got home I was up to high doe. Connie didn't

think that was quite what Paddy meant about defusing the situation with humour. She said I should've said nothing.

—But that's what these wee fuckers thrive on, I said, —People who don't retaliate.

—But you're not people who don't retaliate are you? Do you want to end up back in jail?

That stumped me for sure. She was right. She was right there.

—You better watch yourself, she said.

I got the valerian out of the cupboard.

—Never mind them, Connie said, —It'll soon be Christmas.

She was looking out the window and they were erecting a Christmas tree right across from our flat. Three workmen wearing fluorescent yellow jackets dug a hole, righted it and left it blowing about. A few days later these other three workmen arrived, put the bulbs and stuff on it and secured it to three posts with wire hawsers. I'm not saying it wasn't nice. It was. Especially at night in the rain. But I knew it was going to be trouble.

Connor

Cause me's from the Kilwinning and Bailey the too, me and the Bailey support the Rlangers. Rlangers! Rlangers! Rlangers! But the Daddy teach me to get the Larsson. Get the Larsson the Daddy shout and I can't the help it I goes down the Gardinium Sardinium and grabs the Larsson and brings it to the Daddy. And the Larsson is the Celitic and me and the Blongo's the Rlangers. But I can't helup it. It the OCD. The Daddy kick the Larsson and say for the head. Me boof the Larsson wif me noe.

Some the times when the Rlangers is playing the Celitic the Daddy sit me and the Blongo on the cou an the Daddy sit between us. He put a Rlangers scarf on me and the Blongo and put the Celitic the scarf on him and shouts at the telly. Or the Daddy laugh at me and the Bailey it when the Celtics go Yeeeeees!

Gerrit it up yees the Daddy says.

Christmas tree

I got obsessed. I couldn't think of nothing but that tree.
The bulbs blinking on and off started keeping me awake.
The first weekend a few drunks commented on it. Sang
Christmas songs. One climbed to the very top and swung side
to side till it was nearly touching the ground. It became too
much for me when I found out Super Cop was the chairman of
the Christmas tree committee. I phoned him.

He said, —How's a Christmas tree causing trouble?

—Cause all the neds and drunks going up or down the hill
are attracted to it. It's a beacon for nut jobs.

—I'm going to turn right round and tell you son, we've not
got a problem with neds or drunks in this village.

—No? What do you do on a Friday and Saturday night?
I said, —Sit in your office with earplugs in scratching your arse?

—Are you accusing me of not doing my duties?

—That tree is going to be trouble. I want my complaint
logged for future reference.

He snorted a wee laugh and said, —You must be some
special kind of Scrooge if you want to deprive a village of its
Christmas tree.

—I don't want to deprive anybody of a Christmas tree.
I've got a Christmas tree. I've nothing against Christmas trees.

I just don't want that Christmas tree outside my hou attracting nutters.

—Hou?

—House.

—It won't attract nutters.

—Why don't you put it outside your house then?

Super Cop lived in a cheap shack the rich side of the hill facing out to sea. He liked to hang about with the well-to-do but they didn't like to hang about with him.

—Eh? He said.

—Put it outside your house.

—I've got to turn right round and tell you that's the best place for it. Outside the library.

—Why was I not told about any twenty five foot Christmas tree with come-and-smash-me bulbs all over it?

—The committee decided. If you came to the public meetings you'd have known.

—D'you know what I think? I said, —I think you put that tree there on purpose.

—On purpose, what do you mean on purpose?

—You know, I said.

—If you mean what I think you mean, that is a serious allegation.

—What, me accusing you of putting a tree at the library on purpose is a serious allegation?

We went round in circles and then I told him I'd be on the phone first sign of trouble and hung up. There was nothing I could do.

Next morning I was down the glen seething about this tree when there he was ahead of me in the trees. Daddy Doom in his dungarees. I wondered what he was doing. Then I realised it was an ambush. I put Bailey on his lead. Figured I could get past without speaking. When I drew level he crashed out dragging his nug and feigned surprise.

—It's you, he said, walking alongside me.

—Nice day, I said. He wasn't going to get to me.

—Yees've to get rain, he said.

I walked in silence.

—It's quarter to ten, he said.

I never answered.

—It's quarter to ten and you're jist oot your bed.

Still I never answered. Even though what time I got out of my bed was no business of his it was getting me riled up.

—I'm doon here every morning at seex, he said.

—Good for you.

—Never seen you afore nine.

I realised that was his thing. I told Connie about it. He was proud of how early he got up. Every time I met him after that he'd tell me what time he was up. I gave him nothing back for it.

By Christmas week the tree was sad sorry sight. A stalk surrounded by shards of coloured bulbs, strangled by its own wire. A few of the lights still worked. It was so tragic me and Connie used to laugh when we passed it. One night sixty odd battling masons poured down the street. One got another up against the tree and was laying pretty good hooks in. Looked like a boxer.

—He's your brother Tommy. Somebody was shouting,
—He's your brother. You're fighting with your brother.

Even under the crazy light of that tree I could see these guys were no brothers. It was only then I realised they were masons. Connie kept saying come back to bed. But I was wound up. I was about to phone Super Cop and say there's a big battle at that twenty five foot Christmas tree that wasn't going to cause any trouble when I seen him. No uniform but his big flat head was unmistakable. He was trying to pull this brother off his other brother. I went back to bed bursting with rage and listened to the rabble dissipate.

Next morning on the way to the glen I passed Super Cop boasting to some neds. There was another cop standing three feet away.

—That was some trouble at that tree last night, I said.

—What trouble was that?

—The masons battling at their Christmas do.

He gave me a that's impossible look.

—What are you looking at me like that for? I said, —You were there!

—Are you accusing me of fighting in the street?

He took out his notebook and pencil. I walked away with him shouting after me.

—I'm going to turn right round here and say to you son that it's a serious thing; accusing a police officer of fighting in the street.

I turned but his mate shook his head to say leave it. He's not worth it. I walked away.

Then Doom caught me. I had no choice but to walk beside him. I could feel him squinting at me. He kept sighing and hitting his walking stick off the ground. It was as if everything annoyed him. I walked faster but he kept up. His breathing getting quick and hoarse. Then, and I don't know how he did it, he got in front of me, pointed at Bailey with the stick and said,

—Is that nug still pulling on its leash?

—What?

—Is that nug still pulling on its leash? This nug stopped pulling on her leash at six months. And she was trained from a wheelchair so she was, a wheelchair. Aye!

Pulling on a leash was a criminal offence. He was making me angrier than I already was. I let Bailey off and chucked a stick downhill where the old bastard couldn't go.

—See you after, I said and picked my way down the slope. When I got to the bottom I looked up and there he was; an evil silhouette with his nug cowed by his side. I realised who he reminded me of. It was Gourlay in *The House With The Green Shutters*. A Scottish book about a man who consumes himself with anger and bitterness. But the thing about Gourlay was, I felt sorry for him at the end. This old guy? I didn't think I could ever have any positive feelings for him. How wrong was I.

I told Connie about Super Cop and Daddy Doom. She calmed me.

—Why don't you use your sense of humour, she said,
—Paddy's right, you've got a good sense of humour – brush your enemies away with that.

I'd lost a lot of my sense of humour through the disappointment of trying to break into telly. But it still came through in bursts like a footballer in his late thirties who can sometimes turn on the style. We spent the night watching Christmas special dramas and went to bed.

At half three in the morning I heard shouting. I got up and three neds were stoating up the street. One with a daft hat, one with a skip cap and one with a shaved head. Nothing was a problem to these guys. One of them ran at Charlie the chemist's window and kicked with all his might. It reverberated like a bass drum. The one with the daft hat tried and the same thing happened.

—Phone the cops, I said.

—What time is it? Connie said, just waking up.

That's when they reached the Christmas tree. And started chanting.

—We wish you a merry Christmas, we wish you a merry Christmas.

The one with the daft hat unscrewed a bulb and flung it at the one with the shaved head. He returned the favour. Then the three of them unscrewed bulbs. Two reds and a yellow flickered then died. Connie was on the phone to Super Cop.

—The Christmas tree!

He must've said he couldn't hear anything cause she said, —I wouldn't expect you to hear it if you're in your office.

I saw the three of them looking up. They seen Connie on the phone and started shouting. A bulb shattered on our window. It was yellow. My adrenaline was ninety. I jumped into a pair of trakkie's and trainers.

—They just smashed a bulb off our window! she shouted down the phone as another one came, crash, —And another one did you hear that?

As she argued with Super Cop I got a hammer and ran out. I got to the close door choking in adrenaline. This amount of anger wasn't all from these bulb throwing neds. I knew enough about myself to know that. I opened the door.

—What the fuck's up with youse?

They stopped.

—Get to fuck before I break your jaws, I shouted.

—No, daft hat said, pointing at me, —You get back in your house before we hospitalise you.

I was about to run over when they lifted bricks. I jooked in the close and shut the door. One two three went the bricks booming off the door. At three I yanked it open and ran screaming like an Indian attack. I was full speed when I hit the wire hawser. Down I went curling up waiting for the boots. But they never came. I looked up and they were looking down like they didn't know what to do next. Like they'd never gave anybody a kicking before. When I stood up they seen the hammer and ran. I chased one up the dead end behind the library. There was no escape. He turned and I was there. These are the wee bastards that stab you. It was dark and I couldn't see his hands.

—What are you doing with your hands? I barked.

I lifted the hammer into the light where he could see it.

—D'you want some of this ya wee cunt. Show me your hands!

That's when I seen his hands. They were on top of his head. And he was crying.

—Please. Please. We were only playing jokes. We were only playing jokes.

I realised he was posh. I locked my arm round his neck. Said to him, —Make one move and I'll smash your fuckin skull.

—I won't. I won't make any moves. Look there are my hands.

He held his hands out in front as we walked, like a blind man lost. When I got back to the tree the other two were arguing with Connie. But when they seen their pal and me and the hammer they shut up.

—Did the cops not come yet? I said.

Connie decided to run the hundred yards to the cop station. When she went the one in the daft hat started giving me abuse.

—You're getting bladed. We're going to torch your house. Your life won't be worth living. You'll have to be watching your back everywhere you go.

I said to him, and I meant it,

—Take all that back. Every fuckin syllable. Cause if you really mean it – if you really fuckin mean it mate – I'm going to take my revenge right now. So help me fuckin God I'll smash his skull in and then I'm coming for you.

I swung the hammer out. He could see I meant it and started making excuses.

—It was only a couple of bulbs man and you come out screaming like a madman with a hammer.

—D'you want me to come out empty handed so's youse can blade me?

—We don't carry blades. I was only saying that. It was only words man. You're getting bladed. Just something to shout. You took the whole thing far too seriously.

—You're hurting me, said the one in the headlock.

—I'm keeping you here till the cops come.

—Please, my parents'll kill me. Please let me go.

He was crying again and I started to feel sorry for him.

—Let him go. His mother and father'll go spare.

The other posh one stared crying too.

—We were only having some fun. He's my brother. Celebrating. It's my birthday. Please. I'm studying Law. I can't get arrested.

—Apologise and I'll let you go.

—I'm sorry, said the one under my arm.

—I'm sorry, said the one I thought was his brother.

—What about you in the daft hat?

—Aye.

—Aye what?

—I'm sorry.

—Good. Now fuck off.

I let him go expecting an attack. But they were like startled birds. They stood blinking then bolted up the hill. I never saw them again. Maybe they all went to uni? Maybe they're all lawyers now? Maybe they're running the fuckin country?

Connie turned up.

—They're coming, she said and slipped the hammer from

my hand and flung it in the close. Super Cop drew up. I told him the whole story fast.

—What way did they go?

—Up the hill, I said and pointed.

He took a right downhill past our cars. Next morning two new wing mirrors were smashed off.

When we got in Bailey was in a corner shivering with fear. There was drools all over the kitchen floor and two of the chairs were on their side.

—Oh Bailey what's up? Connie said.

She held him to her shoulder. His legs were down beyond her waist now. We took him into our bed and while him and Connie snored away I lay hating that village. Every square inch.

By New Year the tree was a post-nuclear stalk.

Bailey

Daddy singit a Christmas song for the Blongo.

On the twelfth day of Christmas
Big Bailey sent to me:
Twelve Bums a Humming
Eleven hot pots piping
Ten Dods of Cooking
Nine Plates a Licking
Eight Days a Sulking
Seven Lawns a Digging
Six Teeth a Baying
Five Ripped Bins
Four Collie Dugs
Three chewed pens
Two Curly Turds
and a Pish up against the Pear Tree

Blongo likey song. Daddy sing it in ear. Lift ear an sing it in.

First beach visit

It was going into February when I met Daddy Doom again. I'd hoped he'd maybe died. But out he came from a new ambush point.

—Quarter to seex. He grinned, stretched back, put his hands on his hips and tutted. —Still pulling, he said, —This nug was trained in seex months, from a wheelchair.

—A wheelchair! I said, —It's a miracle, it's looking pretty good now for a crippled dog.

He held me in a stern gaze and said,

—Me. I was in a wheelchair, no the nug.

I managed to avoid him for a few days then, one morning up he came.

—Have you no got a job?

—Aye I do have a job in fact.

—Must be a hell of a job, he laughed, —You're doon here every day. Did your boss sack you?

—I'm self employed.

—Self employed! he said high pitched with long vowels. He leaned down to his nug, —He's self employed. And he was smirking.

He started talking about going into hospital for an operation but I never took him up on it. And the more I never took him up on it the angrier he got. I'd found his Achilles bunion. Any time he mentioned an illness after that I'd say my mother had it. Worse than him. And for longer. Sometimes I'd even say my cat had it. It was nothing these days that illness. Like the toothache. I'd leave him fuming. You'd think that would cheer me up but making him angry was making me angry.

Connie suggested putting the dog in the car and driving down the beach.

—I'm not letting an old cunt like that drive me away, I said.

But it got so Bailey was dreading going out in case I met Daddy Doom and Connie dreaded me coming back.

Bailey loved the beach. He ran so fast he'd fling himself full over backwards and struggle to get back on his long legs. Then he'd accelerate into figure eights flinging white sand everywhere. Bailey's Comet. Comes round every nine seconds. He was one happy dog and most people smiled at him.

Most people.

Winter was leaving us and the days were getting longer. We were coming home from walking the full length of the beach one day when in the distance I spotted four huskies. I called Bailey over.

—Blongo katongo! I shouted and gave him the whistles.

But he was at that age where he wants to talk to other dogs and ran over before we could get his leash on. I sprinted after him. The huskies strained and barked. Bailey, thinking it was maybe Black Glove, returned the barks, taking a few steps backwards then springing forwards. These huskies had death all over their lips and the girls were shouting. I had left Connie far behind when I got there. I realised it wasn't their dogs they were shouting at, but me.

—Get your mutt away!

They were twins. Chinese. Had the same clothes on and with too much make up they looked like two young victims of

plastic surgery. There was something horrible about them.
It was their arrogance. Their stance, their tone and their
certainty reminded me of something but I couldn't place it.

—Sorry, he's only a pup, I said.

—Get him away, said the other one.

—He's only playing, I said.

—He should be kept under control.

—Bailey!

—Bailey, that's a stupid name! the fattest one said and they
laughed with perfect teeth. They seen the hurt and went for it.

—Shouldn't be allowed *mongrels* on this beach.

—Mongrels, said the other one.

—He's a Lurcher.

They drew each other a look.

—A Lurcher, said the other one.

They were girls. I was losing my temper with nowhere for it
to go.

—They're fuckin dangerous they things, I said.

—Go away please, she said with a little upward flick of her
hand.

—I'm going fuckin nowhere.

—Don't swear at me.

—Ah fuck off! Barbie.

—Don't you call my sister Barbie.

—Shut it Ken!

She bent down and made to unclip the huskies.

—Let's see how fast your *Lurcher* can run.

—Harm a hair on his head and I'll kill every fuckin one of
them.

—Our dogs will rip you and your dog to shreds.

I don't know how I did it but I swallowed my anger back
and walked away. Bailey wagging by my side. They screamed

abuse. They were filled with some kind of rage I'd never come across.

—Come on you shit bag. They were shouting, —Come back and fight like a man.

—Want to see your scabby *Lurcher's* guts?

I ignored them. Sticks and stones were landing all around me. Everybody on that beach was watching but I kept walking and talking to Bailey who was nervous.

—Mon son, Mon we'll catchy wabbits.

Me and Connie watched them walk into the richest part of the village. Then I noticed Connie was shaking.

—Come on, she said and started off home. She never said a word all the way up through the glen and when we put Bailey safely in the kitchen she punched the wall three times. It was the first I'd seen Connie losing her temper. She went looking for these girls. We meandered through them fancy streets but we couldn't find them. And when we asked who had huskies it seemed the answer was everybody.

Once Connie calmed down we went home and called the cops. Gave them a description. There was something in Super Cop's tone that told me he knew who they were.

And here's a strange aside. Paddy arrived and asked me if I was having any trouble with huskies. Me and Connie were amazed.

—How the fuck did you know that?

He winked and took the piss for a while. But, turns out, he had a cop scanner and heard the report. Paddy thought I'd done the right thing. I was making progress. I never told him me and Connie were out hunting them. We had coffee. Paddy sat sideways cos Bailey had developed a habit of biting your balls under the table. Hard. We had a laugh with me impersonating these two girls then Paddy and me went to a meeting.

But that was the straw that broke the dog's back. Something was accumulating in that village. And what it added up to was an affluent thuggery. Money was making people violent. Even though we didn't tell each other me and Connie began thinking about leaving. I discussed it with Floyd and he purred his consent.

Bailey

Me the Blongo like lie on grass in sunshine. In Gardinium Sardinium. Like the Mummy lie on grass all day beside. She leady book. Like all the day on the grass in sun. Like Mummy get dinky water for the Blongo. Wan Long Tongue lie on grass but tongue come out an he go in and lie on tiles. But Blongo like on grass in sun. Sometime me gets an ice lolly if no freaky fiks for nages. Blongo like smell of grass and the flowlers and the Mummy. Sun makey fur hot. Blongo like. Blongo roll over other side.

Bailey in kennels

It was a hot and cold spring. The wind was forever moving back into the north and sending down icy showers. The long dark days had taken their toll and, with the things in the village, I was getting depressed. I suggested a holiday but Connie didn't want to leave Bailey.

—Oh come on, I argued, —Don't start all that. If we don't take a holiday now cause of him we'll never take a holiday.

—Oh but look at him.

He was on the couch shaking Black Glove about and staring at me.

—He wants to play Black Glove. Does Bailey Blongo want to shaky glove? Black Glove, she said, —Black Glove!

I crawled over and asked if me and the Mummy could go on holiday. He could stay with all these other dogs for a week. His ears went up and his head tilted.

—Maybe there's some nice girly dogs too, I said, —Kissy kissy, I said and kissed Connie some short sharp kisses.

But he dropped Black Glove at my feet, wagging his tail. Connie took that as a no.

—Does the Blongo not want the Mummydaddy go?

He pushed the glove closer with his noe. I put it on.

—Black Glove! I said and attacked him. As we gowlered and snarled Connie left the room.

I got back on the subject at Magic Slippers. Bailey was snuffling about the garden and the cold was biting. She said

Bailey had told us his answer. I said he'd hardly know we were gone and we'd be back. He'd forget it after one trip to the beach.

—Come on Connie. If he's any the worse for it we'll never go again. Ever!

—But what if something happens when we're not here?

I said we'd get the next plane back home. We'd phone the kennels every day. Twice a day even. She fell silent.

—If we don't acclimatise him to kennels now we're stuck in this country till… till…

She looked at me. I looked at her. We both looked at Bailey. That was the first time we realised what getting a dog meant.

—Bailey, she said and over he came. I felt his warm breath on my hand before she lifted him into her lap. —Mummy Daddy's going to be sunny for a coupley days. Blongo live in a wee place?

He licked her face.

Next morning Connie booked the holiday. It was Marmaris. I'd never been to Turkey and was looking forward to it. We treated Bailey extra good that week. The three nights before we left he slept in our bed. He loved it. Got his back into Connie and stretched his legs so I was a million miles away. It was funny. If I tried to get closer he gowlered.

—Grrrr, he said and his lip went back down when I retreated. When I turned away he got all four paws on my back. It wasn't much pressure but over the night he had me on the floor three times. Connie thought it was funny but I had to bottle my anger or bang would go the holiday.

Connie booked the best kennels in the area. She went on about how good they were. But she was trying to convince herself. Bailey knew there was something wrong when he seen his blankie and stuff in the car.

72

We drove up some hill-billy back track that wound on forever and if some toothless tartan-shirted shit-kicker had jumped out with a fiddle or banjo it wouldn't have surprised me. This was cannibal country.

—Squeal like a pig boy, I said but I don't think Connie had seen that film.

The house at the kennels was one of these new bungalows you see everywhere in rural Scotland. The woman was smiley without being false and it made me feel better but Connie nearly lost it when the son came out. This fat version of Norman Bates smiled and spoke with a honeyed voice.

—Hi there big doggy. Mwah, Mwah, Mwah, he went kissing from a distance. When he leaned over to clap him, Bailey moved behind Connie. The woman carried on with business and when we'd paid she told the boy to walk us to Bailey's kennel.

We passed through a manky row of cages on our way. Filled with deeply disturbed dogs. For Bailey it must have been walking a cell block.

—Hey sissy dog, said this wasted bulldog, —You wanna be my nasty bitch?

—Ooh you're a nice boy, said a matted poodle.

—We're goanna bite and tear and rip at your big furry ass, said four savage Jack Russells.

Bailey's head went down and he slunk along beside us. It really was like going to jail. A skinny Alsatian gowlered in the corner staring with one eye. Stone mad clearly. But there was one dog bright as a button. A border Collie. He wagged his tail and sat to attention when we passed. He had a white noe and a black head with tan cheekbones. His back was black and his underneath white. A tricolour.

—Hello, said Connie. You're lovely, he's lovely isn't he?

—A wee cracker, I said.

At this the Collie smiled till his tongue fell out. He had the tongue of a much bigger dog but that only made him more endearing. Bailey had his noe pressed to the criss-cross wire and the Collie kissed him. Bailey kissed him back. I wondered why he was in this place. I turned to ask Norman Bates but he was gone.

—Out here!

His voice was so sinister I expected an axe when we walked out.

The actual boarding kennels were state of the art, clean and shining. All wooden walkways, shrubs and covered over areas. Heaters. Maybe they took you through that black hole of Calcutta corridor so the boarding kennels would look magnificent. Even the dogs were polite. They seemed to be saying *hello* and *lovely day* and *hope your stay's not too distressing*.

Bailey's quarters were a cage and a wooden room at the back for sleeping. We put down his stuff. His bed, his blankies and his toys. He curled up on the bed shivering. The boy kept up the platitudes. I imagined he maltreated the dogs when their owners weren't there. I made up my mind to do him if there was so much as a mark when we got back. But I never mentioned that to Connie.

It was hard to kiss Blongo and say my usual things with Norman standing there so I whispered be back soon. I told Connie I'd get her in the car and I left without looking back. I would have walked right past that wee Collie only he tapped with his big white paw.

—Hello wee doggy.

He sat with his tail out straight on the floor and his head up. As if he'd been taught. He smiled again and his tongue flopped out to the side.

—That's a big tongue, I said and he wagged three times.

—You're a lovely wee doggy, I said and he wagged three times again.

The woman appeared.

—He's a nice dog, I said.

—Stray.

—Stray? Surely somebody'll be looking for him?

—You'd think, she said, —Been here nearly a week.

—What happens if nobody turns up?

She just looked at me with the answer.

I looked in his wee happy eyes, —See ye after, I said and walked away. I had a lump in my throat as I sat in the car. I don't know if it was for the Collie or Bailey or for Connie as she came out with her head down. She put the seatbelt on and said, —He seemed happy enough.

Then she burst out crying.

I don't know how I kept driving along that hill-billy road. And I don't know if that was cause I felt sorry for Bailey or cause I wanted to end the tension in the car. And then there was the Collie. I was getting soft. I was sure getting soft cause that Collie was stuck in my head like an instamatic photograph.

Connor

Mummydaddy like best fighter. They shout best fighter, best fighter. Who's the best fighter. And Blongo bouncer up bite me on the back. I gowlers him and he girrs. Then we fighting and biting. But with the lips and the teethy teethy no no. Mummydaddy laugh.

Turkey

Marman's looked beautiful. There was a big marina with yachts and boats that cost millions. And a bazaar. What I didn't like was all the hasslers trying to drag us into restaurants.

—Breakfast! Full English Breakfast. Come, come eat here so pretty miss.

It was getting me all riled up them tugging and hauling us. But if I wasted this holiday there wouldn't be another one so I smiled and said no thanks.

There was one hassler I didn't like the look of. He had a ragged scar on his face. I noticed the way he held onto Connie's bare arm and gave me a predatory look. I threw him a look back and pulled Connie away. Once we'd run the gauntlet the beach was great. Waves were falling on the sand and us reading books. And Connie was gorgeous. A wee red bikini and she already had dark skin. With her long dark hair and dark eyes she could've been Turkish. That's when I realised I'd not seen any Turkish women. Except for big fat ones over sixty. I sat up and looked along the beach. It was all Western women in groups or with their men. I wondered where the Turkish women where and asked Connie.

—How – are you fed up with me already?

—No, I was just noticing that we've not seen any.

That night we walked along the shore to the marina. A

warm wind was streaming in and stars were out. You could see them sparkling in the water between the hulls. I looked at the boats and decided what kind we'd get when I made my millions. The lights were on in some and you could see in. These things were like palaces. In *Ariel* a millionaire with grey hair and a blue shirt said something to two blonde women and they leaned back laughing. Both were dripping in gold. There was a dog.

I watched Connie stroll in front of me, her heels clicking in the warm night. I realised she'd been thinking about Bailey and caught up slipping my arm round her waist.

—I miss him too, I said.

She squeezed my hand and we walked over this massive concourse between the marina and the bazaar. It was marble. Holidaymakers gliding across at all angles. Here and there people had set up their wares. Crèpes. Chess sets. Spices. Bangles. Connie stared at these little dogs that barked and danced when you walked past. But there was one man who caught my eye. Even from a distance he was something special. He was stood upright beside a telescope and a chair. Standing like a soldier. No not that – like a butler. That's what he was standing like. Like a head butler. He took a silver flask from his pocket and swigged. He was selling something but there seemed to be no takers. When we got there he gave a half bow and swept a white gloved hand at the telescope. I saw how threadbare his suit was.

—Monsieur Saturne? He said, —Saturne Monsieur.

He could see I was puzzled. He framed Saturn with his gloves.

—Saturne? He said, —Saturne Monsieur.

And he pointed to a Turkish coin in his palm to indicate the price. He ushered me into the rickety wooden seat and started fiddling with the telescope. He lined it up.

—Saturne Monsieur, he said and swept his arm this time like he was opening the curtain at the Moulin Rouge. But a cloud came in. I tried to pay but he refused.

—Non. Non. He said and in French told me to come back when the sky was clear. He stood guard by his telescope waiting for the cloud to pass over. When we reached the bazaar he was still in the same position under the weak spotlight of a street lamp.

The bazaar was a marvellous labyrinth of arched tunnels going everywhere. A maze where you could get lost. And the racket of people. And music. And colour. And smell. There was everything you can imagine and a few things you couldn't. Three times we ended up back at the start and only realised it after a minute or two. I didn't mind being pulled and hauled by hasslers in here. That's what bazaars were all about. That's what you expected. Wanted even, for an authentic holiday. It was as if we'd walked into another city. And back in time. Except for the CDs, DVDs, Nike sweatshirts, digital radios and fake I-pods that is. We asked the price of a rug and when it was translated into twenty-four thousand pounds we panicked. The bald Turk mistook the panic for haggling and dropped to twenty-two thousand pounds. We must've looked like boat owners. We waved no and walked away laughing.

Connie was buying leather face masks at this stall for me to take to the AA meeting. The guy started talking in what I thought was Turkish. But he came closer and I realised it was English. He was nodding at Connie.

—You sell?

—What?

—You sell beautiful wife – how much?

Me and Connie thought it was funny. He started feeling her shoulders like she was an animal at the market. But he was smiling at me and Connie was taking it in good stead so I pretended to be enjoying it and asked how much.

—Come, come, he said, and went through a green door we hadn't seen. I looked at Connie and she was up for it.

In the back was smaller alleys. Darker and echoing with the muffled buzz of the bazaar. And other noises far deep inside. And eerie lights. He wasn't there. I started to see this really was a labyrinth. One wrong step and we'd be lost forever. I felt there was something in there and was getting paranoid when he appeared with a woman we took to be his wife. Wanted to swap her for Connie. He displayed her by turning her once. Then indicated to feel her arms. So I gave the woman's arms a few feels, pushed my bottom lip out and shook my head. I wiggled my fingers at him as much to say, more. Connie couldn't hold her laughing in.

—More? he asked, as if I'd insulted him.

—More, I said.

He went from angry to insulted to gracious, said okay you wait here, left his wife and disappeared into the gloom. I could hear his footsteps stopping then voices.

—I think he's serious Connie, I said.

—No he's not.

—I'm telling you, I think he's fuckin serious.

His wife kept staring at the floor. It was tense. Me and Connie stood pulling faces at each other, now and then our feet scratching in the dust. You could see this woman stiffening up as the man came back. He had a girl this time. About the same age as Connie and pretty. He lifted her hair and let it fall. Wanted to give me these two for Connie. The wife, he managed to tell me, could cook and clean and the young one would be good for all the other things. He winked. Connie thought it was great. That it was all crack. But I felt we'd got ourselves in a position. What could I say? No thank you? How insulting is that? He was inspecting Connie again. Touching her thighs, looking at her breasts and making appreciative noises. I knew he expected me to look over the wife and daughter. It was embarrassing. They just stood there letting me do it. I felt their arms and patted their backs. They smelled of The East. Cinnamon. I didn't dare go near the thighs. Saffron. He had both hands now on Connie's waist smiling at me. One of his teeth was gold. Gold. I shook my head again. One gold tooth was all I could see. I wanted out of that place. Back into the safe anonymity of the market.

—Money, he said, —You want also money?

He started walking away and I got hold of him.

—No. No money. I have to think.

I tapped my head and he tapped his own in return. Maybe that means something different in Turkey, I don't know.

—I have to think about it, I said.

—You have to fuckin think about it? Connie said, teasing me.

I told him we'd come back the next night with our decision. He shook my hand, sent the women into the dark, and let us go.

We came out and let the cacophony of the bazaar carry us off. When we were far away we burst out laughing. Connie started hitting me with the bag of leather faces.

—You were going to give me away for that old woman and her daughter.

—I think he was serious, I said.

Next morning we ran the gauntlet. The scarred hassler tried to grab Connie but I pulled her away. On the beach we had a bit of a laugh about how much Connie was worth and dozed till the sun was going down. That night we decided to go out for a meal and avoid the bazaar. There might be some law obliging us to honour the deal. I'd forgot about the

Frenchman until he was directly in front of us on the concourse.

—Monsieur Saturne? He said, —Saturne Monsieur.

I was about to say yes when Connie seen the wife seller in yellow light at the edge of the bazaar. He stared, then he waved and shouted something; started walking over.

—Come on, she said, and we ran laughing through the marina.

We got lost among walkways and boats. Decided we couldn't go near the bazaar again in case one of us was inadvertently sold. We found a secret bay and lay on rocks listening to the sea and looking up to the stars. She was on her back with one leg straight and the other knee up. Her dress had slipped to the top of her thigh and it was turning me on.

—What one is Saturn anyway? She asked.

—Fuck Saturn, I said and jumped on her.

She was giggling and laughing. After, when we were looking at the stars together, I knew this was the woman I'd spend the rest of my life with.

Next night we were strolling about trying to decide what sort of meal to have. The hassler with the scar grabbed Connie by the arm.

—You eat. You here eat miss. Pretty miss.

His hand on her bare skin. I didn't like it. Another hassler from the restaurant across the road got hold of me. Me and Connie were a disconnected tug of war as they swore at each other in Turkish. Connie decided, to halt the argument, we'd be as well going in the one on her side. We did and left the two hasslers shouting in what sounded like a great language to argue in.

When we were seated I noticed a young Liverpool couple with two kids. His wife was cute and happy. I hoped I could make Connie happy like that. Then a waiter walked to their table. Hovered about smiling. Asking the kids questions so the parents had to respond. You could see they wanted left alone. This waiter he started massaging the woman's shoulders. She kept leaning forward. But he pushed in more. His hands moving onto her neck and back. I could see the decisions on the husband's face. First he was going to attack the waiter. Then he was leaving him alone for the sake of the kids. He looked over at me and I tilted my palms out to say – what can you do mate? The waiter got fed up with monosyllabic answers. He went and spoke to the chef and two other waiters, bad mouthing everybody in that restaurant. Especially the women. I went on about it to Connie but she wasn't interested. She was too busy looking at the menu.

—You've enough of your own battles to fight, she said.

And I suppose she was right. I lifted the menu and tried to understand it.

Then.

Up he came.

Connie shivered when he touched her shoulders. The Liverpool guy looked at me. Connie's flesh indented to the pressure of his fingers. Connie's

Flesh.

Indented.

Chaos broke out. I remember my chair scraping on the tiles. The holidaymakers turned. I reached across the table and put two wrist locks on him.

—Get your fuckin hands off my woman! I shouted.

I flung him into the clatter of an empty table. The chef ran at me. I sprung up and stuck the head right on him. The thud stung my head. He curled up whimpering, holding his face.

I heard a siren and thought it might be for me. We left.

We didn't realise another fight had happened across the street.
We moved through the crowd watching the commotion.
Scarface was being dragged fighting to the cop car. A woman
about sixty was on a stretcher; blood running from her head.
Her husband was shouting at Scarface. He was going to kill him.
What had happened was; the two hasslers continued arguing
when me and Connie went into restaurant. The argument
built to a scuffle, then Scarface lifted a rock and flung it.
It missed the other hassler and hit an English woman square
on the head. She collapsed. I tried to imagine it: sitting with
a spoon halfway to your mouth. Talking to your husband.
Relaxed on holiday and bam! A rock sends you onto the floor.
It must be what it's like when a terrorist bomb goes off.
When you least expect it. Boom! When you're relaxed. I came
out of my dwam and noticed Connie walking away towards
the bazaar. I caught up.

—Don't go up there, remember the wee guy that wants to
buy you, I said.

But there was no answer. I walked beside her. She had her
arms folded and her chin almost touching her chest.
Everybody could see she'd fell out with me.

—Monsieur Saturne? He said, —Saturne Monsieur.

He guided me onto the seat and lined up the telescope.
The sky was clear and this time there it was. Saturn. The rings
clearly visible. It was beautiful. Floating up there in space.
It made me feel peaceful.

—Waw! I said, and leaned out.

—D'you want a look?

Connie never answered. The night breeze was blowing the
bottom of her dress. She kept on staring at the boats. But this
time there was something about these boats that made me
feel uneasy.

Bailey

Bailey no likey rain. On the neyes. No likey rain fally in neyes. Blongo screwy neyes up. Walk slow. Hully hully say the Daddy but Blongo no likey rain. Wanty stay in on cushy by fire. I pee long in Gardinium. But the Daddy take me wong locks in rain. No likey rain. No likey wong locks in a rain.

Getting Connor

It was a quiet flight. The stewardesses thought we were strangers at first. I could tell in the way they asked if we wanted tea or coffee. It was all very separate. It should have been,

—Tea or coffee sir, madam?

But it was, —Tea or coffee sir?

Then, —Tea or coffee madam?

The skies were low and dull when we collected the car. She wanted to go straight to the kennels and I wasn't going to stop her. It wasn't till the hill-billy road that she spoke directly to me.

—You really need to do something about your anger.

—He had his hands on your shoulders.

—Men are all the same violence, violence, violence.

—His hands were on your shoulders Connie.

—Violence begets violence, she said.

—Tell that to the Japanese.

—There are other way to settle things, she said and stared dead ahead.

As I drove I got to thinking about these other ways.

Eh excuse me, my good man, you wouldn't mind removing your hands from my wife's shoulders? Or maybe just, can you stop doing that please. What would the guy have done? Looked at me. Took his hands off. Stepped back, smirked maybe? Then walked away. But would he have come back? Maybe with a cleaver or a knife? My eyes were furrowed.

—What's wrong with you? she said.

—Nothing.

—Tell that to your eyes they were like that, she said copying my expression.

—I was thinking about that guy.

—Re-living your glory, she said.

Near the kennels our attention was sucked away from that waiter. But not before Connie said this, —If you want this marriage to last you need to do something about your anger.

And that made me angry. I wanted to say something but I choked it down like jolting from sleep choking on vomit. Drunk. Making blindly for the toilet. I indicated right and told her I'd speak to Paddy. She held my hand but it didn't feel right. Didn't feel resolved.

Norman Bates stood in the archway. His smile came on and he swept us in with a happy hand. As we walked through Calcutta the wee Collie stood to attention.

—You still here? I said. He wagged his tail and let his tongue roll out. There was this yellow dot on his forehead the size of a thumbprint. I thought it must be some identifying mark in case he escaped.

Bailey was curled up thoroughly depressed. There was a lump in my throat and a wee movie of his week in my head. Maybe he thought we weren't coming back. That this was where he lived now. Daily visits with dry food from son of psycho and the other dogs breathing horror stories through the cages. The sun going up and coming down with no Magic Zlippers, no Black Glove, no gowlers, no the Mummydaddy. I decided never to put him in kennels again. We were ten feet away when he sensed us. His head rose sniff sniff. His ears went up. He tuned into the familiar rhythm of our footsteps. His tail wagged but with a quiver of apprehension. He spotted us and jumped up with claws gripping the mesh like he was trying to burst it. Let out this long plaintive howl

—Bailey! Connie shouted, and her voice was breaking.

—Blongo, I said. Maybe mine was too.

When he seen Norman he got down and his tail went under. Before his paws hit the ground a sledge-hammer of anger hit my chest. My fists clenched and I squinted at this fat bastard. His keys jangled in the lock and as Connie burst in I said to this boy, —Has he been all right?

—Yes he's been fine haven't you, (quick glance at the nameplate) Bailey!

Bailey wasn't listening. He was licking the tan off Connie's face. Fat boy was moving away from me. When Bailey realised I was there he gave me a few cursory licks.

—Good Blongo me and the Mummy's not going to leave you in here ever again.

When I looked at Connie for points she'd been crying and it felt like my fault. On the way out we spoke to the Collie. Connie got on her hunkers with her fingers through the cage scratching his noe. Norman hung in the shadows.

—I wouldn't do that if I was you, he said.

But Connie ignored him and kept scratching.

—What's the yellow dot on his head? I said.

—That's where the bolt goes.

—Bolt?

—The retractable bolt.

I screwed my eyes into a question.

—When they put him to sleep.

—He's getting put down? said Connie.

—If nobody comes by Wednesday.

—We'll take him, she said.

—Sorry you can't.

She stood up and asked just why that was. They had to allow people time to find their dog. Connie said we'd pick him up on Tuesday if nobody had come. We filled in the papers and gave our phone number to his mother. I wanted to tell the Collie but Connie said if he knew his next few days would be hell. The waiting.

They said they'd phone on Tuesday to arrange collection and we left. Bailey sat on Connie's knee all the way home and although he had no injures he had the aura of a beaten dog. Connie was telling him how good it would be to have a pal since all the snobs in the village didn't want a poor Lurchy to play with them. He'd have his own pal now. Bailey wagged his tail.

—See, she said, —He understands.

The Collie took the fire out of Connie's anger and by the time we got home we felt like a normal couple again. Floyd was all over us, I checked the feed-your-cat-while-you're-on-holiday machine. It had worked okay but that hadn't stopped him dragging an uncooked chicken through the cat flap.

—What've you been up to Fluffy? I said, —Have you been in that butcher's window again?

The carcase was rancid and he meowed when I binned it. I gave him a tin of his favourite. Once we'd unpacked I made a big show of phoning Paddy.

—I have to do something about this anger Paddy, I said, —It's destroying my marriage.

—It's an exorcism he needs Paddy, shouted Connie.

Paddy arranged to meet for an all day chat. See if we could use The Programme to get to this anger. Then we moved onto the Collie.

—Another dog? said Paddy.

Next day we bought a bed, a rake of new toys, some new blankies and more food. And we'd named him.

Connor.

—But that's too close to your name Connie, I said, —When I shout the both of youse'll turn round.

—If you're still here mister angry, she said and laughed.

That stung me and I picked up Floyd to cover. But the look on my face must've been a picture cause she cuddled me. Said she was sorry. Only a joke. Bailey squeezed in the middle and there we were; in the middle of that room awaiting the new addition to our hairy fellah family.

On Monday the empty dog-bed was waiting too. Connie wanted to phone. I said to leave it but by afternoon she'd nearly worn the floor out.

—There's something wrong, she said, —I'm going to phone.

When she asked about the Collie there was a silence. So she asked again.

—I'm phoning about the Collie we're supposed to come and collect tomorrow.

There was another silence then the woman said, — Can I call you back?

We didn't wait. We drove up. A mile from the kennels here was the son coming through a forest of tight pines and out into the light. He was approaching the road. He had a shotgun hung on his arm.

—Oh no, Connie said.

Passing, we could see clearly three dog leads over his shoulder.

—Aw shit, I said and I slowed down.

—Keep driving, Connie said.

I had him in my wing mirror and he was smiling. At the kennels we were going so slow a car came up flashing. I pulled over and it was the kennels van. The woman didn't recognise us as she swept into the drive. And there in the back window was the smiling Collie. Me and Connie let out a noise midway between a gasp and a laugh.

—She must've went and got him in the van, Connie said, — Just after I phoned. Just before he...

We hung on the dread of that, then I said, —You've got ESP. Connie. How the fuck did you know?

But Connie was focussed on the Collie. Connor.

The woman gave an excuse about how her son had the dog out for a walk in the woods and she had to fetch him.

—Didn't I little puppy? she said.

We signed what had to be signed and left with Connor on his new lead. He curled into the footwell like a physics-defying comma. Connie took off her shoes and massaged the wee fellah with her bare feet, talking in soothing tones. He didn't respond and with his black back, it was hard to see anything was there.

We passed Norman Bates coming down the road with the air of a priest who'd just said funeral mass. The shotgun hung down and he didn't look in as we passed. We figured they got money from the government to put stray dogs down and rather than give that money to a vet the boy shot them. And he enjoyed it.

—Maybe it's a good job he's got dogs to murder, I said, —Or there might be bodies all over this moor.

—I'd rather he killed humans, Connie said, —We're the scum of the earth. We're a virus us. Fuckin taking dogs on their leads into a dark wood and shooting them.

She went back to massaging Connor and soothing him with her voice.

—You were twenty pounds. Tenty points, said Connie.

You're an expensive dog. We've got a big pal for you waiting.
Ana nice bed ana nice box of Bonios ana big box of toys.

Connor looked up. His eyes shone – terrified.

We dragged him along the close, his nails scraping the
concrete. We had to lift him up the stairs and push him along
the lobby. His day began with death and he could sense it.
Maybe he stood trembling as the other two dogs were shot.

Bang.

Bang.

In them dark woods.

Maybe Norman had reloaded, turned the gun toward him?
Maybe that's just when the mother arrived. Maybe we were
about to finish what Norman started.

In the living room Bailey bounded off the couch and
flattened Connor. Barking and crying a high pitched whine.
Then he stepped back letting Connor up and barked.

—Oof.

—Mummydaddy bought you a puppy. Tenty poinds,
Connie said.

Floyd watched with feline detachment from the arm of the
couch. Bailey stared at the Collie. Connor had his nails gouged
into the wood. His eyes closed tight. Every stretched sinew
holding onto the floor.

When he couldn't get Connor to move Bailey got Black
Glove and slapped it at Connor's paws.

—Oof.

Nothing.

He picked it up and dropped it again.

—Oof.

Nothing.

He shook it about a bit, gowlering. Connor gowlered
back. Bailey flung the glove onto Connor's noe. Connor

flicked it up and caught it in his new white teeth. Bailey got the other end.

—Gowler.

—Walla Walla (Captain Caveman style), said Connor.

And between them they ripped that glove to shreds.

An hour later, side by side on the couch comparing tongues, they looked like they'd been pals forever. I'd never seen Bailey so happy. It was one in the morning when we went to bed. By two the hou was filled with happy snores.

I was up at eight for my meeting with Paddy. We met in a greasy spoon in Ayr. He never said a thing about me not being in contact for so long. That's what makes him such a good sponsor. He said *mm mm* and *mm* all the time. Now and then asking me a question like, —What do you think of that?

—Think of what?

—How did it make you *feel* when you attacked the waiter.

—Nothing at the time but guilty after.

—Mm.

He talked a lot about the way Floyd purred on my chest. I felt better just speaking to him. He got me to admit my big resentment for telly and film people. Pointed out that my whole demeanour changed when I spoke about them. My body tensed and my eyes glinted with something.

—Something?

—Mm mm. Something.

—Maybe you should cut yourself off from that world? He said.

But I wasn't ready for that advice and when I ranted about how I had great ideas that they just didn't have the talent to see he calmed me down.

—Okay, that's fine, let's move on. What about relaxation. Walking the dog – or dog – zz. Does that relax you?

I told him about the glen and Daddy Doom and all the pedigree dog people giving us a hard time. Paddy shook his head.

—Do you know what the common denominator is in all these stories?

—What?

—You!

I ranted about the nutters in the village. Getting myself further and further into angerworld. I knew I should've stopped but I couldn't. I just ranted. Paddy only spoke once I'd finished.

—Maybe you need a hobby, he said, —Do you like music?

I did like music and he suggested I take up an instrument. He was a musician so I asked him what was the most relaxing instrument. But he shrugged. So I asked him to suggest one.

—Trombone, he said.

—Fuckin trombone?

—See, there's that anger again, he said, —You suggest one, he said.

—Guitar.

—You must have tried the guitar before, he said, —Everybody's tried the guitar before.

I nodded and he said it was better to start afresh. With a new instrument. Open the curtains on a new day he said. And I understood.

—Violin, I said. I don't know where it came from.

—Violin? And he raised an eyebrow.

—I don't know what it is, I said, —I've got this feeling I could play a violin.

—It's quite emotionally expressive, he said and left a gap for me to say something into. I didn't say a thing.

—The violin symbolises all that's civilised in the world while still having a wee bit of the devil flung in. Perfect choice

Manny, I'd say. And, research shows involvement in The Arts has the effect of making you a more empathetic, well rounded human being.

—Good, I said.

—And how are you with the neds these days?

—Neds? Don't get me started on neds Paddy. I'll be back in jail again in jig time.

—Still make you… rage then?

—What do you think?

I told him about Duane and his bird and when he'd stopped laughing he said I should work on my ned-rage. We spoke a bit about AA and I left with a sense of direction, got home and gave Connie a hug.

—That's me cured I said. Paddy's fixed me. Says I've to get a violin.

—A violin?

—That's what Paddy said.

She shook her head and put the kettle on. When we'd had a coffee and I'd wrestled a bit with Bailey and Connor I suggested going down the glen.

—Test me out, I said, —See if Daddy Doom's there.

The glen was empty. Bailey chased Connor but could he catch him? This wee Collie turned like a dodgem. Even though Bailey was twice as fast Connor left him barking with frustration.

We were soon in the woods beside the burn. The water was high and fast. You learn every day. Connor was racing high speed in and out the trees and Bailey, having realised he'd never catch him, was hoping he'd pass close enough for a wee bite. He got nearer and nearer to torment Bailey. Then gruff! Bailey got him in the side and, trying to regain his balance, Connor skidded into the burn and swept downstream with his head bobbing and his body turning.

And the roar of the waterfall a hundred yards away.

Me and Connie sprinted along the edge and we were catching up, I think we'd have caught up, when Bailey jumped in, got Connor by the neck and held on as they flowed down-river. We thought we'd lose both of them but Bailey's big Lurcher legs found a foothold. He struggled to the edge with Connor yelping. I don't know if it was the water or the teeth. Bailey got solid ground and dragged Connor out. Connor came to us shivering. He's been wary of water ever since. Bailey plodded up knackered and we made a big fuss of him.

—Get him a medal! we said.

Connie found a wee bit of tin-foil and made a medal, bent it round Bailey's collar.

—Blongo the lifesaver! we said.

We were all cold and wet and happy.

On the way home Bailey needed a pee. He doesn't lift his leg to pee. He crouches down like a lady dog. He splashed all over his paws and seemed to be liking the warmth. I sang him a wee song to the tune of the old lady that swallowed a fly.

♫ I know a wee doggy
    That peed on his paws
    He peed on his paws
    To empty his baws
    Dibbidy daws.

Just couldn't get a last line. And I know it's not biologically sound but it's a good wee song and he likes it to this day. As I sang it for the second time Connie nudged me. Dalmatian Woman was behind me raising her disgusted snout. I waited till she was away, lifted Bailey's ear and sang in a whisper.

♫ I know a wee doggy
That peed on his paws
He peed on his paws
To empty his baws
Dibbidy daws.

Connor wanted some too so I had to sing it into his ear.
And in the distance Dalmatian Woman met up with Fat Labrador
Woman and Patterdale Woman. They were pointing and
discussing.

—You're crazy, said Connie.
—But not angry, I said.
As if I was cured.

Bailey

Some the times Bailey bad. Some the times when Bailey have the fleaky fiks Bailey put shengus on all the fings. Come out Bailey's boppums. On the walls an the Mummydaddy's got to clean it up. The Bailey sit on his cushy with one nye open. Mummydaddy make the noises. Eee! Yuk! One day Bailey fleaky fik and put the shengus all over the tluck. Mummy fell out with the Blong. Got me shengus all over jumpy tluck. Put the Blong innnit his room like bad doggy. Blongo not mean it.

The Gift

But I wasn't cured. Far from it. A few weeks after meeting Paddy I got an old violin for sixty quid and started terrorising the house with it. The first time I ran the bow along the strings Floyd leapt in the air and shot out of the room. As I practiced I noticed this background noise. Bailey was howling every time I played the B. His head was tilted up and he was howling like a wolf. Connor had his head buried under a cushion.

—Jesus Christ, said Connie and banished me to the back room.

All I could get out of this thing was a succession of squeaks and squeals. I came out the room angry with myself. Connie was laughing. Said it's not something you can do on your own. Even Mozart took lessons. I went for some valerian but it was finished.

Charlie was harassed. There was a sick gypsy with his daughter, three old ladies in a row collecting their monthly supply for all things poorly and two junkies for methadone. They looked like a couple. But whereas a normal couple might holds hands or cuddle; these two stood with their baseball caps touching like whispering ducks. I nodded at Charlie and he nodded back, flicking a look of disgust at the junkies.

Story was, he'd stood up for himself when the methadone programme was introduced. He was in all the papers and on the telly. There was no way he was giving junkies the very thing that was destroying Scotland. The only thing he'd like to give them was a kick in the backside and three months in jail. He wasn't allowing selfish scum into his shop. He didn't exert years of effort at university to let junkie wasters get their kicks for free. When were the law-abiding citizens going to be rewarded? The law should protect ordinary people – not neds and junkies. The papers loved him. They knew when the time came he'd have to give in or give up. He was more-news no matter what happened. There was even a petition. Ninety percent of the village signed it. They didn't want junkies in their chemist either. But the junkies won. They had rights. And the day Charlie poured that first plastic cup of green liquid his heart broke. Junkie bastards. He was an angry man I could identify with.

Just before my turn I noticed this junkie stuffing sunglasses in his jacket. If there was an award for bad shoplifting he would've won. Everybody in the queue was signalling with looks and coughs. It was only a matter of time before Charlie...

—Hey! said Charlie.

—What? said the junkie, with elongated nasal vowels.

—You know what.

I was expecting him to run. But he never. He stood and his bird stood beside him. Two skeletons in solidarity. Charlie came out from behind the counter.

—Give them back.

—What?

—The sunglasses.

—What sunglasses?

—I stood and watched you stuffing them into your jacket.

—You accusing me of shoplifting?

Charlie tugged the Berghaus out and five pairs clattered to the floor.

—What ye doing? said the junkie.

—Aw, what you aw about, said his bird. But so slowly I don't think she remembered the beginning by the end.

—You're embarrassing me in front of this whole shop, says the junkie.

I felt the rage explode inside Charlie, like a soft grenade. He grabbed them.

—Right.

—What ye doing? she said.

—Paws off – that's assault that so it is, he said.

—Out.

—Ye canny fling us out, he said, —We're on the mefadone programme.

—Aye, she joined in, —We're on the mefadone programme.

—You're getting no methadone. Out.

—We've got a legal right to that mefadone.

—Aye, she said, —We've got a legal right to get that mefadone.

—I'll get you done, said the junkie, poking his bony finger in Charlie's chest, —I'm phoning my social worker. Mon Shantelle.

Outside they called their social worker on an ultra expensive phone. Explained with flailing arms how the Chemist had embarrassed them. Accused them of shoplifting just cause they were junkies. Refused them their legal right to methadone. Their legal fuckin right. They kept giving Charlie, and us, the fingers and the your-throat's-getting-cut gesture. We all commiserated with Charlie. I mean what can you do? Everybody had a ned tale. The gypsy, loaded with adrenaline, said if he had his way he'd kill them all. They're worthless. A scourge on society. Take take take but give nothing. We're protecting them at the expense of everybody else. We pay for their protection.

—Aye, with more than just money, we pay, said an old woman with the gravity of a philosopher.

—Give me the rights they've got and a bloody Uzi and I'll sort them out, said Charlie.

He's *that* off it he said. An inch. And although another old woman didn't want to kill anybody, she wouldn't have minded a kick at them. Just a wee kick with her gardening boots on. On the rump. Not the head or anything. Just enough to give her satisfaction that something, at least something, had been done.

I kept my mouth shut. The last thing I should be doing is talking about violence. I got my valerian, wished Charlie well and went out. As I left a Smart-Car drew up with a hippy hippy shake, baggy eyed twenty-something, sandal smoking do-gooder. Her posh *hi there* got a hail of complaints. She calmed the junkies and marched into Charlie's: her chest out to its full legal might. The junkies slouched in behind to watch Charlie's dressing down; sniping from behind her back. A rush of bad desire came over me. To pound the junkies to a pulp. Maybe with a sledgehammer. And all the time I'd be shouting about rights. Who's rights? Sorry? What's that you're saying? You've got rights? Well not anymore ya selfish bastards. You've no rights now. Not a one. The world has changed. The pendulum has swung back.

Stop right there, I said to myself. *Violent fantasies.*

When I told Connie I could see her anger rising. Especially when I told her about the bead-chewing, rope-haired, social worker with the posh accent who took them back in for their rights and their *mefadone*.

—Methadone programme, Connie said, —It's a big word for going in and swallowing a plastic cup of green shite. Where do they get off calling that a programme?

I looked out the window. The junkies were thanking the

social worker. They even gave her a pair of sunglasses. She slipped them on, adjusted her mirror and purred off to save the world. Connie recognised the junkies.

—They got their wane took off them, she said, —Left it in three nights on its own. It was in the paper. Nearly died of dehydration.

My valerian was taking effect so I tried to feel compassion. But I couldn't. They were selfish manipulative bastards. Care for nobody but themselves. No that's wrong. Care for nothing except where the next hit is coming from. Don't care for themselves at all. I was all compassioned out for neds and junkies.

—Maybe we could have a slap-a-junkie week? Connie said, —Boot-a-ned?

I burst out laughing and we pretended to be political candidates with an anti-ned manifesto. The whole country, except for the *I do nice things so that you'll think I'm a nice person* do-gooders, would vote for us. It would've been full on funny if we didn't half believe it. Bailey and Connor joined in running round about us barking. I feel asleep that night a happy man with Floyd on my chest.

Next morning I spotted Daddy Doom in the same ambush. I put the dogs on their leashes. He stepped out of his bush.

—Half past five, he said.

—Good for you.

—Is that another dog you've got?

—More the *merrier,* I said, and I emphasised the word merrier. I let Connor off and he headed downhill. He pointed at Bailey.

—Is that nug *still* pulling on its leash?

The lead was thrumming with strain. Bailey had his neck twisted and all his paws dug in trying to go forwards.

—No, I said.

—Whit!?

—He's not pulling on his leash.

Blue rage flashed across his eyes.

—Whit's that then?

He tip-tapped the taut lead with his stick.

—Oh that. Aw – I see what you mean now. No – that's not him pulling – that's me actually pushing. Watch, I said and keeping the lead tight I leaned forwards letting Bailey drag me a few steps.

—See. I'm knackered. I've been pushing him all the way from the house. In fact...

As he raged and folded his lips over each other I let Bailey off and he ran down past Connor into the water with his legs splayed and his mouth open waiting for sticks.

—He wants me to throw a stick, I said.

—Oh – he's got a talking nug noo, he said and marched away, —A talking nug I've heard it all noo. Aye. I have that. The man's got a talking nug.

Although he'd made me a bit angry with his talking nug remark I felt like it had been some sort of victory. I went up the road and told Connie. But she could see though my smile.

—You're still letting him get to you, she said.

Bailey

Me flakken the Daddy he comes in flom the alkies. Flakken me flakken me shouting he. The Daddy go on the cou an me go oof oof an flakken him. Big long paws on he chest an lickty lick his fay an bite his noe with teethy teethy no no. Nages Blongo goes like that for and the Connoroo gets toy an give toy to the Daddy. An the Daddy says to Connor good tacked on at the end doggy. An I flakken. No let go.

Whole lot of nutters

But it wasn't just Daddy Doom. A whole host of nutters frequented that glen and none of them liked Bailey. That dislike bled onto Connor so that individuals went out their way to give us grief.

Patterdale Woman's instamatic smile took me in for the first couple of months but one day I seen it flick off when she looked at Bailey and when I turned she flicked it back on.

Scary.

One day here she was wearing a cream suit. It wasn't a Sunday. It was a wet Tuesday afternoon. Bailey bulleted towards her and Connor followed. By the time I arrived she had paw marks smeared down her trousers. Looked like a dog had been hanging on and slipped off.

Bailey looked up for claps but her smile fell off and hit him on the head. He took two steps back. That's when Colin skidded to a mud-sloshing stop rattling a line of dirt across her shins.

—Are you okay? I said.

—Do I bloody look okay?

—Apart from the mud you mean? I said appealing to her sense of humour.

Her smile tried to come on but it had no chance. Serious lip failure. She grunted and pointed at Bailey.

—If you ask me. That dog needs a good kicking.

—Nobody asking you but are they?

She looked as if she was going to spit. Bailey got behind me.

— I'm telling you then. If he was my dog I'd give him a good kicking.

—Aye and if you did I'd kick *you* round the place.

— You wouldn't have a legal leg to stand on, she said, raising her head and letting her chin fall with a sarcastic gasp, — That would be assault.

—I know it would be assault ya nutter. Did you think I didn't know that? Ya patronising snob. I know what assault is.

She snorted, gave her little dogs a tug and dragged them towards the big houses muttering posh obscenities.

There were other less annoying people but time helps them grind you down too. Like Five Collie Woman, forever wrapped in the leads of her Collies and although she was stressed and angry she never took it out on us. Or anybody else. Nor did she speak. She'd found her niche between anger and communication. Maybe Five Collie Woman manufactured her stress and fankle so she could walk through the glen alone. And that's partly what was wrong – we'd upset the equilibrium and couldn't find a niche. The glen was all niched out.

Or take The Dog Trainer who gave out tips on how to hold a dog's leash etc.

—No, no, no, don't hold the lead like that, you have to do this, do that.

Her dog wouldn't sit if you whacked it on the head with a shovel. But that didn't matter. I stopped being angry when I realised she wasn't right, the woman. She had that shell-like look people on heavy medication have. Like there's nobody in there. No, that's wrong – like there's somebody in there but they're cowering in a box in the cupboard under the stairs.

Felt sorry for Fat Labrador Woman and her divorce. She

was beyond her sell by date and a constant note of panic hummed in her voice. A kind of high pitched plea for help. She was done for and knew it. She wasn't fat but her big brown Labrador was. She was on the desperate for a man and gave me the chat before she met Connie. She talked to salve her grief and it was hard to get away from her. But I suppose she'd eventually get into the hate groove.

One day, out with Connie, Bailey ran away. At that time we thought it was Catchy Squirrelers. But now we can see it must've been fits. Connie and Connor couldn't find him. If she'd let Connor off he'd have found Bailey. But we were naïve then. We didn't know how smart dogs were.

Connie came home crying. We both searched. We searched the glen. We searched across the main road to the beach. We checked with the vet but no reports of an injured dog. We wandered on.

Searching.

The third time we passed the vet gave us an address.

I had this unexpected lump in my throat when I saw him in a garden. It was a nice couple in the rich part of the village on a month's holiday. They were making a big fuss over Bailey and when he seen us he burst free. We smiled and that whole family smiled; the man, the mother, the two girls and the boy. Bailey had bolted into their garden and crashed into the fence. When they got to him they thought he was dazed cause he walked in circles for a few minutes. But his first straight line was into their kitchen ripping open boxes.

—Funny doggy, said the three year old lassie.

We thanked them and if that moment was a microcosm of life in that village I would never have left. But as we turned, there she was in the garden across the cul-de-sac; Patterdale Woman. She got a glare in before her smile blinked on.

The family said hello and platitudes crossed through us. As we walked up the street I could feel Patterdale wishing us all bad things.

—I hate this place Connie, I said.

—Me too, she said, —Me too. And she squeezed my hand.

It was a few weeks later when we realised what had happened. Patterdale had a pal. Dalmatian Woman. She was so full of anger even I noticed it. Her anger was against men firstly, women with men secondly and then the rest of the happy world in general, thirdly. When we passed she never spoke. She'd give her Dalmatian a heavy tug and heave it away. Our early *hellos* were met with grunts. We could sense her coming even when leaves were thick on the trees.

Problem was, Bailey and the Dalmatian liked each other and sometimes it would find us. First, you'd hear her in the distance shouting,

—Spot!

Yes – that really was its name.

—Spot!

It wasn't the name that echoed, it was the rage. And when she seen Spot with us she'd scream with her fist tightening round the leash. When Spot came back she'd give him a trouncing. You'd hear him yelping all the way back to the big houses.

So, me and Connie were down the glen this day and up comes Spot. We said hello and let Bailey off. Connor played catchy with us cause he's not a dog person. Bailey and Spot ran circles in the field. We seen her across the other side. I knew she had a dog whistle cause she was standing to attention then relaxing, standing to attention then relaxing. And as she did Connor stopped and looked up and there was a blip in the perfect rhythm of these two running dogs. Eventually Spot lolloped towards her. And so did Bailey. We shouted across the field but Bailey couldn't hear us. Off Dalmatian Woman went blowing her whistle – with Spot and Bailey following.

It was a long way round and she was gone when we got there. With Bailey. We didn't know where she lived exactly. That's when I first came up with the idea of sending Connor. I got down and looked into his eyes.

—Find Bailey, I said.

He was gone for a while.

—Great we've lost him now an all, said Connie.

But Connor came back, stopped ten feet away and bounced about till we moved towards him. He ran away again. Disappeared. Came back till we knew what he meant.

It was the same cul-de sac but drained of friendliness. The nice family's windows were like bereavement. Bailey was tied to the lamp post crying. And he had a strange look that we couldn't fathom. But we know now. It's how he looks after a fit. Post-ictal.

It took ages to untie the knots. Two figures moved in Patterdale's window. Her and Dalmatian Woman.

—Did youse tie him to that lamppost! Connie shouted.

—Connie leave it, I said.

—Get out here now! Connie said.

It was exactly when I noticed two gashes on Bailey's head that Connie noticed the stick. Connie made for the door. It was locked.

—Open this door.

Connie wasn't shouting now. She was quiet. The quiet that comes with focus. I really believe if that door was open them two women would be dead.

The knot sprang open.

—Connie! I said and that's when a cop car drew up. It was Super Cop and a younger guy.

—Aye, said Super Cop, —It's you. Trouble from Glasgow. The Celtic man.

—They tried to kill my dog, said Connie.

—That's funny, he said, —I just had a call telling me the dog attacked them.

Patterdale and Dalmatian were out now. Connie didn't know I had a hold of her wrist. Her force jarred my shoulder when she went for them.

—I've a report this dog attacked…?

Dalmatian Woman stepped forward helped by a push from Patterdale.

—Me. It attacked me, she said and gave us a childish grin.

—Get the dog, said Super Cop to his pal.

—No, hold on! said Connie, standing in their way, —Where's the marks?

—What marks? said Patterdale on Dalmatian's behalf.

—Did he bite you? Connie asked.

A mumble.

—Did he bite you?

—Not bite exactly, said Dalmatian.

Patterdale couldn't hold it in. She burst out with this, —It needs a good hiding that dog. A bloody good hiding and she swung a kick at Bailey.

The young cop stepped in and moved the women into the garden. He asked about bite marks and when they didn't have any he took Super Cop aside. The two women stared and we stared back. How human beings could ever get to this I don't know. But it was all hate. Everybody and every inch. All I wanted was left alone. Peace.

The cops let us go with a warning. Super Cop went into Patterdale's house to take statements. As we left I nodded a thanks to the young cop.

—I'm leaving this place, I said, —Soon as I get the money.

—Me too, said Connie and we kissed making a pact of it. Then I got an idea.

—I've got a great idea Connie, I said.

—Kill them all?

—No – write a script about all these nutters.

But she'd heard it all before. About writing scripts. She was up to here with my ideas about scripts. But I thought it was great. To show Scotland in its true light. Filled with bitter envy and snivelling spiritual midgets.

I wrote it in three days and it was a cracker. I called it Daddy Doom. Connie read it and said it was good. That was a first for her. I made ten copies and sent them off to producers. I never expected replies really.

Connor and Bailey

We hate the vlin. Me an the Blongo. Vlin go in Blongo's ears make him howl.

Hoooooooooooooooooooooooooooooooooooooooowll.

Colin stuffy head under cushy on cou. Daddy killit the vlin cause it scream and scream and the Mummy is in the baf. When Mummy come out of baf Daddy stop vlin.

First Violin Lesson

My first violin lesson showed me just how hard this was going to be. It was all about holding the bow and the instrument. Instrument, that's what she calls it, my teacher. She showed me the basic finger pattern and I spent that whole week practicing. A B C# D. A B C# D.

Every other living being in the hou spent that week hiding. But after two months I was playing *Wild Mountain Thyme* badly and they began to tolerate me.

Me and Connie had started looking at the property pages. If we could get the money to leave this god-forsaken place we would. Find somewhere with no people. In the meantime we kept to the paths less travelled keeping a lookout for Dalmatian Woman and her secret silent whistle. But we didn't see her for a long time and when we did she'd veer off. We managed to evade all the nutters till one day when I was counting the money I'd make from my Daddy Doom scripts there he was.

—It was raining at seex o clock.

—Hope you didn't get wet, I said.

He mined that for insults then came back.

—Have you no got much work on then?

—Eh?

—You said you were self employed. You can't be getting much work I was saying to the wife, cause you're doon here at half nine every day when you should be grafting.

—I work in the house.

—In the hoose! he said in his high pitch, —You canny get a lot of work done in the hoose.

—I do alright, I said and shook him off when Five Collie Woman appeared.

—Morning, she screamed.

As I sneaked away I heard him saying to her, —See that fellah there...

And it wasn't going to be anything nice. But it was all good material for my project so I noted it down.

One morning Daddy Doom asked just what it was I done in the hoose.

—I'm a writer, I said.

—A writer! he said, and just what is it that you write in that pokey wee flat of yours?

—I write for television! I said, and I'd have been as well doing a boom boom at the end.

It stopped him in his tracks. He turned on the path and gave his nug a tug

—Television? he said, and he took a long time saying it.

—Aye, I said, —Television! And gave him a big ego smirk.

—That shite!!!

I tried to make it look like it was nothing. But he'd rocked me and he knew it.

—There's a lot of people watch that shite, I said.

—Aye and there's a lot of people in the loony bin.

Sensing victory he walked away.

—Television he writes. Oh my. Is that what kind of writer he is. Writing shite like that. Television tee hee. Wouldn't watch it if you paid me.

I was so angry I dragged poor Bailey home and swore to Connie I'd kill the old cunt.

—You must admit, she said, —Telly is shite, you're forever saying it yourself.

—What! I said.

Summer was coming in and I woke up one morning at half past ten. I got a coffee and took Bailey down the glen. It was all women in flowery dresses and people going for summer strolls. Then I seen him coming up the path with his wife. I'd never seen her before but she had the same run down air their nug had; wearing an old lady dress and old lady hair but get this – a pair of brand new white spongy Reeboks stuck to her feet.

He seen me and the look on his face was glee. He pushed his arms out to put the brakes on the world and bellowed.

—Whit kind of time's this to be walking your nug?

I drew my eyebrows together and he closed in. This time swinging his arms from side to side, shouting even louder.

—Whit kind of time's this to be walking your nug! It's nearly eleevin o clock man!!

He tapped his watch with his finger nail. The clicking annoyed me. The whole glen waited for my answer balanced on that long crooked nail. I pretended not to understand his question then:

—Aw. Right, I said, —I see what you mean. No – this is the second time I've walked the dog the day.

—Whit?

—I was down here at six o clock this morning. Never seen you.

—I... I was here at seex, he spat.

—No you weren't.

—I... I was.

—Aye!!! I said like he was a lying bastard. The crowd grinned at him and he stormed towards the post office.

So there I was gathering material for my new smash hit

black comedy starring Daddy Doom and a host of Glen psychos thinking this could be it! My turn for a breakthrough! My anger lifted with the prospect of success.

And there would be money. I fantasized to Connie about what kind of house we'd buy. But she'd heard it all before. So I told it to the dogs. They liked it. When I described the hou beside the sea with a big Gardinium Sardinium and a beach with nobody on it, they pointed their ears and wagged their tails.

I spread a map on the floor and we, the dogs and me, searched for perfect places to live. That's when I first noticed Galloway. A few small towns here and there and a massive expanse of land with

Nothing.

No

Thing.

Hills, moors and forests. Lochs. Cliffs. Sandy beaches. Islands. River estuaries.

But

No

People.

And under two hours drive from Carlisle where I could catch a fast train to London for my Daddy Doom meetings when somebody signed it up.

—There's bound to be a hou there for Mummydaddy baileyconnorfluffy, I said.

They sat with their paws straight out looking at the map. When they realised they couldn't eat it they got on the couch, let out a wee gowler each and slept. Floyd padded the map like Giant Cat From Planet Zog and sat on Galloway Forest Park. It looked remote. Connie came in and asked what I was up to. I told her we could be doing with a day away in the countryside. Chill out.

—There's a big forest park under Fluffy's arse, I said.

I moved Fluffy. When I lifted him he felt light but I never thought nothing of it at the time. Connie thought it was a good idea to get away from that village.

Two days later we went down to Galloway. Once we broke out of Ayrshire it was single track roads. On and on they went, through some white villages with scattered houses. It looked more like Ireland. We came onto a high moor with the sea shining away in the distance. That road wound down to another valley. It was then we felt we were in another place. We passed a Dumfries and Galloway sign. I remember being surprised that somebody, somebody and a van, had come all the way into this wilderness with that sign.

We'd not seen another car. Nor person. That's why we were surprised when we passed a few houses in quick succession coming into a village. Glentrool. We took a left there onto another single track.

—Keep going, see where it goes, Connie said.

It came to a dead end seven miles along Loch Trool with high mountains each side. I couldn't get my head round the Highland scenery. Except it wasn't Highland scenery. These mountains were different. A rusty yellow. More rounded than sharp. Like the hills of Donegal. When we turned off the engine there was silence.

Silence.

Absolute.

Just us opening the doors. The dogs moved in circles in the heather. Connor found a worn wooden signpost to piss on. It pointed up a burn. To The Summit Of The Merrick, it said.

—Fancy it? said Connie.

The first part was boulders and puddles of black glaur, right up the side of the burn. But just as I was getting fed up the path changed to soft peat and meandered towards a forest. Now and then; the summit through clouds. The dogs were in and out the burn; all teeth and tongues. It was the first Connor had been in the water since the stream washed him away. As I watched the sun came full out and I had to go down for a drink myself. I laid on my belly and sucked in clear water. That's when I felt a rush of something. I know what it is now; serenity. But then it felt like drugs. It must've showed on my face cause when I came back Connie asked what was up.

—Nothing.

She squinted and smiled before walking away. That water was so refreshing I stared laughing and didn't stop till we came to a forest. We took turns at impersonating Daddy Doom and other assorted Glen nutters. The dogs were our audience.

—Is that nug still pulling on its leash?

—I'd give that dog a good hiding.

—You don't tell a dog to sit like that you tell a dog to sit like this – and – sit.

In the forest we came to a wee bothy. Like a cottage left to rot. It intrigued me somebody had lived up here. A half-hour's walk up a mountain. Two from the nearest village. That sort of solitude appealed to me but Connie wanted to know where I would get a loaf.

That shut me up.

At the top we huddled in the cairn listening to the wind shearing over our heads. Holding onto each other like castaways and the dogs pressing tight. As we stood to go back down it buffeted our clothes and the dogs' hair was perpendicular. It was wild.

We stopped at the bothy and Connie opened two tins of dog food. Popped them onto flat rocks. Connor scoffed his like the sheep were coming in but Bailey only ate half. I nudged

Connie cause he was picking up twigs and piling them around his food like a wigwam. And he was on automatic. He went back into the forest and we could hear him cracking about. Out he came dragging a log. Sat this log across the pile of twigs. Looked at us and snarled.

—Bailey, Connie said.

He sat sniffing at his treasure. Connor was bellyflopped taking everything in at safe Collie distance. Connie stood up but Bailey snarled and she sat back down. Not out of fear; out of curiosity. His hair was up so that he looked heavier.

—He looks like a wolf, I said and left my mouth hanging open.

—I know, Connie whispered.

We stared at this wolf till he shook himself back to Bailey Blongo. Never looked at the food again. Connie and me agreed it was one of the most amazing things we'd seen.

When we got back to the car I realised we'd not looked at any houses. When I suggested it Connie knew that's why I'd got her down here. We were moving if we ever got the money. She'd live in a shoebox in Galloway, she said.

We got home refreshed and able to take the glen. For the first week anyway. I was still gathering material but the lack of response from telly companies was starting to get to me.

I cracked one morning through a combination of Patterdale Woman, Dog Trainer, Duane and Daddy Doom. I got them all on top form. I flung the leads on the floor and was just about to rant to Connie when the phone rang.

—Yes, I said – but my tone was *who the fuck is it*?

I got this Irish accent.

—Hi, I'm looking for a Manny Riley.

—I'm Manny Riley.

—This is Peter Donnelly. I'm a producer. BBC? he said, pitching his voice up into a question.

—Aye? I said.

—I'd like to talk to you about your Daddy Doom idea.

—Aye? I said.

—I think it's fantastic, he said.

—Thanks.

—Is there any possibility you could come to London any time soon?

—I'll have a look at my diary and get back to you, I said.

I spent a few minutes basking in the praise he was heaping on my writing, slipping in the odd famous name and big film or telly show he'd worked on.

—Are you buying a diary? Connie asked when I got off the phone.

I told Connie the guy loves it, absolutely loves it he said, it's sharp and original and it just leaps off the page, I really think we can get this made, he said, Connie, this is it. He's from the BB fuckin C. This our big break. She hugged me. But it was half hearted hug. Part of it was ice.

I called Peter's PA Pippa in the morning and made a meeting for the next week. I buzzed till then. Dreaming about money. Maybe I could write a book to go with it.

—We could be millionaires, I said to Connie.

—It's only a meeting, she said.

—It's not only a meeting. He's going to make it, he said.

—He thinks he can get it made, you said.

I didn't let Connie get me down.

—I'll have to get a mobile phone, I said to her.

The day of the meeting Connie walked the dogs. Just her luck, the rain was fizzing down and she was soaked. As she came out the trees who did she bump into but Daddy Doom. He looked at the dog, looked at Connie and bleated,

—Has he sent you oot cause it's raining hen?

She never flinched.

—No. He's got a meeting in London.

—A meeting, he said, —In Lon-don? You should get him to buy you an umbrella all that money he must be making! In Lon-don!

—I'll get him to buy you one too, she said, —You better get home before you catch your death of cold. It's not good for somebody your age.

She smiled and walked on. But he caught up and looked her right in the eye.

—Hey. He says to me he's doon here at seex some mornings with the nug? And he let a little blast through his teeth, — Seex in the morning!

—Aye. That's right, Connie said, —He gets ideas, for his writing you know, and can't rest till he's sorted them out. Gets right on my nerves, down the beach in the middle of the night, down here at six in the morning – he's always doing that.

—I've got a funeral to go to, he said and stormed away.

She phoned me on the train and I scribbled it all down

—Episode five that'll go into, I said.

—We'll see, she said.

Connor

A big buziz. Mawnlower cable. Teethy teethy chew chew.
Burizz it say to me shaky my head. Teefies go yak attack
attack. Mawnlower got wire. Bad wire. Colin go yelp yelp.
Mummydaddy come out pully cablers Collie fall they fink
dead. But Clunks no dead. Clunks live and shaky shake.
No more mawnlowers. Bitey bitey wires no no.

Connie's first fit

The BBC paid first class to London. I stood at the first class section while the hoards piled up for the other carriages. It was only me and a couple of well dressed business men. Even the guy on the ticket barrier raised an eyebrow. I savoured it for a bit before stepping on.

And the seats. It was like hurtling over the countryside in your own living room. Air conditioning and the pleasing hum of silence. And waiters forever coming up. More food sir? Everything all right sir? Water sir? Drink sir? I nearly forgot I was an alky.

London. It was people everywhere. And it was dirty. I mean bogging. I couldn't believe it. It wasn't what I expected. The whole place was in a hurry. Peter gave me instructions how to get to Mr Wu's. 56 Old Compton St, Soho. We were going to do lunch.

I expected a big bog-hopper type of Irishman, but he was the same height as me and skinny. Could do with a feed I was thinking, good job we're meeting in here. His head was shaved with one day's stubble and he wore a black polo neck. Looked like somebody from the control room of a spaceship.

—Manny? he said with a three hundred watt smile.

—Thought it was you, I said.

He shook my hand and checked me out like I wasn't what he expected either. He clicked his fingers.

—Two, he said and the waiter grabbed two menus guiding us to a seat Peter obviously didn't like.

—Not here, said Peter.

The waiter took us to what must've been a better table. He pulled our chairs out and I tried to look like chairs were pulled out for me every day.

—So? he said.

—So?

He tapped the menu.

There was no chicken cashew nuts. No Sweet and Sour Hong Kong style. He read like he knew the quintessence of Chinese food. He asked how was the journey and where did I live exactly and how did I get into writing scripts.

It was only after sending the main course back to be properly cooked he got onto Daddy Doom. He repeated everything he said on the phone. How original it was. Insightful. The sharpest dialogue he's read in years. But what he said at the end made my heart sink:

—Of course it does need some work.

—Work?

—Well, who can get things right first draft? he said and hit me a poofy wee punch on the shoulder.

—What bits do you not like?

—We'll come to that later, he said and started eating.

But that little exchange set up a camp-fire of anger in me. And although I couldn't give it a name I know it now: it was Peter manoeuvring himself into a position of power. He noticed my discomfort and started praising again remembering bits. Quoting.

—Oh is that nug... is it nug?

—Aye, nug.

—Is that nug still pulling on its lead?

134

He laughed a vacant laugh. I wasn't sure what I was eating or how I should eat it. But he sensed my mistrust and got onto money.

—A hundred K you should get; at least, once it's made.

—K?

—Thousand.

I nearly choked on whatever I was eating. I asked him how much I'd get up front. That was over forty K. Forty K. He said it like it was money you'd drop running for the bus. But I was thinking forty thousand fuckin pounds. And when would I get it? As soon as I signed the contracts. He advised me to get an agent and gave me a name. Zoe Metzger-Brooks. I was about to pump her number into my new mobile when it rang. Connie. Peter left the table to let me talk.

—Manny, Manny, there's something wrong with Bailey.

—We've to get forty grand.

—He's on the floor and he shaking all about.

—We've to get forty grand, right up front.

—Bailey's on the floor shaking about.

—Shaking about? What d'you mean?

—I don't know. He's shaking all about. And he's doing something funny with his jaw.

I could hear this noise in the background like a washing machine with a bad load. I could hear her shouting, —It's okay Bailey Mummy's here. Mummy's here.

—Have you phoned the vet?

—I can't phone the vet, I can't leave his side. I think he's dying, Manny, I think he's going to die. She screamed *Bailey* and the phone went dead.

When Peter came back he asked if everything was all right.

—Dog's sick, I said.

—Oh, are you still okay to stay until tomorrow?

—Yes, I said, —Of course. But I felt sick when I said it. As soon as I got away I called Connie but it was engaged. I thought she must be calling me. I was in the foyer of the Copthorne when she rang.

—I'm just calling to let you know how Bailey is. In case you're interested.

—Of course I'm interested.

—Aye, you sounded like it.

—You hung up on me.

—No wonder.

There was a long pause and I was about to ask if she was still there when she spoke.

—The vet said it was an epileptic fit.

—An epileptic fit?

—That's what he said.

—Can dogs have epileptic fits?

—That's what I said.

She told me the vet said these things can happen. Stress usually. They pick up stress dogs and it affects them. Connie thought it was the aggression in that village. The vet said chances of it happening again were very slim.

—Are you coming home? She asked.

—It's four o clock.

—Are you coming home?

—I've got to meet Zoe Metzger-Brooks in the morning.

—Who?

—The agent. To do the deal, Connie we've to get...

She hung up.

Next day I met Zoe Metzger-Brooks in an office in Wells Street. She knew Peter and listened as he introduced me. She was always on the lookout of course for new writers but she'd have to read my work first before making a decision.

She was sure I'd understand. I nodded. So we chatted about the project a while and she *mm mm'd* and *really'd* and nodded her head while reading emails bleeping in every few seconds. Peter droned on but she wasn't listening.

Then her eyes lit up at a word: Commissioning.

—We're commissioning this, said Peter.

—Commissioning? Has Jane okayed it?

—Yes, Jane absolutely loves it.

Suddenly Zoe Metzger-Brooks loves it too. Suddenly she's all smiles and buzzing through for contracts to be brought in. Explained to me that the forty K was for three one hour scripts and what they called the bible. Peter would keep me all right on what that bible was.

—So all I have to do is write three one hour scripts and this bible thing?

—Three first drafts, she said.

As I signed, she told me, in front of Peter, that she'd squeeze the first forty K out of the BBC within the next four weeks.

When I got home Connie wouldn't let Bailey out of her sight. She took me through what happened over and over. I said it would be a one off. Just like the vet said. Four weeks passed with Connie and me not believing the forty grand.

On the big morning I gave Bailey the letter to give to Connie, following him in case he ripped it. Connie let out this wee amazed squeak when she opened it.

—Forty grand!

We'd never seen money like that.

—Forty grand, she said again.

—God bless Daddy Doom, I said.

—And other assorted nutters, said Connie.

We were at the bank at half-nine and they lit up when the read that cheque. Took us into a wee room and tried to sell us mortgages and insurances. Me? I would've bought the lot but Connie's great with money and good at saying no. We came out wondering if it would actually clear.

And it did.

Clear.

We took Bailey Bounce and Colonel Connor to the beach elated. Connie believed in me at last. She kissed me and told me she was proud of me. I remember turning into the wind to hide the tears. She was proud of me. Connie. We got four burgers from the mobile café. One each. Made them sippy boppums in the sand.

—Sippy boppums for a burger!

Bailey tried to grab his.

—No, sippy boppums.

They must've looked like good dogs as they sat to attention. When we dropped them in they scoffed, sand an all. It was the last sunny week of that year and people were windsurfing and kite-surfing and riding the wave-tops on wee highly coloured kayaks. This was a different Scotland from the one we met in the cul-de-sac.

—That looks great, I said.

We watched them skidding along the water and coming in on the crests of big waves. A south westerly was blowing and you could taste the ocean. We walked the full length of the beach skimming stones for the dogs. It was a great day. The first time I felt financially secure. Connie was calculating the interest and telling me if we didn't spend and managed to get this much and that much from other jobs it wouldn't be long till we had enough to buy our dream house by the sea.

Later, we were sitting on the sand wondering how to celebrate with us two not drinking. There was a couple with kids and they'd cracked open a picnic. The woman was talking with a roll on roast beef close to her mouth. Bailey snuck up and gently took the roll scoffing it in two bites. I was ready for a fight but her husband laughed. So I laughed. And Connie laughed. We all laughed. Their kids clapping the dogs. Running away with Connor rounding them up. I have to say we walked away feeling good about people for the first time in ages.

—Ach, I said, the people here aren't that bad!

—I know, said Connie,

We spoke too soon.

As we walked along a white transit came through the dunes and seven people got out. Two men in their fifties and five neds. They were shouting about who was going in the sea first. But their shouting was nothing to do with the sea and everything to do with attention. The two older men went to the mobile café and the five sat on the beach passing a joint. People ignored them but they didn't ignore people.

—Hey you ya fat bastard.

—Haw baldy!

—You ya old hoor.

This young kite-surfing dude went past with a good looking bird. All blonde and gorgeous both of them were. These were two people with a life. Looked like graduates in the first years of a great career. Lost in each others company and to tell you the truth I don't think they even noticed the neds.

—Hey! I'd shag your bird!

The kite-surfer turned and stared at them.

—Aye, your bird! said the ned, jumping up.

The kite-surfer was for going ahead but his bird tugged him away. The neds gave them abuse as they left. By this time me and Connie were passing with the dogs. I noticed one of these neds was Limpy and he'd spotted us.

It was inevitable.

They stared, passing the joint ostentatiously. Limpy spat for my benefit. Then he said it. Right to Connie's face.

—Show's your minge.

Connie, thinking quick, grabbed him by the neck.

—What did you say!?

He squeaked *show's your minge* and they all laughed. And as they laughed the two older men appeared with bags of food and hot polystyrene cups.

—What's going on?

I told them and he swung, catching Limpy such a slap he fell backwards, thump, into the beach. The other four went silent. The man couldn't apologise enough. But he was from another age. The time before...

Before something happened to this country.

On the way up through the glen, expecting trouble but not getting any, Connie suggested we should use the money to move – now.

—But what can you get for forty grand?

We got on the internet and found out. There was two places in Scotland you could get cheap houses. Buckie.

—I used to drink that, I said and she laughed.

And Galloway.

Typical afternoon

Afternoons are Mummydaddy walks. Here's how yesterday's went;

Colin shifted soon as I saved my file, before I closed the programme, before I closed down the pc, before I pushed the chair back, before I switched out the light, before I said,

—Gardiniums Sardiniums?

I came down from the attic holding Bailey by the handool. When me and Bailey got down Connie was saying tousers n boots to Clunks.

—I got him by the handool Mummy.

—Did Daddy get you by the handool?

Bailey wagged his tail.

—Tousers n boots?

—Oof, said Bailey. And bump said Connor.

♫ Putting on the boots Daddy, Putting on the boots Daddy, Putting on the boots Daddy, the boots Daddy oh!

—Hurry up the Daddy, said Connie standing at the door.

No Spewy today. When we meet him he manages to twist the conversation round to Bailey's brain scan.

—You paid a thousand pounds for a scan. I can't believe that. For a dog.

We tell him we'd sell our house to cure Bailey but his last

word is always *a thousand pounds* and a shake of head. But we like him. The people are different here. They lack that Scottish bitterness.

—Street clear Daddy, says Connie, —No Spewy.

—Captain alert Mummy!

Captain was tottering up South Street.

—Collision course Daddy.

Two or three times a week we meet Captain. He always says he envies us our dogs. Tells us he had a dog in Barbados. That he's too old to get another dog and then asks if we're on holiday. His memory self destructs every twelve hours.

—I envy you your dogs.

Connie said, —Pardon? and he shouted even louder

—I envy you your dogs.

We stopped to let him clap the dogs.

—I had a dog in Barbados. I loved that dog, he says.

—Could you not get another one? goes Connie.

—At my age. I'm ninety!

He stares at me through his cataracts, then Connie.

—Are you on holiday?

—We live here.

—Live here? In this village?

He stared at us walking away, presumably with an itching deep in his brain that there's something he's overlooked. We keep them on the lead till we're well beyond the harbour house where Bailey's got a habit of making sculptures.

One day he caught me this guy. Or caught Bailey. I was thinking of ideas for movies when I heard a shout. Bailey was producing a leg shuddering sculpture on the guy's lawn. I should've apologised and scooped the poop. But it was making me angry him shouting and his wife folding her arms at me. Bailey finished with a big satisfied sigh and lolloped up to me happy.

—Did you see what your dog just did?

—What did he do?

—He just bloody… defecated… in my garden.

—Not my dog.

—Pardon?

—My dog's not left my side.

—He did, said the wife and refolded her arms.

—Must've been somebody else's dog.

—I stood there and watched him, he said.

—What are you some kind of weirdo?

—Pardon?

—You must be some kind of weirdo standing watching a dog having a shite.

And while he was unwrapping his rage I walked away. But the same as with Daddy Doom; making him angry had made me angry too.

When I got home that day Connie sent me back to apologise and clean it up. It was humiliating but strangely enough, once I'd done it I felt good. He even laughed this guy, said he thought the whole weirdo thing was funny. I promised I'd keep Bailey on a lead. When I got home I kissed Connie and told her she'd hit on something. It felt great to apologise.

—I thought they taught you that in AA.

—No they don't.

—Paddy told me that's what AA is all about.

I shrugged.

—You need to keep in touch with Paddy, she said.

When we passed harbour house yesterday Connie said, —What are you some kind of weirdo? and we laughed.

We let them off. Connor likes crashing through the trees and Bailey likes plodding beside us like an ancient dog. Connie adjusted Bailey's new camouflage collar.

—Blongford like his new collar?

He wagged his tail.

—Daddy, Bailey likes his new camel fladge collar.

Connor crashed out of the trees like a hundred tons. Spun on a pound coin and crashed back in. Poked his black and white head out.

—Catchy Deers the Collie, I say.

—Chasy Deers Daddy not Catchy Deers.

—That's right, I shout into the trees, —Chasy Deers.

We listened to Connor in the rhododendrons then walked on with Bailey. He walks like an old man away from the house and a puppy on the way home, towards food.

—Daddy where Bailey go to? said Connie.

I panicked cause he's got a habit of quietly disappearing.

—There the Bailey there Mummy ya daftie.

He was still between us.

—No – Daddy, where's Bailey? She said, —I can't see him for his camel fladge – so Daddy, where the Blongo?

—He's not there, I said, —Can't find him Mummy.

—That's cause he's camel fladged. He's disappeared.

—Maybe he's down at the end of that lead somewhere? I said.

Me and Connie travelled inch by inch the length of that lead and started patting Bailey's face and body like two blind people.

—He's here. He's here, she said.

—I can feel fur, and lips Mummy, I said.

—And two big sticky up nears Daddy.

—And teeffles, and ton gues.

—But I can't see him Daddy where is he?

—Kissy lips, I said.

Bailey gave my lips a bashing.

—He kissed me. He just kissed me! You try it Mummy.

—Kissy lips mommy.

— We've found him Daddy, she said, —We've found the camel fladged Blongo!

Connor bumped into our excitement and we gave the two of them barrow loads of attention. But two people, a man and a woman, were coming so we shut up.

—Afternoon, said the woman.

—Hi yi, we said with a slight overlap.

—Lovely day.

—Beautiful, said Connie.

—Nice dogs.

Boom, they were all over this woman cause *nice dogs* means claps.

—What kind are they?

—He's a Collie I said, —And he's a Melancholy.

There was a beat before woman laughed. The man smiled.

—Melancholy, oh he's lovely.

She gave Bailey a right good clapping. He always gets the most claps. That's his job – to make people feel sorry for him.

—Who's a lovely old doggy, said this woman, —Who's a poor old dog? Who's a poor old melancholy?

The man gave me a look that tells me he's embarrassed. I nod back as if I understand.

—He's only seven, says Connie.

—No.

—He is. He's looked like that since he was six months.

—No.

—Poor old dog, she said and we chatted about how beautiful it was here. Then all four of us scanned the sea. And in that silence they said their goodbyes.

Connie had brought a ball and they chased it about Cruggleton Bay till they were flopped. We sat on the benches and I did terment with Connor.

I shove a feather through the slats on the back of the bench. I pull it back as he bites it. He can't get his noe though and it drives him crazy. I stick it though one two three four slats and he bites one two three four gulps of thin air. His snout jamming at the eyes. That's when I tickle his nostrils.

—Terment! I shout. Terment.

He barks, I'm sure he's saying *give me that fuckin thing*. But on I go one two three four. Snap snap snap snap.

—Terment! Terment!

He jumps over the bench to get the feather. Soon as he's in the air I terment him from the other side. We repeat the exact mirror of terment. When he's fed up he digs his nails into my legs – usually drawing blood. I shout terment and throw the feather away. He's a savage animal; ripping this poor feather to shreds. When he's finished he sits puffing the scattered remains to a cloud round his paws.

—Mon Lurchy Collie home for cooky dinner, said Connie and we started the trek home. Bailey was up like a new dog. Biting me then Connie. There was shooting yesterday too. The dogs get edgy at the bangy bang.

—Mon Mummy'll tect ouse.

In they went to Connie as the sporadic cracks ripped through the trees. Connie soothing them.

—There was bangy guns and he did not like it. Oh bangy guns mon Mummy'll tect you. Mon get tected.

I had some forgotten biscuits in my pocket.

—Nurrawan? I said.

That got them cause they're not used to nurrawan in the afternoons.

—Be nice. On the boppums. Mummy they're not sipping on the boppums.

They sat and got their biscuit each. It took their minds off the shooting and I made up a new song as they chewed.

♫ Pardon me Daddy – is that the crunchy thing you chew chew.

On the way home Connie ranted about the shooters. And I agreed with every word.

—Big brave macho men with their guns, she said, —Killing them terrifying birds. Oh watch they don't get a hold of you they pheasants. Tear you to pieces, the most vicious things on the planet. You just need your four by four and shiny shotgun. Oh the danger of it all. The manliness. Have you seen them taking off? You could hit them five good slaps and a kick before they're higher than your shoulder. You could grab one and insult it to death. You could stick the head on them. Oh we're hunting for our food! ASDA you can get two chickens for the price of a shotgun cartridge. There's something wrong with men that need to kill.

Bang bang a shotgun went off in reply.

—Pricks, she said and never meant anything so much in her life.

She got into an argument once with a city bumpkin. Accused him of being a coward. He looked at me to do something about my wife. But I was as ready to punch him as Connie.

—It's a sport, he said.

—Why don't I chase you through trees with a shotgun, she said, —That would be a good sport.

—They're only animals

—No – we're only humans.

He didn't know what she meant by that.

—You like killing don't you?

—It's sport, to do with accuracy, skill.

—So if I gave you a gun that was really a camera that would do?

—What?

—A gun that takes photographs.

—You mad?

—You need all the skill and accuracy to get that photo. Creep through the trees, a pheasant struggles into the air at no miles an hour, click – you take a photo – you take ten photos – accuracy? You take a photo where your cross wires cross its eye. There's skill. You don't get more skilful than that.

The guy had nothing to say. He walked away.

I remembered that yesterday as me and Connie walked home. And I realised she was a Buddha.

My first fit

It was a wee fishing village right on the sea and if the devil lived there it didn't matter cause it was so beautiful. Set on a horseshoe bay a half a mile or more across. Forest right down to the sand. There was ten houses for sale all under thirty thousand. Every house we looked at we asked the dogs.

—Blongo likey hou?

—Roo roo like hou?

But they didn't seem that interested till we took them into the biggest wreck of all. They sniffed about in the dank derelict smell and seemed to like it. I looked out the back window.

—Connie, c'mere over here and see this.

We stood holding each other.

—Does that belong to this house?

—Must.

The garden ran a hundred feet to cherry trees at the bottom. We found the back door and went out. It was closed on all sides by old houses and trees. The sky was blue. Connor and Bailey chased each other round. They loved it. Connie kissed me.

—Buying it! she said like monopoly.

—Much is this one?

She shuffled through the papers and showed me the price.

—Twenty.

Four weeks later we moved in. Using the other twenty grand to start renovating. We lived in a dust filled room with a camping stove as we renovated and over the years we've spread out through the house. Two weeks after moving in we met Barnacles. I was walking along the shore and he came up with Springsteen, his dog.

—Ye on holiday.

—No. I live here.

—Y leeve here? Whaur do ye live?

—Yellow house on Cowgate.

—You've bought that oul thing?

—Doing it up.

—Is it a holiday home?

—No.

—So you're gan to leeve here, permanent like?

—Aye.

This guy passed.

—That's your neighbour said Barnacles. Kenny Crusty. He's a hippie.

Barnacles paused, said hi to this Kenny Crusty as he passed then said, —Fuckin nutter. Wan to be avoided. Knows everything about everything in a hippy sort of way.

He was right. Crusty Kenny was full of saving the planet by himself and mad esoteric ideas. He was special. If only you knew what he knew you'd be a better person.

I'd meet Barnacles on the beach taking the dogs their last walk. Got to know him and he got to know me and passed the information on to the village. Barnacles looks out to sea between his sentences. In Galloway there are long pauses between sentences. And it's nothing to pick up on the next line hours or even days later. For instance;

—Fuckin drainers it was, he says this night.

—Eh?

—Drainers. The four quare fullahs. They were stealing drainers. Cast iron's worth money these days.

He was talking about four guys hanging about the harbour three days before. Sometimes I'd be sitting on my favourite rock watching the stars and I'd hear *aye*! He'd be leaning over the wall above me. He could see me but I couldn't always see him. I was from the city and my eyes weren't used to it yet.

The work on the house was hard and it was October before I was able to look for an AA meeting. It was a Wednesday night in Kirkcudbright and even though they were all quite posh my thinking was we're all alkies. We're all in the same boat. I phoned Paddy and told him I'd finally found a meeting.

—About time an all, he said.

It was a good meeting and I was enjoying going there. I thought they liked me an all. But they didn't.

One day in late November, the afternoon was getting dull and the dogs still hadn't been out. I'd been sitting fretting at the lack of progress with Daddy Doom. I'd had one phone call from Peter saying the BBC were looking at it and would get back to me. It sat like lead inside my chest.

There was an easterly. Rain was coming in off the sea so the beach was out of bounds. The coastal paths would be mud. The Gardiniums Sardiniums would be sodden too. I decided to take them Runny Forest cause the paths are ash with only some mud where they've corroded. And the trees shelter that easterly.

It was the usual when we got to the car park. They pressed against the back hatch and before I let them out I shouted.

—Man giving away free biscuits; apply within.

I opened the hatch they flew up the path. Connor eventually snapping at Bailey to stop him going past. Lurchers are faster than most dogs but Collies have got to be first. It's a recipe for bitey-bite.

I soon overtook them cause they were snuffling about.

There wasn't a soul in that forest. It was mainly a summer forest and by winter it was empty. We had it all to our selves. It was birches and beeches and Caledonian pine. Oaks and all sorts. Bright yellow leaves shivered on some trees and a kaleidoscope covered the ground. And the mulch smell of early winter. It was a wonderland. It sent me into my rhythm sooner than usual. The dogs kept catching up then shooting off in the same direction, or different.

And we plodded on.

The endorphins kicked in and this mellow high came over me. My disappointment with film and telly lifted into the air waiting for me like a balloon.

The endorphins is when I start talking to the dogs.

—Runny forest. Who's a good boy, who's a tlever?

Or I make up a wee rhythmic song. That day it was this:

♫ Bailey Blongo Connoroo, running through the trees.
Bailey Blongo Connoroo, running through the trees.
Bailey Blongo Connoroo, running through the trees.
On a wet and windy morning.

—I know it's afternoon! I shouted at them as if they'd just remonstrated.

But maybe they had.

By the wooden gate Bailey had come into my side. He's good on short sprints but once you've done two miles he flags. And to conserve energy he gets beside me and stays there. Meanwhile Connoroo's off in the trees appearing sometimes a hundred yards ahead

—Yo Scout! I shout.

And sometimes a hundred yards to the side.

— Who's that in the trees? I shout as if he's gave me a fright.

By the Barking Spaniels I was done in. And so was Bailey. He didn't even look at them when they ran out. He kept up that steady four legged plod. They snarled and oofed and barked but made no impression. So they got cocky. Closer. Their teeth coming out for real. That's when Superroo crashed out the trees, dunted one with his big stony head and gave the other a wee chewing. They skittered back to their house in the middle of the forest where a line of smoke came to the top of the trees and bent into the wind.

—Roo roo to the rescue! I shouted.

Connor ran backwards taking the plaudits with a big open mouthed Collie smile.

—Roo roo to the rescue! I screamed.

The sky rained ice-cold bullets. We ran down the slope gathering speed. By the bottom we were in two inches of water. But halfway through the run we got our heads down and got on with it. I felt great running with a red line of sunlight going down in the west and my dogs at my side.

Then Bailey stopped ankle deep in a muddy puddle. I thought he was just knackered so I crouched down, put my arm round and tried to coax him.

—Mon the Blongo. Go fast with your big paws like this.

And I showed him how to make his big paws go. But they felt strangely rigid. Then I realised he couldn't hear me. He was looking dead ahead.

—Bailey, ye alright son?

He fell to the ground, slumped onto his side breathing heavy. His lips tightened over his teeth and his jaw opened. Wide it opened. And wider. So wide I thought it would crack apart.

—Oh fuck, oh fuck, Bailey! I said.

Connor knew something was wrong. I could smell the metal.

Bailey's front leg twitched and I thought he was coming round. But then it was a pure electrical storm. His whole body shuddered like a just caught fish. Flopping about that muddy puddle. I tried to hold him down but he was too powerful. His legs started going. Paddling. Like he was swimming, but fast. Swimming away from sharks or piranha. He was dying. I knew he was dying. All sorts went through my head. And fast. That he ate a mushroom and what the fuck did I bring him up here for? Cause I didn't want to get muddy, or wet or blown away with the wind on the shore. Selfish reasons. I lay down along his back and wrapped my arms round him. His legs were flailing and his head was coming back knocking me hard in the face but I held on.

—Daddy's here Bailey. The big Daddy's got you. You'll be all right. You'll be okay son.

He gnashed and he must've bit his tongue cause blood was arcing and spattering onto dead leaves. But I held on. I wanted to be the one to carry him into heaven.

Connor barked once. There they were, four people, looked like winter tourists, standing feet away. They were wearing them expensive but useless outdoor clothes. I'm lying in a puddle behind a vibrating dog with my t shirt spattered in muck and blood. They looked like they thought it was some local sexual perversion.

—Are you all right? the woman asked

—Do I look all right ya fuckin maniac.

—I only asked.

—Well only get to fuck and mind your own business.

—So – reee, she said and the rest of them tutted and muttered *well* and *really* in the same accent I'd heard in London.

I closed my eyes and held onto Bailey telling him it was all going to be all right. When I looked again they were gone.

154

Then, as sudden as it had started, the vibrating stopped and he struggled up. I crouched beside him wiping slabbers and blood from his chops. Connor padded over and sniffed. There was something he didn't like and he backed off two steps.

That's when Bailey ran.

I mean bolted. Shot off. Lightning he was. But in a straight line. Through bushes. Into trees. Over ditches. Into walls. His legs kept going on automatic. His brain was still in a kind of coma but his body was going at maximum. Post-Ictal they call it. In seconds he wasn't there. And I couldn't hear him. Just a hissing above the trees. The easterly. And night closing in.

—Connor, I said, in the most serious tone I'd ever used, —Find Bailey!

Whoosh. Off he went. Down that path like a... like a Collie. I followed through rain so heavy it was hard to see twenty feet. Connor came back to tell me to follow.

—Good boy good roo roo, I said and he went back into the rain.

The next time he came back he looked more certain. He turned and galloped off and I followed. When I came to a crossing they were there. These tourists.

—Did you see my dog? I said.

—What did it look like?

—The one I was...

—Oh he went that way, said this tall guy with grey hair.

—That way?

—Yes, they all agreed.

But Connor appeared on a different path.

—You sure. Big dog, hairy?

—That way, he said.

I started down that path and Connor raced ahead. There was a fleeting thought these bastards had sent me the wrong way. And I'm certain now, cause since then Connor's never been wrong. Not once.

Connor was trying to stop me. To turn me round. He wasn't running so far ahead as usual. He was going thirty yards, stopping, watching me a second then running at me, past me in the other direction, nudging my leg as he passed.

When I got home Connie was already getting into the other car to look for us. I blurted out what happened. But I was filled with anger. Anger from so deep inside I couldn't say where. She spoke into this anger.

—That's exactly what he did the day I phoned you, she said.

—No, this was horrific I said, you've not got a fuckin clue.

—That's exactly what he did the day I phoned you, she said.

I explained it all again. But she kept saying that's what he was like when she phoned me crying. And within that explanation was a dig. I'd fuckin brushed her off in London. When she was looking for comfort I was in a posh Soho restaurant with that big Irish poof of a producer.

—Take two cars, circle the forest, said Connie and she was off.

We met three time on the dark road. Our headlights making a pool of fear and unspoken blame on the tarmac. When we left for the third time I felt our marriage depended on finding Bailey. All I could see was the darkness beyond my headlights. It was useless. I parked up and walked.

What would I do if I was a dog? If I was a dog who had just recovered from a fit what would I do? I'd sniff. I'd smell. And what would I smell? Things? Yes but what things? Things strange and things familiar? And then what? Then what? Follow the things familiar? The wind was still coming in from the east. The east. The village. The smells of the village. I closed my eyes and sure enough there was smells. Smoke. Food? Cars.

The forest. Go back into the forest.

The forest was pitch black but I found that exact puddle. I closed my eyes and sniffed. I don't know why I sniffed cause I knew the direction of the village. I moved off. I was soon passing through the deepest parts of the forest.

—Bailey, I would say every now and then. But I did say it. I didn't shout. And I stood listening with my head tilted down. I'd maybe hear something and say his name again, —Bailey?

I burst unexpectedly onto the road. The road. Hadn't thought of the road. A car whizzed past. Shit! Fuck! What would I do? If I was a dog? A car would go past whiz. I'd get a fright. I'd be terrified in fact. I'd stay to the side. No. I'd get off that road. I crawled through the hedgerow and found myself in a field. Ran along the edge shouting Bailey's name into the immense space. The moon came with some light at last. Even though I'd been running for hours something kept me going. I felt like an animal. All my human frailties were overcome. Switched off. Transcended by a need to find Bailey. Find Bailey.

Find

Bailey

Then, there he was. An unmistakable shadow in the corner of this field. Soaked through, shivering and he didn't recognise me. His head was hanging down and it was clear that he'd lost his way.

—Blongo?

His head came up slowly. He turned and tried to make me out.

—Blongo, I said, —What you of doing here?

He crept up. Closer. Peered through the darkness. His tail started. Just a wee wagging. He sniffed and pushed his head against me. I knew then he was drained. It was as if we'd swapped energies.

—Mon son, it's alright, the Daddy's here. The Daddy was

looking all over the place for you. And the Mummy's looking for you too. Want to go the home for the cooky dinner?

I lifted him so that his head an paws were hanging over my shoulder and carried him. He was utterly exhausted and I'm sure he slept some of the way. When I got in the car I realised I'd been crying. All the way home he rested his head on my leg.

Connie was happy to see Bailey. But underneath was an icicle reserved for me.

That night the dogs slept with me and Connie, under the blankies. And in the morning when I woke expecting to see Connie a big hairy Lurcher was staring at me. I felt he'd been staring a while. Thinking about yesterday. About how I found him shivering and cold, and lonely in that moonlit field.

He kissed me.

Bailey

Bailey jealous the Mummydaddy. The Mummy on the cou and shout Bailey Bailey Bailey. The Bailey get on the urra cou wif the Daddy and sit my head on the Daddy's legers. Shovy mcgraws under my noe and stare at the Mummy. Jealousing her. I get the Daddy to clappy head and scratchy noe. Some the times but no a lot the times I jealous the Daddy but that's no good the Daddy laughs when I jealous him. Some the times I jealous the Mummydaddy same time. Mummy shout Bailey Bailey Bailey and I go to the Daddy and when the Daddy grabbers I slink and go on my cushy. Bailey stare at Mummydaddy. Jealousing.

Dog bites balls

Bailey's fits came periodically. Unpredictable. I slung a hammock at the bottom of the garden where I could lie and chill out. It became my haven. It was only once a week at first but soon I was down there daily. I perfected lying under the cherry trees not thinking about anything. Not Bailey's fits, not the renovations and not Daddy Doom. The BBC would send me piles of notes, I'd re-write the scripts and send them back. Then they'd send me more notes.

I was getting fed up with everything but down at the bottom of the garden I'd stare maybe at a twig. Or a cloud. Or follow a bird in its circumambulations around the cherry trees. I'd lose myself in something small. And here's the strange thing; after half an hour I'd be chilled. That's when Bailey came down. When I was chilled. He could detect it.

—Ham hok, I'd say and lift him in. He'd lie there with his noe in my neck and his legs hanging out. Or sometimes with his neck hanging out and ears trailing off the ground like a mad giraffe.

In that calm state I began to understand my personality. Unpredictability would turn to anxiety, anxiety would turn into fear, fear would turn into anger, anger would turn into aggression, aggression would turn into violence, violence would subside and I'd be left with guilt and remorse.

—Manny! Manny come quick! shouted Connie this day.
I heaved Bailey off the ham hok and ran up. She was just back
from the vet with Fluffy guy. Connie burst into tears.

—He's dying, she said, —He's got FIV. It's only a matter of
time.

I held her but I couldn't send out what she needed. She
sensed I wasn't sincere, pushed me away, and went into the
garden with Floyd. I smashed a few plates off the wall but
that didn't make things any better. I felt useless. She'd a lot of
memories tied up in that cat. Stuff that would never be easy
to let go. I tried to think of solutions through my anger.
Maybe there was something on the internet about FIV?

Three days later I found a web page recommending this
concoction of herbs and vitamins. When I got back from town
I mixed the stuff up and put it in a syringe. Floyd shook his
head and let out a noise that said he didn't like it. He looked
up at Connie and winced. He let out this horrible noise. It was
probably this concoction hitting his gut.

—Oh my wee boy, said Connie and held tight as she could.
I clapped him light on the head but my heart wasn't in it.
I wished I could go away and come back once he was gone.
But it could take months before he... I tried to comfort Connie
but my heart wasn't in that either. I was useless. Fuckin useless.
I went into the garden. There was an electricity of anger all
about me cause the dogs wouldn't come near. I couldn't cope
with any more sick animals. Instead of helping Connie I was
getting angry. As if it was her fault.

I retreated to my room and worked on Daddy Doom.
Except it wasn't called Daddy Doom any more. They didn't
like that title and were trying to come up with another one.
In fact they didn't seem to like anything. They'd asked me to
take some of the swearing out. Then they asked me to take

more of the swearing out. Then they asked me to take all of the swearing out.

Peter the Producer couldn't have picked a worse day to phone. I told him it was all over. They'd made so many changes to my original idea I didn't know what it was anymore. I wasn't even sure I would be able to write it. In fact I'm rapping it. He wanted to come and see me. He was sure he could sort this all out. They were on the verge of green lighting it, he said.

He arrived in Galloway three days later. Connie hadn't recovered from Floyd's shock news but she smiled and made a great meal. She was the perfect hostess but when he went to the toilet she said, —What a pure wanker.

Bailey was under the table waiting for scraps and Connie was keeping an eye on him. She was sure the fits were caused by eating the wrong things. Connor was looking strangely at Floyd.

At dinner Peter told us they'd come up with a new title.

—Like what? I said.

—The Gym.

—The Gym?

He nodded and raised his eyebrow like he was a genius.

—But it's not about a gym, I said.

—Ah. We've had a meeting. Jane and I. And the script editors.

—A gym – oh I can just see it now – I'm walking my dog through the aerobics and Kaiser spin bikes. Out comes Daddy Doom with his fuckin bunnit and dungarees. *Is that nug still pullin on its leash*? he says, all these young babes turn as the trainer pumps up the volume and shouts, Last sprint Guys!? Is everybody up for it?

—We think it would be excellent to set this in a gym.

—It's set in a glen. With a bunch of old crocks.

I sighed and he told me about the extra twenty K they'd

give me to rework the whole thing into a gym. Make Daddy Doom the cleaner who annoys people.

—What about the dogs?

He leaned back in his chair and sighed.

—Can't do dogs I'm afraid. Directors would shit a brick.

—Directors? What the fuck've they got to do with it? Know what Peter – fuck it! I'm jacking it!

He played his trump card.

—We've decided this would be our choice this year for the TTVW.

I couldn't speak. The TTVW was the award for the best new writer to television that year. Winners went on to great things.

—I knew that would cheer you up, he said, —I think you've got the potential to win. Especially once it's moved to the gym. People love precinct dramas. And everybody's going to the gym these days. I'm a member myself. Three times a week. Never miss it. Personal trainer the lot.

He shook my hand and told me not to worry. The last thing they wanted to do was interfere with my artistic integrity.

That's when Bailey bit his balls.

Peter's face changed ever so slightly. Like a man who's just wet himself and is scared to stand up. His lips went tight together.

—What's up? Dog bite your balls? Connie said.

—Mm mm, Peter squeaked.

—He's always doing that, said Connie, turning away smiling, I'm sure I heard her cry *yes*!

—Right Bailey, let Peter's balls go, I said.

Bailey came out with a smile on his face. Peter the Producer had a late plane at Prestwick and was glad I was in agreement with the direction the project was taking. He'd report all that to Jane.

—Twenty grand, I said, when I closed the door.

—Let's order the heating, Connie said.

We listed one wood burner, twelve radiators and a hot water boiler. Floyd came up. Me and Connie exchanged glances, she picked him up and put him over her shoulder.

One weeks later I handed in the script re-set in a gym. Two weeks after that I got the nod I was short listed. I was fuckin short listed! I couldn't believe it. They loved it Peter said. There was a good chance I'd win. That was the buzz in London anyway. They were talking. My name was out there. I was a hot ticket. He'd read the opposition – it was shit. The ceremony would be in Bafta, Piccadilly. I said *yes* and *mm mm* as if I knew it. Like I was never out of Bafta, Piccadilly. Like I had tea and scones in Bafta, Piccadilly of a Tuesday afternoon.

Connie wasn't as excited as I thought she would be so I printed a list of past winners from the internet. Showed her all the telly shows they'd written. All the films they'd done.

—This could be it Connie, this could be fuckin it. Mega – bucks.

—If you win. And then maybe, she said.

—Oh put a dampener on it!

—I'm putting some reality on it.

—I've got a good chance – Peter said.

—Peter – every time you're in contact with that patronising poof you go up high as a kite and then crash down.

—But I'm one of the top four new writers in Britain now Connie!

She relented a bit but only cause of my excitement, asked me when it was. I told her two weeks, got down close beside her and described the great time me and her could have in London.

—We could be doing with a break, Connie, and if I win we can come back up with the future safe.

—The future is safe, Manny.

—I mean money and...

I stopped but it was on the end of my tongue. I had to say it before it fell off, —Fame.

—Fame, she said and let out a little hiss through her teeth. I backed down by saying I meant fame equals money. That nobody takes you seriously unless you're famous. If I won my name would be ringing in film companies all over the West End.

—Come on Connie, a break in London.

—What about them?

They were on the couch listening to every word.

—Take them with us, I said.

—To London?

—Get a hotel that takes dogs. We'd only leave them in a couple of hours.

—They don't allow you to leave dogs in.

—Don't tell them.

But she wasn't risking the dogs in a hotel on their own. Nor travelling all the way to London with them. Nor walking them in London. The dogs were

not

going

to

London.

I suggested to take somebody to stay in the hotel and watch them but that was shooting myself in the foot.

—So it's not about a break away for us then?

She had me. It was all about networking. About milking as much as I could from this prize. Meeting the right people. Who knows, Daddy D... The Gym, might only be the start of it.

There might be some big American film people on the lookout for new talent.

—It's my big chance Connie.

—What? To soak in the glory of all them *important* people.

—Fuck – what if I didn't go and I won it? I'd be throwing away the chance of a lifetime. It would be insane to pass off a chance like that, I said.

—You are insane, she said, —Why don't you take your Spielberg letter.

Ouch! That went through me. I sulked away in the room till she came in and explained she couldn't put Bailey under that sort of pressure. If it was Connor it would be okay. He's a Samurai.

And then there was Floyd.

We said nothing more but the next day I went to the vet and asked what the best kennels were in the area. She gave me a list of three. The first two were adequate but the third one, a few miles away towards Stranraer, was like the Hilton. Each cage had a padded floor. And a piece of grass to go on. That was cleaned by two girls who patrolled constantly. The food was top quality names. Pedigree Chum and bags of every doggy biscuit you could think of. Their sleeping quarters had heaters and blankies and toys and cushions. It was so good I wanted to move in myself.

When Connie asked me where I'd been I said, —Kennels.

There was a silence then she said, —Oh no way.

—You have to see this place Connie.

—Why? We'll never be using it.

As I described it she pressed her hands over her ears. I tried to tell the dogs but she took them out the room.

I left it a few days. But when something came on the telly I'd check the writer and if they were past recipients I'd let her know. I mean big movies. Big telly series. It slowly got to her. I'm not saying it changed her mind but the wheels started turning and one night she said,

—London Creatives – that was a TTVW winner?

—Aye.

—London Creatives?

—Aye – that's what I'm saying Connie. That show sells in every country in the world. The writer's a millionaire. A billionaire maybe.

I snuggled up. Tickled her till she laughed saying billionaire over and over. Told her I didn't want to be alone in London on what could be the biggest day of my life. A day that could propel us into another world. I wanted to share it with her.

—You could start a dog sanctuary with the money.

—Could I?

—Aye, that would be a good thing to do, I said.

—You'd run a dog sanctuary?

—Once we got the money we'd need something to do with it, I said.

When we went to bed I could see this dog sanctuary glowing like a hologram inside Connie's head. I fell asleep and dreamed they called out this other writer's name but I walked onto the stage. Some famous actor handed me the trophy. But this other writer was standing on the stage like Oliver. The crowd stared booing and hissing but I held it to my chest and ran. But as I ran the whole Bafta building chased me down Piccadilly. Then the award started dissolving. I realised I was dreaming but still I held onto that award. I tried to bring it into reality. It fell away like sand and I woke with immense loss. When I flung my arm out Connie wasn't there.

It was the middle of the night and I could hear her talking to the dogs. I couldn't hear what it was exactly but it was low and melodious. I drifted in and out of sleep hearing her move from the kitchen to the living room. And when she woke me in the morning this is what she said, —What if Bailey takes a fit in the kennels?

—He won't. It's a million to one chance he'll take one precisely when we're away.

She needed more.

—And if he does they'll just send straight for the vet.

—So long as you promise on your life this will be the last time ever.

I grabbed her and hugged her.

—Promise Connie. Just this one time.

We put Floyd in the vet's quarantine for the two nights and headed to the kennels. They were the best kennels Connie'd ever seen. The owners were nice and the two girls loved dogs. They were uneasy, Bailey and Connor. Real uneasy. And when we went into the cage Connor belly flapped and dug his claws in. Me and one of the girls had to push him. Bailey followed Connie and she held onto his neck. When they seen Connie crying the girls said they'd leave us to it and stood outside.

—Mummy's going away for a wee two nights just. You be a good boy and don't take freaky fiks?

I had to heave Connor's head from the ground to kiss him.

—Daddy be back soon. You look after Bailey.

I kissed Bailey, —Be a good Lurchy, I said.

I put my hand on Connie's shoulder and leaving the cage, I walked past the girls and down the path. This sense of loss was bigger than in my dream. When Connie eventually came out she was crying. I tried to talk to her.

—Don't talk to me the now, she said, —Just leave me. I'll be all right.

To cap it all we both had the flu coming on strong. As we

drove away I knew I'd put a darkness over our relationship. And this darkness, it grew exponentially with the distance we travelled south.

Bailey

Me head it hangy down. Me look the sad cause get the more claps when look the sad. Colin get the clappy clappy no no off the peeps in the trees but the Blongo get all the clap and some the times if the Mummydaddy no see Blongo get a biscuit flom the peeps. The Daddy meet the peeps in the trees and they asking what kind of the dog is they. And he says he a Collie and he look at me and the Daddy say and he's a Melon Collie. And the peeps laugh and say Melon Collie a lot of the times and laughing the still. They give me big claps so me like the Melon Collie laughings. Me like Melons.

Award

On the M6 Connie had a bad feeling. I told her it was just this flu messing with her head.

—Makes you depressed, I said, —I'm the same.

The stress got so thick there was no point in trying to talk. It was even interfering with the radio. My shoulders were tightening and there were times I was for turning back.

We pulled into Westmoreland. For the first time we felt like a married couple. Silent over expensive coffee. Orphaned comments about the stone wall being nice and then nothing. Nothing for a long time. Other couples coming in chatting. Holding hands, laughing at the price of things. But Connie's head was sideways looking out onto the moors. There was supposed to be a lake but for the deep fog we couldn't see it. I half expected a werewolf.

Tearing down the motorway she turned the music down and fell asleep. I knew she was dreaming of the dogs. I tried to think about them too but all I could do was dream of fame. Of walking onto that stage the winner. I ran over the list of previous winners. They were writing their own shows. Raking the money in. Hundreds of thousands a year. Me and Connie, we'd be made for life.

She woke up in a traffic jam and asked where were we.

—Birmingham. Another hour, I said and she went back to sleep. Her face was puffed up. The next time she woke we were leaving the M25 for Boreham Wood. Peter booked us into a hotel there so we could leave the car and get the train into London.

After the Copthorne, this was a let down. It was more a guest house with this toilet crammed into the corner and shoddy workmanship everywhere. Connie wasn't impressed.

—Peter didn't spare any expense, she said. —That's what these people do, she said. —Big flashy hotel when they want your signature, dump once they've got it.

I went for two kebabs and a box of high powered Lemsips. We had a Lemsip each and tore into the kebabs and a two litre bottle of coke. And even though we had another Lemsip before bed we tossed and turned all night. A strange room, in a strange place, the flu and Connie's worry about the dogs. It felt like coming off drink.

I stared at the ceiling stains thinking it wasn't supposed to be like this. It was supposed to be me and Connie in a fancy restaurant in a posh hotel. Low lights and her radiant and proud. Proud of my achievements. Leaning across the table and saying it. Actually saying *I'm proud of you* and a wee kiss. Aye, a wee kiss. And back to bed to make the kind of love you make in that situation. For us to sleep the sleep of angels and wake singing. Me in the shower, her applying make up and I come out and she's a million dollars. What a babe, I'd say. Then off to collect my prize.

But I woke with a banging head and made for the Lemsips. Connie rolled about in bed. The room was more tatty in the light of morning. When I finished the Lemsip it was getting late so I woke her.

—We've got to be in Piccadilly for one, I said, —The awards are at two.

When she opened her eyes she was ill.

174

—I can't go, she said.

—What?

She said, —I can't go. I'm not even sure I can get out of bed.

I wanted to explode. Fuckin go mental. Ruining the biggest day of my life. But I held it in.

—I'll make you a Lemsip, I said.

My temperature was a hundred. I'm sure it was. Sweat pushing out. That horrible little room made me feel I had a horrible little life. When she'd finished the Lemsip I asked if she was okay.

—I don't know.

—You don't know? Look what time it is.

—I don't know.

—You either are or you aren't.

—Let me get out bed first, she said.

She got out. Slow. I was sure she was doing it to annoy me. In the shower for ages. I remembered back to our wedding day on Skye and wondered how it all came to this.

Time was ticking by.

—Connie it's nearly twelve o clock! I shouted.

But she never answered. I paced the room till she came out the shower. She sat at the mirror. Looked at herself.

—Maybe you should go yourself, she said.

—What? We come all the way down here and now you want me to go myself?

—Look at the state of me.

I told her she looked great, but she didn't and she knew it. Her eyes were puffed, her face was red and she was tired. She said she didn't want to go. She didn't like these people. She didn't like the person I became with these people. These people only bring stress and bad karma.

—Karma?

—Aye – karma!

—But if I win this, I said, —We're made for life.

—If you win it they'll give you a wee trophy.

—It'll change our lives, Connie!

—Who says we want our lives changed?

That stumped me. Then I said, — Connie, this could make me... famous.

As soon as I said it I knew it was the wrong word.

—Famous? she said.

—You know what I mean.

—Aye, she said, —I think I do.

—Fuck it! I said and got on my knees, —Connie, you're my wife, I love you, I want you to be there with me. If you loved me you'd come.

—And if you loved me you wouldn't have forced me to leave the dogs in they kennels.

By now I had the shakes. It really was like I was coming off the booze again. It was quarter past twelve.

—Fine. Fine, I said and finished getting dressed. The crisp white shirt grated on my skin. The tie strangled me. The suit was a straightjacket. As I turned to go I could feel sweat run down my ribcage.

—Will you be here when I get back?

—Maybe, she said, —But if I can find a way to get home I'm going home. There's something wrong with the dogs. I can feel it.

She stared at me.

—Connie what the fuck're you doing this to me for?

She must've seen the tears of frustration cause she sighed and asked if we could drive back to Scotland right after the ceremony.

—Aye! Aye! Right away. Straight back here and up the road, I said.

—Give me five minutes, she said.

176

I'd wanted to hang about and network. Meet a few honchos. But now I couldn't. At half twelve we walked towards the train station. I started getting paranoid. The dogs this and the dogs that. Connie ignoring me. Parrying every time I tried to raise the scenario of me winning. From some deep resentment it rose.

—You fuckin resent me being short listed don't you?

—What?

—You resent me being short listed for this prize.

—Leave me alone, I'm not well. And she sneezed. I even thought that was deliberate.

—You've got to ruin everything I do.

—I thought we'd sorted all this out?

—Well we haven't!

She walked on.

—What do you do it for Connie? Eh?

She walked faster. People were staring.

—All that shite about the dogs, you've done everything you could to make this trip a fuckin misery!

I knew I shouldn't be doing it. I knew I should've stopped. But I kept going. It was the same when I used to drink. I'd start smashing up some pub or house and a part of me would be saying stop. This is the wrong thing. This is the exact wrong thing. But I was possessed when I was drinking and I was possessed here. Connie started crying. But I still couldn't stop. I'd used up all the insults and all I could come up with was,

—You even gave me the fuckin flu.

She kept walking, leaving me in a cloud of rage. I shouted it and I shouted it loud.

—I'm fuckin talking to you ya ignorant bastard!

The whole street turned. I stood there for five minutes. I was so angry I was going to throw myself under a bus. Or jump through a plate glass window. Or do... something.

But I came down. I wasn't calm, but I came down. And as my rage subsided I started walking. And as I walked a ray of clarity came into me. Her dogs in the kennels. Her husband giving her abuse on the street. I started running.

I seen her long before she seen me. Trying to look like a commuter. But I could tell she was lost. I had guided her into some place where she couldn't see the way out. I thought of the Connie I saw in the casino. What the fuck was I doing all this for? She spotted me and I walked up. To this day I couldn't say what her look meant.

—We'll go in, I said, —See what happens and come straight back for the car, I said. —Be home by tonight.

She never said no so I bought two return tickets. When the train came it was so full we stood at the door, not talking.

At the next stop this guy got on with a pal. His aftershave hung about trying to kill us. Once the train was wheels and murmur and newspapers this guy started up. Loud like an intercom. Posh as they come he was. Not like Royalty. No – this accent was advertising its poshness. Like a red Ferrari or a fancy yacht that stays in the harbour. He was telling the other guy about Cynthia asking when they'd get married. He was quite handsome but a few weeks in some shitty job, some ill fitting clothes, a hefty dose of boredom and frustration and he'd not be nearly as handsome. Nor as blindly confident. He had long vowels.

—She was twittering on, practically begging me to tie the proverbial knot. Said her mother was pushing her. Cynthia darling, I said, you know perfectly well I still have to do Argentina – she knew that. It was on my bloody itinerary. When we met. It was Africa, Australia, United States, and I still had to do my year in South America.

To spark up a conversation with Connie I whispered that the

other guy must be either a work colleague or a neighbour who couldn't avoid him. Then he started telling the whole train about this recent trip to Scotland. What an interesting geological land that is, of course, if one can stay away from the locals. If it wasn't for the locals Scotland would be the most super place. And he laughed three staccato laughs through his nose.

I had a lot of rage looking for a victim. And Connie knew it. She took my hand and squeezed it. She whispered to imagine I was under the cherry trees. On the ham hok with Bailey. I concentrated.

A bird flew overhead.

A bird flew overhead.

A bird

flew

overhead

through the cherry trees.

I was in another place when I heard the carriage sigh. An announcement and it wasn't liked. Connie told me the train was experiencing mechanical problems. We'd to alight at the next station and board the following train. The next station had hundreds waiting. It was obvious they hadn't got the announcement as our train emptied into them.

People from our train.

People waiting for our train.

People turning up for the next train.

Me and Connie stayed at the edge of the platform. I remember the faces on the approaching train pushing back into the carriage. We stood at the door again. The train was so heavy it made slow progress but Connie was holding my hand and that felt good. When we drew into the next station I saw a woman's lips say aw fuckin hell and she walked away. The doors opened but too many people were in the doorway.

—Clear the passage please, he said, —Come on, clear the passage.

And they were obeying him. He guided people out from the carriage. But they were coming up against a glut next to me and Connie.

—Off the train, he said.

There was plenty of room so I wondered who he must be talking too.

—I said off the train – are you perhaps hard of hearing? Excuse me! Ex – cuse – me!

Everybody was looking at me and Connie.

—Ignore him, she said, —We're not blocking anybody.

—Perhaps they're deaf, or foreign, he said to the carriage and stood in front of me.

—Hello!? He said, and some people laughed.

At me.

Laughed

At

Me.

He flicked his right hand twice in front of my face.

—Off the train, he said.

Instant werewolf. I grabbed his neck.

—No! You get off the fuckin train!!!

Everybody leaned away. I squeezed and he choked. I pushed him and his back hit the silver handle. His neck was red. He was white and shaking. He tried to explain.

—There are people trying to get off, he whimpered as he re-adjusted his tie. But I had tunnel vision now.

— Keep off the moors, I said and I heard a snort of laughter from Connie.

— P... Pardon?

— Keep off the fuckin moors!

When he got back on the train was quiet. You'd have thought everybody loved rattling wheels. It was a while before they started talking. And he started talking.

About me.

Connie tried to stop me going over but I slipped from her grip.

—Did you go to Glasgow when you were in Scotland pal?

His arms came up crooked to his chest in case I took a swipe.

—Pardon?

—Have you ever been to Glasgow?

—No.

—Well don't cause you won't last ten fuckin minutes.

Connie looked at me and shook her head. I was relieved to see Farringdon drawing in. When we poured off chummy was watching me.

—Avoid him, Connie said.

We took a left and found ourselves in a narrow tunnel onto a quiet street. Thank God for that quiet street in a city of seven million.

—I'm just going to say this, said Connie, —You need to get help for your anger.

—I need help?

—That's all I'm saying. You're getting worse and I think it's your involvement with these telly people.

I tried to speak but she said she didn't want to argue about it.

—I've seen things in you I don't like, she said, —You're mentally ill, Manny.

—I'm mentally ill now?

—You're breaking up.

—I'm breaking up?

—Aye, and your breaking up's breaking us up.

—You want to break up? I'm going for this award and you tell me you want to break up?

—No. I don't want to break up, but if you keep this up who knows. I want peace, Manny! That's all. Fuckin peace.

I knew she was right. It went through me like radiation. And I was still buzzing when we seen a man up ahead.

—Guess who? said Connie giving me a nudge in the ribs.

His briefcase took a swing and off he went, fast but not actually running. We slowed. But it made no difference. He was glancing behind every few steps. It reminded me of *American Werewolf in London* again. And come to think of it, the American was quite a nice guy when he wasn't werewolfed up. But it was hard for him not to be a werewolf when everywhere he went he was an outsider. In the end they had to give him the silver bullet. And I sure wasn't going to let Connie give that to me.

Connor

Me Collie clunks dog likes to pee pee ploppy in the bushy. I goes in the bushy an pee pee poppies. Collie's got lot of the dignities. But the Lurchy he pee pee poppies right onit the pafta. Onit the pafta. Big ploppies and smells they do. Stinky. Not stink like metal boppums. And he pee pees not with the leg lifters he pee pees with the going down like a lady. And the Daddy he laugh and the Daddy he sing

Hey – hey dude pees like a lady! Song the Daddy play in the tluck an the man sing hey hey dude look like a lady. But I Pee Long carey carey no no. He I pee longs and ploppy on pafta and bouncer up to the Daddy goody goody yes yes. And the Daddy clappy him goody goody yes yes. And the Daddy look for the dog warden. Daddycallcunt.

TTVW

In Piccadilly the whole world was going somewhere. The flu and all that movement was making me dizzy. We got something in a burger joint that tasted like nothing. It was dry and meaningless.

These guys with suits and bow ties ushered us in and scored our names off. In the David Lean room the film industry swung wine glasses from their fingertips. I seen more black polo necks that day than the rest of my life. Me and Connie sat in a corner with orange juices. I suppose we must've looked like two people coming down after a heavy night. Now and then a couple would speculate who we were. You could see them wondering if we were important, then deciding we weren't.

The volume of chat rose till the place was one continuous shout. Everybody seemed to be growing taller. Even filled with Lemsips the churn of nausea came in waves. I was shivering. So was Connie. I felt a pang of guilt. Like it was my fault she was shivering. I felt paranoia I'd not felt since my drinking days. I wanted to get up and go.

That's when Peter found us. He had a Chinese girl with him.

—Manny! Here he is, he said, —I've been looking all over for you. He gave me a hug and introduced Pippa.

—So you're Pippa! I said.

She kissed me on each cheek.

—Hi Connie, Peter said, leaning in to kiss her.

—Don't, she said, leaning back, —Flu.

—Oh, stay well back, Peter said, making a Dracula cross with his fingers. We false-laughed at that then, in the following silence, scanned the crowd.

—You must be really excited, said Pippa.

—It's great, said Connie with no conviction and Pippa threw Peter a glance.

—Can I drag him away for a few minutes? Peter said.

Connie nodded and we slunk into the crowd leaving Connie with Pippa.

Peter said Zoe Metzger-Brooks couldn't make it but she'd sanctioned him to promote me on her behalf. He'd get a cut but that wouldn't affect me. Peter took me through I don't know how many introductions. The names should have impressed me but I was no good at names. It was films I remembered. Stories. I got the feeling Peter had been an up and coming producer and *discovering* me sent him up the rankings enough to have his calls returned. When we reached the windows my head was swimming. I wanted to jump down into London and get lost. Peter told me to wait there till he located some people I really *had* to meet. He'd bring the mountain to Mohammed.

As I watched them yakking I seen the people were shells. But not the shells you get with poverty. Not the veneer of personality that negotiates you to work and safely home.

No.

These shells were stainless steel. A façade of power. Armour plated. Impenetrable. Yes – they were all polite. Too polite. But there was a hint of dismissal in everything they said. I looked at all these beautiful people and thought what's the point in lavishing all that attention and money on

186

your body? Lip jobs, boob jobs, thigh jobs, bum lifts, face lifts, eye lifts.

It's never going to repay you, your body. Never. It's going to keep needing more jobs as it gets older. There's no permanent fix cause there's no permanent anything. And one day it's going to break down and die, your body. This whole hall will one day be empty. Disintegrate. Dust.

A bell rang. The place fell silent. Drinks an inch from lips.

—Would the TTVW award delegates please make their way to the Princess Anne Theatre.

There was a rush like church and people funnelled out. I waited where waiters collected unfinished drinks. There must've been three hundred people before Connie arrived. She looked ill.

—Manny, I'm really worried about Bailey, she said.

—Don't be daft.

We were in the hall by then and the place was hushed. I met the other candidates when we were guided to our seats. One had a shaved head, a black polo neck and a black leather jacket – I swear on that. There was a nervous woman about forty, dressed in purple and black. And an ordinary looking guy. None of them looked like the winner in my dream. I nodded as I made my way along the row.

There was a speech about how vital writers were to the industry, about how important it was to nurture new talent. Then they gave out a load of regional prizes. It was an hour before they got to the TTVW drama award. The big one. My heart was beating so hard I'm sure the guy behind could feel it in his knees. Shortlisted writers' work was individually praised before they announced the winner.

I had always imagined Connie would hold my hand. Squeezing tighter as we closed in on the announcement.

The others' partners had their arms round them. But me and Connie had drifted these last two days. I think I was wiping a tear.

—Manny Riley.

—What? I said it out loud.

The clapping was thunderous. The candidate next to me pushed me up and I walked bewildered onto the stage. The guy handed me a trophy. Manny Riley – Writer Of The Year it said. It was like a car radiator. He was talking but I couldn't hear. The lights were hot and I didn't feel right. The radiator was getting heavier. His palm guided me to the microphone.

—Manny Riley.

Ripple of applause. Then I was

Falling

First face I saw was Connie's.

—Manny, Manny, ye all right?

Space was clustered with floating heads. I don't know if their bodies were obliterated or they were wearing black. As Connie tottered me off the stage I got a thunderous clap. Some whoops and I'm sure I heard a *bravo*.

Peter said it would be better if I left early. He would set up meetings with the top head honchos all over London. As I left he slapped me on the back.

—This is it, he said and winked.

—It is, said Pippa to Connie.

Connie kept her arm round me along Piccadilly. I bought a bottle of Lucozade and some Solpadine and asked for a carrier bag. The trophy was making me sick.

We filled ourselves with Solpadine and drove north in silence. Waves of sickness washing over me. The trophy lay in its carrier bag on the back seat.

It was the look on the guy's face that sent Connie running

to the kennel. He followed saying he'd got the vet and everything was okay. He'd called our home number but it was a machine.

—Open the door, said Connie.

The guy tried to speak.

—Open the fuckin door.

Connor was curled in a corner but Bailey was pacing. He looked thinner. Connie got on her knees and held him.

—Oh Bailey, Bailey, she was saying.

But he didn't recognise us, her, or that place. He looked like a dog after massive trauma.

—He had some kind of fit, said the guy and Connie glared at me. Bailey's back end was matted with something.

—I'm sorry, the guy said, I'm really sorry, —We've never had anything like this before.

Normally Connie would have told him it wasn't his fault. Let the guy off the hook. But she put their leads on and left.

—He took some kind of fit, the guy told me, —We got the vet, he told me, —We did everything we could.

It was my fault. My ego was to blame but what good would it do explaining all that to this guy? I paid and left. Connie had put the seats down, put the dogs in and was leaning over holding Bailey. Soothing him.

—It's okay Mummy's back. Mummy's never going to leave you again. Can you hear me Bailey?

He was looking about as if he expected an attack. And there was another feeling in that car too.

Blame.

Halfway home Bailey started releasing all this stuff from his arse. Connie screamed and I pulled over. A lorry bleated its horn. I wanted to kill that lorry driver. It was red – coming out of Bailey's arse. It was blood!

—Oh no – Oh God, Connie said and climbed in.

The smell was awful. She held onto him.

—Well what are you doing? Get to the fuckin vet – quick!

I hammered it to Whithorn with Connie talking to Bailey like a dying dog. The vet was shut.

—Fuck fuck fuck, I said and kicked the car.

—What is the use in kicking the car, she screamed, —Do something.

I memorised the emergency number and ran to a garage.

—Can I use your phone?

—Well – we… don't usually…

—Can I use your fuckin phone – aye or no!

He took me away in the back of the workshop where this ancient black phone sat on an oily workbench. I got through to a machine.

—It's an emergency, I blabbered, —you have to come quick, I'm outside the vet's, my dog's dying, there's blood coming out his back passage.

When I hung up the guy was standing beside me. Looking.

—My dog's dying, I said and left.

Connie had the hatch open. She was covered in this stuff. Bailey was on his side panting. He didn't look like he had much time left.

—You and your fuckin award.

—I didn't know this would happen.

She went back to soothing Bailey. I don't know how long it was but when the vet arrived I opened her door before her car stopped moving.

—My dog's dying, I said.

She opened up and invited us in. I carried Bailey in and laid him on the table. Connie kept her palms on his head and spoke to him. If the vet thought this was strange she never let on.

When she started asking Connie questions I went out and sat with Connor.

An hour later Connie came out with Bailey walking. Her and the vet were chatting and smiling. Like they were old pals.

—See you later Eileen, she said, —Thanks.

—Bye Connie.

Connie got in and laid Bailey across her lap. Said nothing so I started the engine and drove toward home. Eventually she said, matter of fact,

—It's some kind of reaction to dried food. A digestive disorder. She thinks we've caught him in time. She's gave us her home number in case...

And she burst out crying.

Connor

Mummy finks urra peeps is crazy cause Mummy knows me and the Blongo can municate. But none of the tlever peeps finks that like science tests. So Mummy finks if we cant municate wif aminalies on our own planet, what chance have we got of municating with aliens from urra part of the universe? None chance that's how mucy. Municate municate no no.

Windsurfing

I was sidelined the next two months as Connie nursed Bailey back to health. She spoke to me in distant tones. Bailey's fits became more frequent, as if the kennels triggered something. He was having them weekly. One day running into two. Connie was never away from Eileen's but the medication wasn't working.

By then I'd been to London and met who knows how many producers and heads of Drama. By April none had got back to me. There was one I was sure would get back. Her office was like walking into an old romantic horse-drawn gypsy caravan. It was a shock coming from the Ikeaesque office landscape into hanging carpets and candlelight; stained glass windows and joss sticks. And there she was, long hair, a face that must have been beautiful before the wrinkles set in and who knows how many long flowing garments. Her arm was hanging out the slightly opened window. When she pulled it in she had a joint. She took a tug and offered it to me. I shook my head.

—So you won the TTVW, she said, —Congratulations. What have you got?

I ran a few ideas past her and she was truly interested. She offered me a line of coke and when I mentioned AA she got off the subject quick. I got the feeling she'd been there. When I came out of her caravan into Ikealand I felt we'd connected. But when Peter called her she couldn't remember me even being there.

—What about all the other ones Peter, I said, —Have none of them got back?

—I'll put in some calls.

By May they still hadn't returned my calls and Bailey's fits were two days a week. It was getting to me. Summer was coming in and we'd no plans. No holidays.

Connie said —Look around, we're on holiday, we've got a beach and mountains and countryside and all the things.

I couldn't argue but what I meant was get away from our lives for a bit. Everybody needs to get away from their lives. And when I had that thought a stone sank inside me. Cause I knew we weren't getting away from ours. Somewhere along the line Bailey became our life. He was the love of Connie's life and a big resentment in mine. I talked it over with Paddy and he said you've got to stick by your wife. He reminded me who it was that got the dog in the first place. Me and my fuckin impulse that's who.

—The vet's got puppies, he said. Bailey was my responsibility.

One day we were on the beach and the sky was turquoise. There was a strong wind coming in warm from the south. Big rollers crashing on top of each other.

It was only us on the whole beach and the temperature was over seventy. The sand hot to touch. Connie was in a bikini on a towel with sunglasses and I remembered Turkey. She was right, it could be anywhere. And it was good to be away from the phone. I was always bursting to call Peter about my big break. Somehow on the beach it didn't seem so important.

Bailey was on his side in the sand. Now and then he stretched and let out a womble womble. Connor was sneaking up on a flock of gulls. They were in the air a moment before I heard his bark. And he ran into that confetti of birds. I was watching that when somebody said hello. It was Eileen and her husband.

—How is he?

—Just the same, said Connie, lifting her sunglasses.

—Thought you were James Bond and his wife, I said to Noel. They were wearing wetsuits and they had a board each.

—Going surfing?

—Windsurfing.

I'd heard of it. Connie said to let Daisy onto the beach and we'd watch her while they were in the water. So down she came, Daisy. It was the first time I'd seen her close. A beautiful big Irish wolfhound. Movements the exact same as Bailey. She was a massive version of him. And they liked each other. They nuzzled and smelled and eventually lay down and slept face to face in the sand.

Eileen and Noel meanwhile pulled all sorts of apparatus off their roof rack. They clicked poles together, tugged at ropes and pulleys, unfurled big lime-green sails. I said to Connie it was lot of bother just to float about in the sea. But I soon changed my mind.

They stepped onto their boards. There was a crack as their sails curved out. They boofed through five or six breakers and were far out in the bay when they turned side-on to the southerly. That's when I changed my mind. One of them, Noel it turned out to be, leaned away from his board and he went

He went

He went

Faster.

Then he was flying along the surface like a skimmed stone.

—Fuck sakes Connie check this!

I'd stood up without realising it. Eileen was planing across the bay now. And you could hear the thrizz and boof of her board as it left the water and landed.

—That looks fuckin magic! I said.

They turned at the rocks where Connor had chased his gulls and off they went skimming towards the harbour. Noel was first to turn. He gathered speed and was coming towards us. He hit a wave and

Up

He went. In the air three, maybe four seconds before he boofed into the sea again and headed off towards the rocks. Eileen was next. Speed. Wave. Up in the air. But she came crashing down nose first. There was a big splash of silent white water. Eileen and her gear disappeared.

—Shit.

Me and Connie were worried. We looked at Noel. He had turned and was making his way back. But he went right past where we last seen her.

—Noel! I was shouting and Connie joined in but he wouldn't have heard. The dogs were up now and panicked.

That's when she appeared. Up out of the waves came her sail and then as she gathered speed, she came over the top of a crest. She waved down to us cause she must've known what we'd be thinking. And she jumped a wave.

They came in an hour later with big smiles and red faces. The dogs barking at their feet.

—That looks magic, I said.

—Would you like a go?

I got down to my shorts and they fitted me out with a buoyancy aid. I stepped onto Noel's board, he lifted the sail and told me to hold the boom. When he let go a tug of wind somersaulted me into the sea. I came up glugging salt water. Everybody was laughing.

—Easy isn't it? said Eileen.

She suggested we should take it up. But I asked the price of the gear and my face fell when she told us. Not to worry. They had some old gear in the shed. We made a date to learn next time the wind was in the west.

—The sea will be flat then. Flattish. Better to learn without waves.

That was a Wednesday and I felt good on the way to my AA meeting. When it was my turn to share I ranted about windsurfing. At the tea High Speed Mary asked if I had to swear so much. But I didn't remember swearing. I was only talking. Only being myself.

—Try to cut it down, she said, —We've been worried about your language since you came here, she said and tapped me on the arm twice.

By the time I got home I had built up a resentment. Who the fuck was she to tell me how I should talk?

A week later when Connie was out in the garden with a fitting Bailey I phoned Peter. Demanded to know why these people hadn't called back. Listed him all the previous winners and what they were doing now.

—Is it cause I'm Scottish? I said, —Do they not want Scottish drama?

—It's not that.

—Or do they want middle class work. Is that it?

—Let's not allow chips on our shoulders to come into play, he said, —Let's concentrate on getting The Gym made.

—But Peter...

—Can I call you back, he said and hung up.

I got his machine that day and the next three days. Bailey's round of fits had stopped by the time I got Pippa. She promised she'd get Peter to call.

—When?

—Soon.

—When's soon?

—Pardon?

—Is it in five minutes an hour a day a week a month or a year?

—He's had a meeting with the execs about The Gym.

That cheered me up. I told Connie Peter had a meet the execs. The Gym must be going ahead. You don't meet the execs for nothing. The door went. It was two people in wetsuits.

—It's a westerly, they said.

—I'm waiting on a phone call.

—The phone can wait, said Connie.

Eileen threw us two old wetsuits.

—No point splashing out on wetsuits and then not liking windsurfing, she said.

My mood lifted on the beach. The three dogs ran about catchy burdies until Bailey and Daisy found a place to lie in the sun. Connor watched as Noel named the parts. Board. Mast, click it together. Run the sail on. Check the battens in the sail. Click the sail on. Downhaul...

Hey – I won't bore you with the details. I'll just say it took us half a day to stand on the board with the sail up and go twenty feet. But that twenty feet was the best twenty feet I'd ever travelled. At one point I stubbed my toe and kicked the board in anger.

—That's right, said Connie, —Get angry, that'll help won't it Eileen.

—Yes. Anger helps a lot.

When they were teaching Connie I played with the dogs. Connor was a laugh. He watched me walk backwards into the sea, barking every time I sunk down a level. He was wary of water since he was washed away in the stream. But when the sea reached my mouth he charged in to save me. Diving through the waves. Jumped and held me with his claws. In a real situation he'd have drowned me. But it was funny. I showed Eileen, Connie and Noel, every time the water got to my mouth Connor came charging.

That was the day we invented Torpedo Rockets, me and Bailey. He came swimming in. He likes swimming. Up he came with his noe in the air and his ears flattened. The water licking at the tip of his ears. I could see his big paws trundle under the surface. I turned him away and, lifting his head, gave his arse a heavy push. He travelled through the water like a torpedo.

—Torpedo Rockets, I shouted and he swam back for more. This time I gave him a bigger push and shouting louder,

—Torpedo Rockets!

By the end of that me and Connie had taken a step towards each other again. We, all four of us, had a meal at ours and when Eileen and Noel left I realised we'd inadvertently made friends.

—That's cause of him, Connie said.

—Who?

—Bailey, he's gave us windsurfing and friends.

I couldn't argue.

I was still talking about windsurfing a couple of days later when Peter called. Said the Beeb had some notes on The Gym. Thought it could be more contemporary.

—Like how?

—If we go with the gym thing, he said, —And that's what the Beeb want, Daddy Doom doesn't quite fit. As a character.

—What?

—He's not contemporary enough for a gym. Can we make him a younger person? Jane and I think we should base him on a personal trainer.

—Who the fuck is Jane? A nutter?

— She's got this really interesting personal trainer.

—Can I call you back Peter? I said.

And hung up.

Bailey

Blongo watchy telly. See wolifs. Big Daddy wolif eaty deers.
Urra wolifs stand in snow sticky tongues in and out. Tongues
in and out. Asky for bitty Daddy wolif's food. Now Blongo
sticky tongue in and out all the times asky Mummydaddy for
the food. Lick lick lick feed me now.

Swearing

By the beginning of June we were coming on at the windsurfing and could go across the bay and back without falling
in. We'd even planed in a strong wind. It was the first time I'd
felt exhilaration since I was a kid. We spent the whole of this
Wednesday windsurfing. I asked Connie for some advice about
the AA meeting. Every week one of them mentioned my
swearing. I'd explained that when I get into a flow, when I am
myself, the language is the language. They said it was foul
mouthed but I said maybe they had to look at their tolerance
cause it's not foul mouthed where I come from. Jean said
surely I was more articulate than to resort to swearing. I told
her I didn't resort to it. It's part of a complicated articulacy.
Connie said I should tell the whole meeting my views soon as
I got the chance. But don't let them know it's bothering me.
I went to my meeting on a high.

Connie took the dogs to the beach at ten. Springsteen
came up and then Barnacles.

—Wuar is he the nicht then?

—Kirkcudbright.

—Kirkcudbright? He never told me he was gan to
Kirkcudbright.

He looked out to sea and was about to ask what I was
doing in Kirkcudbright when I arrived back. The dogs ran up
jumping and crying. Once they'd licked me to bits I sat beside

Connie on her favourite rock. She had Bailey on her knee and Springsteen was trying to get Connor to play.

—Did you do it? she said.

—Didn't get a chance, I said, —The way it went the opportunity never came up. They were all too fuckin nice.

—Maybe next week.

—Aye.

She chipped a stone. Connor and Springsteen chased it. Bailey bounded off her legs and the three of them tumbled into the sea.

—Aye, said Barnacles from the tide. It was the first I'd noticed him.

—Alright Barnacles, I said and went over. He was looking at the moon. It was nearly full.

—Big oul moon the nicht, he said.

—Aye.

Then there was a Galloway pause. I could hear Connie talking to the dogs and doing her best to include Springsteen.

—She says ye were in Kirkcudbright?

—Aye, I said.

I still hadn't got used to the pauses. The moon was good but not that good.

—Ye never told me ye were gan to Kirkcudbright, he said.

I thought I could hear Connie laughing. But if she did she covered it up by talking to the dogs.

—You never asked Barnacles, I said.

—No. I never, he said, as if that was okay then.

I think the tide was on the turn cause it moved away from our boots and even after seven waves didn't come back up.

—What were you doing in Kirkcudbright like?

—AA meeting, I said as if that explained everything. He came back after ten seconds.

—AA?

—Aye, I said, —It's not that I'm a chronic alcoholic or anything. It's just that when I drink I'm crazy. Violent.

—Aw. Wan o' they cunts. He said, —Better no drink then.

That's all he said. He changed the subject even though it took him twenty seconds to do it.

—They got caught.

—Caught with what?

—The drainers. Gan to Stranraer. In a white van.

—Did they?

A long pause.

—Aye. Cunts that they are. Springsteen nearly fell down yin o' the holes.

Connie was up off her rock and that was time to go. Barnacles walked away talking. He never ever said cheerio. He walked away talking so that his voice faded. This time it was Sellafield and what we'd look like if it blew. Only forty miles due south.

—We'd be walking like that, he demonstrated, —With our skin hanging off like that, he said. He flung in a few deathly moans. Oooh! Aaah! There would be no hope for them that lived closer.

In bed Connie suggested I phone Paddy to come down next Wednesday. Go with me to the meeting. Maybe I'd be able to say something easier with him there.

—Say what has to be said to the snobby fuckers and leave. You'll feel better once that's done.

—I can't ask him to travel a hundred miles to go to a meeting with me.

—He's your sponsor, she said.

Next day I phoned Paddy. He tried to talk me out of it. Said to be sure I wasn't acting on resentment. I was. But if I didn't do this I would explode. In the end he thought it would be better to go through with it. He'd arrive next Wednesday.

That Wednesday the sun was blazing. We had a late lunch in the garden with Paddy. I called it Drunch. It was like being in Italy or something. When the meal was finished we had a laugh setting the dogs on him. Paddy was terrified of dogs. You should've seen him running round the garden half laughing, half afraid. The dogs grabbing at his trouser legs.

—Get they fuckin things away from me, he was shouting.

But every time he came near me I'd grab his arms. Make it look as if he was attacking me.

—Horsey Horsey, I'd shout to the dogs.

Don't ask me why it was *horsey horsey*. You'd think one word would be the same as another but it made them go bananas. They chased Paddy up the cherry trees. Me and Connie were doubled up laughing at the table. It was good to have Paddy down and I was looking forward to the meeting.

—See if these cunts rip my jeans, Paddy said, —You're fuckin paying for them.

As I coaxed them over with a biscuit Paddy jumped down and sat on the grass smoking a fag.

—I'm fucked, he said and lay back blowing smoke up through the cherry trees. The smoke looked beautiful in the heat haze.

—Is the sky always blue down here? he said.

It was an hour's drive to the meeting. Paddy kept commenting on the scenery. I told him to wait till he seen it on the way back. Everything turned pink. Even the mud at the side of the river. He couldn't wait.

—Just be yourself tonight, that's all we're asked to do, he said.

It was the usual suspects at the meeting. Some faces fell

when they saw me. Whispers. I introduced Paddy and they tried to find out how long he was sober. When Paddy told them thirty years you could feel the awe. He was practically a guru. I sat down but Digger Kenny sat next to me. When I moved to another seat I seen him glancing at High Speed Mary.

They were on the fourth step. I won't bore you except to say it's about looking at your own faults and not other people's. High Speed Mary read the step out and then everybody said what that step meant to them. It got to Paddy.

—My name's Paddy and I'm an alcoholic. Aye fourth step. Nearly blew my fuckin mind that. I mean getting all that shite out my head onto paper. Cunt of a job it was. But when I did that and step five I was spiritually uplifted.

I had to admire Paddy. Although he knew about my big trouble with them he came and was himself. But he'd created a bad feeling and I was next.

—Manny, said High Speed Mary. When I started talking I could feel them all leaning back. They were shaking their heads by the time I had finished.

—Kenny, High Speed Mary said.

He wasn't next in line. I knew right there and then it was a set up.

—Well, he said, pushing his cup away like he was about to stand up. He didn't. He leaned back tapping the fingers of both hands on the table. —Well, he said again scanning the room, —I don't know where I'm supposed to be. But it certainly doesn't feel like an AA meeting.

He looked directly at me and said it,

—Your language is atrocious.

—What language? I said.

—That sort of language isn't acceptable at an AA meeting.

—What language is that Kenny?

—Swearing.

So here it was. Paddy widened his eyes at me. This was my opportunity.

—I didn't come here to stop fuckin swearing. I came here to stop drinking.

—And become a better person, Kenny said.

—You've got to stop swearing in order to become a better person?

—Yes.

I lifted the AA book and let it drop with a thump in the middle of the table.

—Somebody show me where it says I can't swear and I'll stop.

There was no takers for that one. I let the silence sit a moment before I spoke,

—Well, I'm not changing one fuckin syllable.

Bang! Kenny slammed the table with both hands. That's when I first noticed the gold rings and expensive watch. As if he'd power dressed for the occasion.

—Group Consciousness Meeting! Kenny shouted and shot his hand up in the air.

The group copied him except for one or two allies. The Group Consciousness Meeting was held. The vote was taken and it was decided swearing would not be tolerated. I said that was fine they don't need to swear. But I'm not a member of their group so I'd swear to my heart's content.

—You leave us with no option then, said Kenny, —We'll have to ask you to leave. You're barred.

—Barred from an AA meeting? Are you fuckin mental? I said.

—Please leave, he said, getting out of his chair. Maybe he was going to get physical. I don't know. Paddy whispered it was time to say my bit. I asked if I could say something before I left.

—So long as you don't swear, said Kenny and sat down twisting his watch on his wrist.

I opened an AA book and read this section on how it was absurd for one alcoholic to judge another. We're all the exact same. Recovering drunks. Some of the punters got the gist and knew they were wrong. But Kenny and High Speed Mary sat bolt upright letting it wash over them.

—Finished? he asked when I closed the book

—No. I'm not, I said, —I've been coming to this meeting for nearly a year. And I've listened to everybody in here. And do you know something? Everybody in here swears.

I gave them all examples of how and when they swear. None of them denied it cause I had their voices and mannerisms off to a T. Some of them had the grace to bow their heads a little. I looked directly at the instigator.

—D'you know what the problem is here Kenny?
He didn't.

—What the problem here is that I swear with a Glasgow accent. Well yous are a bunch of fuckin snobs. Yees can shove your meeting up your arse. I'll not be back.

—Thank God, said Kenny.

—No – thank fuck! I said and left.

On the drive home Paddy calmed me. He said they were scared when I shared. Especially the ten years in jail. They thought I was still that same guy. But he knew, and I knew, how far I had come. He was proud of me. I have to admit there was tears in my eyes. Paddy ruffled my hair and told me to stop greeting like a big lassie.

—Fucksakes look at that! said Paddy, —Pink!

I pulled over and we got out. Ripples of pink and red and ochre. All my anger flooded into that pink river. When we got home Connie was making French toast and spinning it into the dogs' mouths.

—How did it go? she said.

Paddy told Connie what happened as she made us some.
Then me and Paddy went down to the tide with the dogs.
The moon was on the water like a silver road back to
Kirkcudbright. Or coming away from it. I thought Barnacles
would be out but he wasn't. We walked along talking. I was
telling Paddy that when I first went to AA if they didn't swear
I wouldn't have went back. I'd have thought it was some kind
of holy joint. He said just as we get sick from time to time,
meetings get sick too.

They seen us before we seen them. The three Hannay
Brothers leaning against the harbour wall.

—Hi Manny.

—Is that you John? I said.

It was and his two brothers. I introduced them to Paddy
and we chatted under that big moon. John must have been
sixty or seventy or eighty. It's hard to tell down here. Age.
His brothers were younger. He started telling us how his family
had been fishing this sea for hundreds of years. When the
brothers were young their father would take them to the
islands off Carrick shore. Leave them there with a row boat
and lobster creels for three days and come back for them.
They slept in a wee tin hut on the island.

—What islands are they John? I said.

He pointed over to the Kirkcudbright side.

—See them there? John said.

—I can't see anything.

—Och come on man – it's a full moon surely ye can see them.

I peered at the shore five miles away but couldn't see any
islands.

—Where? I said.

He even stood behind me and lined up my head.

—Fuck sake – there!

The brothers were trying to show Paddy. But me and Paddy were city boys. Our eyes were used to light.

—Sorry John I can't see them.

He stepped back and this is what he said,

—Right. See when you're gan to Kirkcudbright next Wednesday, to your meeting? Take the first cut off. The Sandgreen cut off. Then you'll see a sign for Carrick Shore. Gan doon there and at the road end you'll see the islands. That right boys?

—Aye John.

I agreed to go and as we walked away Paddy wondered how come they knew so much about my AA?

—Barnacles, I said. And I imagined him telling the village what I'd told him on the beach that night with Connie and the dogs.

—He's an alky. Not a chronic alky. Just wan o' them that gans crazy when he drinks like. Wrecks the joint. Fells folks an the likes. He gans to a meeting in Kirkcudbright on a Wednesday.

Paddy didn't know if that was a good idea. But I felt great about it. I didn't feel like they were judging me. To them it was just a matter of fact. Like being a plumber. That night I felt as if I belonged to something.

Connor

Daddy's got the angry. I see the Daddy's angry. It go about him round and round yes yes like colours. Like the fing comes out the telly and the cooker. Like the fing what was round the bad mawnlower wire. It goes bizz. Daddy got that yes yes when he got the angry. I nuzzle the Daddy till it goes away. Stopy spinning. The Daddy can break fings wif his angry.

Bailey's Scan

By August Bailey was bad. Connie was worried he might have a brain tumour. I broke my silence with Peter and squeezed a couple of grand out by agreeing to all changes no matter what. The Gym would have no Daddy Doom. It would all be young and trendy people.

I remember he asked if I was up to writing about young and trendy people living where I did among all them geriatrics.

—They could teach you a thing or two, I said.

The vet school gave Connie an appointment for the next week and we celebrated with a kebab. We felt a sense of hope. A sense that something might be able to be done.

We were both on a high. There was nothing we could talk about that didn't lead back to this upcoming appointment. I was sure they'd find the cause of his fits. But as time went on Connie started to worry.

—What if it is a tumour?

—If it is it could be just benign.

—But what if it's dangerous? What if he needs brain surgery? I hugged her, till Connor gowlered us apart.

—Maybe us flitting gave him the tumour, Connie said.

—How could flitting give him a tumour?

—Sellafield's just forty miles down there. Barnacles says it affects people.

I started thinking there might be radioactive particles on the beach. I looked it up on the internet. That's when I found this fungus stuff that was a cause of epilepsy. And guess what? Cause of the gulf stream and the lack of frost it grew here in abundance. I went on a downward spiral too. Connie knew there was something wrong and got it out of me.

—What? It grows here? she asked, —In the ground?

We decided if we had to, we'd leave this area. Even though we loved it we would leave.

On the Tuesday before the scan Connie had to go to Morrisons in Stranraer. She was only just away when Connor barked and pointed at Bailey. Bailey was watching something move about the room. And this something was moving in jerks. It was like he was following ghosts. I put his harness on and sat him on the couch.

That's when he went. Big time. Started vibrating. Connor sat in the corner watching till the last wave of electricity fired through Bailey's body.

—Big Bongo's epilectric, I said to Connor and he barked once.

I stood him on his legs. He was wagging his tail, watching flying ghosts with a happy smile. Panting. I started imagining they were real these ghosts. Maybe spirits were flying through him. Maybe that's what fits were. That's when I felt something flying through me. But I didn't have time to react cause Bailey's legs started going like the hammers of hell and he tugged me right off the couch. He ran, with me holding his harness, towards the wall. I was just thinking he was going to split his head when he ran up the wall.

yes

up

the wall.

With me still holding the harness. I pushed my left hand

out and held his arse in case he fell. But that gave him extra torque and next thing he was on the ceiling.

Yes

On the ceiling.

On the ceiling.

I had one hand on his harness and another on his back and he ran halfway across before the weight gave way into my hands and he fell. I caught him and heaved him onto the couch. His legs were still paddling and his claws ripped at the leather. So I turned him onto his back, taking a few scratches and watched the paddling slowly die. As he lay with his tongue hanging long and pink down towards his ear I felt a rush of pride. I hadn't lost the head. I got a towel, wiped his chompy jaws and we lay on the couch talking me an him. All about how I was going to be a better Daddy from now on when big Blongo has the freaky fiks. He was looking in my eyes as if I was someone he recognised but couldn't place. He fell asleep nuzzled into my neck. I had things to do but he was so peaceful I couldn't move him.

That's when I saw them.

The paw prints.

Halfway along the ceiling they went. Evidence of a dog that could defy gravity. I laughed and Connor came over.

—Look up there Roo Roo, Bailey Blongo's a magic death defying anti-gravity dog.

I sang a wee song. And as I sang Bailey had the strength to open one eye and watch us.

♫ Blongo, the magic dog ran upside down on the roof oof oof.
   upside down on the roof
   oof oof

Blongo, the magic dog ran upside down on the roof
Here's the proof:
His paw prints are on the roof
His paw prints are on the roof
His paw prints are on the roof
So there's the proof ya hairy oof!
Oof oof.

Connor laughed and jumped up beside us. We all fell asleep.

When she came in bundled with Morrisons bags Connie didn't believe me. I took the bags and let the dogs flakken her. I pointed to the ceiling. She couldn't make them out at first but when she did she sat down. I acted out the whole thing with Connor barking beside me.

—Bailey, she said, cupping his face, —We'll have to take you to the circus.

They're still there, these paw prints.

The night before the scan Connie had to stay overnight in Glasgow. Connor knew there was something wrong. They don't like change, Collies. She phoned from the Travel Lodge. Blongo was on his cushy. We spoke about how the future could be if they found a cure and left each other that night glowing with hope.

I let Wan Long Tongue sleep on the bed and woke with him breaking my legs. On the beach I realised Connie would be walking Bailey in a park. By breakfast she'd be in the Vet Hospital. Connor and me went up to work withy biscuit and as I tried to understand Peter's notes I realised Bailey would be in the scan machine.

I don't know what made me do it but I knelt down and said a decade of the rosary that he'd not have a tumour. But they'd find something and it would all be okay.

Connie clapped Bailey as they drugged him. He had to be perfectly still in the scanner. They put this breathing tube in his mouth. Positioned him and Connie kissed him before leaving the room.

—Mummy's here Blongo, she whispered.

She was in the café lost in worries when she heard the voice.

—Hey!

—Eileen.

—You went for the scan then?

—Mm mm.

—I would've done the same.

They had a coffee together. Eileen was there with Daisy. She was ill and Eileen was up for tests. That shocked Connie although she didn't say. How a vet was powerless too. She hadn't thought of that before. And neither had I. She asked how we were doing with our windsurfing and laughed as Connie explained just how bad we were. They arranged to meet up back in Galloway.

There was nothing wrong with Bailey's brain at all. Connie felt like crying with relief. The scans were all clear. They had them up on the wall. It was strange looking at slices of Bailey's brain. Blood tests showed nothing and they said he had idiopathic epilepsy.

Connie came home the next day happy. She showed me some of the tests they'd done with Bailey. Holding one of his legs off the ground and seeing how he'd walk.

—Imagine trying that with Roo-Roo, I said and Connor came over.

I tried it and he gave me a Collie nip for my trouble. The vets had a lot of advice on three sheets of paper. Take him off dog food completely. Nothing with additives. Nothing in excess. Don't let him get stressed. Simple diet. Fish and chicken and the like. Cook vegetables.

That's when the morning pot was invented. Every day Connie chops a load of spuds and turnip and onions and carrots and simmers them in a pot. Throws in some chicken. On other days it's a pot of rice and we microwave some white fish. Bailey and Connor like that grub. They munch away making these mmm noises.

A week went past and no fits.

Then two weeks.

Then a month.

Eight weeks passed and we thought he was cured. He was a different dog. Happy and bouncy like a big jalopy of a puppy. We almost forgot he was epileptic. That's why it was such a deep rooted shock when, one day in late October, Bailey had another massive fit.

It was one of them days when the sky is grey and there's no wind and the horizon seamless meets the sky. If we weren't in such a light mood it could be depressing. But Bailey was well into his tenth week. We were already talking about getting somebody to dogsit and get away for a couple of days. Paddy maybe? Eileen? Life had brightened up.

There was nobody on Cruggleton Bay and the tide was in except for thirty or forty feet of sand. The trees over hanging were throwing out colours.

It was me and Connie and the dogs and nothing between us, nothing near us. Then I found an amazing skimmy. It went ten before dissolving into mini skips impossible to count.

—Twenty, I said

—Twenty my arse, says Connie, —Ten it was.

—Fifteen then.

Connie skimmed one. Twenty before it dissolved.

I said, —Ha! Nine.

—Twenty and you know it.

She uncoiled another one. Away into the distance it went with Bailey and Connor pounding after it.

The water's not that deep. You could walk out a hundred yards and only be up to your chest. They looked way out in an ocean when they stopped. I skimmed one alongside them and they went barking after it. When they got to where they last seen it they started ducking under. Bailey submerged his head and come up coughing then Connor did the same. But Connor was more determined and stayed under so long he looked like a rock. Connie was getting worried.

—It's not deep, I said, —They're probably still standing up.

—But what if they go the wrong way?

I burst out laughing.

—How the fuck can they go the wrong way? They're not daft. They're not going to say I know come on Connor let's go out there where there's fuck all but grey.

—They might.

So we shouted but they stood. We whistled and still they stood. Waiting for another skimmy. Even when I put my hand in my pocket for nurrawan they didn't move. Connie got an idea. She skimmed a stone between them and us. In they came with bows of white across their chests. They stopped where the stone sunk and began dunking.

—One two free! Connie shouted and skimmed another. They came closer. When she skimmed one along the sand they tumbled over their feet wondering where the water went.

—Ya pair of dafties, I shouted and over they came. Connor calmed down and Bailey walked with his tail and ears pricked. We should've known that was a bad sign. But we were still inexperienced then.

223

He went off like a box of fireworks. But this time he didn't fall. He ran about the beach kicking like a horse.

—Bailey! Connie shouted and made after him.

But it was no use we couldn't catch him.

—Get him Connor, get Bailey! I shouted and Connor went.

But when he got there all he could do was bark and try to round Bailey up.

When we were yards away Bailey stopped and we thought it was all over. Then we realised he was watching something out at sea. Ghosts. We were almost there when he shot in. On and on went as if he was chasing a skimmy.

He was a hundred yards out with Connor catching up before Connie ran in shouting his name. I followed and it was like the nightmare where you're trying to flee but you're walking through treacle. I powered through. Bailey went under. Connie screamed.

—He's went under, he's drowning! Bailey, oh fuck Bailey! Connie was shouting.

Connor swam round the spot barking. I closed in. I could see something in his teeth. What is that? What the fuck is that? He was pulling Bailey's neck. Keeping his noe above water.

—He's all right, Connor's got him, I shouted. Connie pushed on, her arms going from side to side above the water. I could see the rest of Bailey under the surface.

—Good Connor, good Collie, clever boy. Did you save the Bailey? I said as my feet left the sand and I had to swim. I got to Bailey and Connor let go. I lifted his head out and he spluttered. He was breathing and his big brown eyes were exhausted. He had the same look as when I found him lost in the forest. Connie arrived and grabbed him.

—Bailey! Is he all right? Is he okay?

—He's breathing.

When we could stand again she took him off me completely. Held that giant dog in her arms like a baby.

—It's all right Bailey, Mummy's here. Mummy's here.

Connor was swimming in circles clearly stressed. I clapped him as he went.

—Connor saved him Mummy. Connor's clever. Did you save the Blongo Connerroo? Mummy, Connor's a life saver.

He smiled and swam to Connie.

—Tlever Connor, she said, —Did you save the Bailey's life?

We were in shallow water now and Connor could jump up. I expected her to put Bailey down but she never. She wasn't letting go till we were far from that beach. Some people had appeared on the shore watching. We came out of the water and walked past them.

—Afternoon, one of them said and we nodded but kept walking. I don't know what they thought but sometimes embarrassment isn't possible.

In the Gardiniums Bailey struggled to get back onto his feet. Connie let him down and he asked for flingy stone. We realised that to him, nothing had happened. He'd been walking along the beach next thing he was in Connie's arms in the Gardiniums.

—I wish life was like that for us sometimes, Connie said.

—Like what?

—When bad things happen we wouldn't remember them.

She was right. Things pile up. And I got to thinking about Bailey's fits. How he'll never know. His life, if he can look back on it, will have holes where the bad times were. Like a film with bits edited out. Maybe he'll think that's normal. That life takes wee leaps forwards? Who knows. But I knew we'd remember. Me and Connie. And Connor too. The best we could do is don't let them pile up.

Then I noticed Connie crying.

—What's up?

She looked at me and her cheeks were glossed with tears.

—Nothing.

—It's not nothing, I said and put my arm round her, —What is it?

—Och it's stupid?

—Good, I'm stupid so I'll understand.

—I was just remembering the time Bailey jumped in and dragged Connor out of the stream.

That brought tears to both our eyes. Tears of a certain kind of joy. They released our strain these tears. When we got home we built the fire big and strong. It felt like we were battening down the hatches for the winter.

Connor

When the Mummy fall the out wif the Daddy she talk to me and the Blongo more. Nice nice talk talk. And when the Daddy talk she talk short. Aye. No. Talky talky long no no. Me feely sorry for the Daddy some the times when Mummy talk talk to him no no an me go and nuzzle him neck till the Daddy laugh outside an the inside. Me know when the Daddy laugh inside. He some the times try to laugh just the outside but me know he not laugh the inside so me nozzle and lick an sometimes kissy lips and when the Daddy laugh in the inside me big Collie smile. Waggy tail.

Nightmare

We took him to Eileen and she prescribed more phenobarbital and added on bromide. She smiled when I said he was hallucinating.

—How do you know he was hallucinating? she asked.

I told her about him following ghosts like this, and imitated Bailey. She didn't say she believed me but she was considering the possibility.

Back home we tried scooshing bromide in his mouth but he coughed it up and spat it out. Then he clamped his jaws shut.

—Open you mou for Mummy.

But he wouldn't and I had to prize it open so Connie could scoosh it in. It became a chore but after three days Connie put it in his food. He munched the lot without even looking up.

Bailey didn't have any fits for two weeks and we thought the medicine might be working. But he wasn't right. He'd stopped bouncing. Stopped flingy stone. Stopped catchy burdies. Didn't kiss me for putting on the boots Daddy. Connor went through the usual games but Bailey plodded beside us. And he was getting fat. Even after two weeks we noticed.

Then he went into the worst series of fits ever. Two days and a full *grand mal* every fifteen minutes. We tried more medicine but that didn't work. We tried less medicine and that didn't work. When he wasn't in a *grand mal* he was watching ghosts and when he wasn't watching ghosts he was trying to run up the wall. When he wasn't running he was walking, when he wasn't walking he was pressing against a wall. He liked corners. Corners and any small spaces. I remembered finding him in the corner of that field. He got into the space behind the fire. Connie prized him out as I chucked basins of water in the fire to cool it. We took ten minutes each controlling him on his harness but it was a strain. A complete overall strain. Connie could see the anger rising in me.

—Away you to your bed, she said, —Take Floyd with you.

I lay clapping Fluffy guy and I could feel the bones jutting out everywhere. It was terrible. It was all wrong. He'd been pushed aside just at the end of his life. I chinny chinned Floyd but it was more for my own benefit. In the morning Connie was in some state. Bailey was still wired and padding about. Connor stayed well clear and Floyd was nowhere to be seen.

I took over and let Connie get to bed. It was nine o clock but by eleven it was getting to me. Bailey on the end of my arm like an anchor. Even making a coffee was a nightmare. He was pulling and I snapped at him. When I tried to drink it he jerked and I spilled some on my t shirt. The phone went and it was Peter. I had to let him leave a message. I couldn't call him back. By twelve it was really getting to me. Fuck this! I went into the garden and let him off the leash. He ran straight down and crashed into the wire fence with a big orchestral clash. That clash shook through me. In that moment I managed to blame everything wrong in my life on Bailey. Even my telly show grinding to a snail's pace was Bailey's fault.

That's when Kenny Crusty's head appeared over the fence.

—All right?

—Do I look all right?

—What's up with the dog?

—You're the fuckin psychic Kenny, you tell me.

—Bad vibe.

—Mind your own business.

—I've got a pal who cures things.

When I got rid of him I looked up to make sure the blinds were closed, left Bailey against the fence, went in and drank my coffee. Connor wagged from across the room.

—Come on over tacked on at the end dog, I said and he understood. He wagged his tail and shot onto the couch shoving his noe into my ear.

—Kissy lips, I said.

His lips brushed against mine just so I could feel the touch. As I clapped Colin my anger subsided and I started feeling sorry for Bailey. Out I went.

—Bailey, I shouted nice and low.

It was half past one and he wasn't in the garden. But there was no way out; when his epilectrics started we'd fenced the place off. He wasn't down at the cherry trees. He wasn't hiding at the kitchen door. He wasn't at the greenhouse. He wasn't anywhere. I snuck back through the house, opening the front door like a burglar and walked round the village. But he wasn't there.

The tide was in.

The tide

was in.

—Shit fuckin shit.

A few villagers nodded and I figured if a dog had ran into the sea somebody would've noticed. You can't do anything here without being spotted. I went back to the house hoping he'd reappeared in the garden. But he hadn't. Then I thought – Connoroo!

—Roo-Roo, I said, —Find Bailey.

He circled a few times sniffing the grass. He broke away and shoved his head into the gap between the shed and the dyke. Six inches.

There was Bailey's arse. And his legs still pushing forwards so his head and neck were up the back fence.

—Good Collie, good Colin, good Roo-Roo.

Connor rounded up his own happiness and I dragged Bailey out by his back legs. He was still paddling forwards when I got to his chest. When I turned Connie was looking down from the window. Her face was ghostly. I don't know if she blamed me but I felt guilty just the same.

I walked him round the garden and when the rain started I put on my otterpoofs and sat at the table with the parasol up, Bailey straining on the leash at something I couldn't see down at the ham hok, Connor curled up at my feet.

I must've looked a picture by the white table, rain running from the faded blue parasol onto my head, a wet Collie at my feet and a mad Lurcher straining at nothing. I don't know how long it was before I nodded off but I came to with my back soaked and Bailey on his side panting like a hundred mile run. It was dark and the rain had stopped. When I went in it felt like an alcoholic's house after a weekend on the drink. Soulless. I listened and Connie was still in bed. It was seven o clock. I thought about putting the dinner on but Bailey went into another fit. Flinging furniture everywhere. Smashing ornaments.

I ran through in a flush of rage.

—What the fuck're ye doing? I shouted and got him by the neck.

—Stop it Bailey, I said, —Stop it, stop it, fuckin stop it! and flung him down.

He hit his head on the stone floor. But kept vibrating.

232

There was a flash in my mind. Like a bomb without the boom. I lifted a chair above my head. Bailey had blood and saliva on his face. And Connor was in the corner. And the chair shook.

The chair

shook.

I lowered the chair and cried with rage and guilt and frustration. I let Bailey bounce all over the room and that brought Connie down. I waited for her anger but she put her arms round me.

—I can't take much more of this Connie, I said.

She just hugged me.

—Go'n make something to eat, she said.

As I left the room I felt like I'd been on the drink. Like I'd lost it and smashed up the house. I'd made no progress at all with my anger. I wasn't fixed. Rage was just buried deep. I would never be rid of it. I was a failure.

When I brought two bowls of pasta Connie and Bailey were on the floor like Yin and Yang. He'd stopped vibrating but was still panting. We managed to eat with her holding the lead. We talked about what to do.

When I said, —What do you want to do? she knew exactly what I meant but she skipped past it. Pretended I meant now and not eternity.

—I'll stay up tonight, she said, —You come down at seven?

The alarm went off at seven. I found Connie in the garden with dawn coming up. She didn't kiss me or speak. She was dead to the day and shuffled past handing me the lead. Bailey didn't seem as bad as I sat on that white garden chair. He was panting and watching the odd ghost but otherwise he was okay.

By the end of that day he was sleeping and we got back to normality. We tiptoed about the house and when he came round he wanted fed.

The following week fits weren't mentioned. I was doing the latest set of changes for Peter and resenting every fuckin one of them. But there was money dangling at the end of it.

What we did notice was Bailey's clumsiness. He was fat and lethargic. And the bromide was making his paws dry so that he slipped on smooth surfaces. The medicine was all side-effects and no cure so I suggested taking him off. Connie asked Eileen and she said to give it a bit longer. I could tell Connie wasn't sure what Eileen exactly meant by *give it a bit longer* but I didn't say anything. Part of me already believed we'd be better off without Bailey.

It was on my mind that whole week about holding that chair above my head. I told myself it was hunger, tiredness and frustration but no matter what the excuse was I couldn't find a way to forgiveness. All I could see was a man I didn't like.

I phoned Paddy but he kept saying *mm mm* and *right*. I thought I was going to get nothing out of him when, at the end, he asked, —Do you think it's only the dog you're angry at?

—What's that, a fuckin Zen riddle? I said.

He just said *maybe* and went on to talk about me finding another AA meeting to go to.

That week, cause of my guilt, I was extra nice to Bailey. In the trees at Cruggleton Bay when I was sure nobody was looking I crouched down and apologised.

—Bailey, I said, —Daddy was going to hit you with a chair, but Daddy wasn't right in the head. Daddy needs his head fixed. Just like you and your epilectrics. Daddy loves you.

I don't know if he understood but he licked my lips and wagged his tail. I hugged him and kissed him, slapped his back a couple of times.

One afternoon when the tide was way out I took him catchy burdies. There was crows dotted among a thousand gulls. He loves chasing black crows.

—Catchy burdies, I said.

Nothing.

—They burdies is laughing at you! I said.

Nothing. Connor was padding towards them. One leg then a stance, then another leg, then a stance. When Connor took off I pointed Bailey's head to the birds.

—Buuuuuuuuuuuuuuuuuurdies, I said, long loud and drawn out.

But he dropped his head and kept plodding through the sand. It was getting to him too. I hadn't thought of that. The fits and the drugs and the dark feeling in the hou was depressing him. He looked like a dog fed up with living. We had to get him off these drugs.

On the way back home Barnacles was climbing over the harbour wall from his boat.

—How's the big fullah? he said, clapping Bailey and saying, —All right big fullah. Springsteen ran about with Connor and Barnacles gave me a couple of cod and asked if I liked langoustines. I said aye. He said he'd bring me some in the summer. I never even knew what they were, langoustines.

—They're great with a chilli sauce, he said.

Bailey was at the edge of the harbour wall. It's a bit of a drop when the tide's out. I didn't shout in case I scared him. Next thing he was behind the railing. I spoke calm as I could.

—Hello Blongo, what you doing in there?

Instead of bending down to come under he took a step back. His back legs slipped off and there was a look of shock as he span back over the edge. I heard an almighty thud and I thought he was dead.

—Jesus, said Barnacles and the look on his face was the end of Bailey.

The full weight of wishing him dead last week hit me. But when I looked over he was in the stream bed looking up.

I shot down the ladder, inexplicably happy. He had stalactites of that black grunge you get in harbour streams hanging off him. Creature From The Black Deep.

—Bailey! I said, —Bailey! Are you alright?

I felt him all over for broken bones. But he seemed okay. I clicked the lead on but when I looked up I realised there was no way back up the ladders. I had to walk up the stream to the slipway. Where Connor was waiting. And as I did Kenny Crusty came along with his wee Jack Russell.

—Aye! he said.

—All right.

—But you're not.

—Obviously, I said.

—Thon's a quare place to gan walking your dog, he said.

—He fell in. Off the harbour wall. He's fuckin stupid.

—Aye, he said, —They say dogs take after their owners.

—Is that why yours is a wee nippy fucker Kenny?

And as I looked up, Barnacles was smiling and Kenny knew not to say another word. We got out at the slip and people stared as we made our way through the village. This oily black *thing* and me and Connor.

A few days after Bailey fell in the harbour Barnacles took me fishing. You notice things about people when you get up close to their life. He had a Bible open in the wheelhouse and a Christian fish on the window. As we steamed out I could see him actually reading this Bible. I went aft and watched the prop churning the water and the village shrinking to a postcard. When he closed the Book and came on deck, I didn't mention it. And neither did he.

It was a warm day for the end of October. The sea was slow and had formed all these large triangular swells. Some were reflecting the blue sky and others the sun.

236

—This is a good spot, he said and he turned the engine off. In the silence laced with lapping water on the hull, the trace of iodine in the air and the far-off cry of gulls, Barnacles set up two rods. No bait, just hooks with feathers. It was mackerel we were after.

The rirr of the reel as Barnacles cast out.

Plip in the distance.

I did the same.

Rirr. Plip in the distance.

His rod went down straight away. And I gave a gasp of surprise.

—They're daft these mackerel, he said, —they'll be queuing up to get caught.

He made a funnel with his hands and shouted into the water, —Form an orderly queue down there ya wee stripy fuckers.

He reeled in five shuddering mackerel, twisted them off one at a time and cracked them dead with a priest. It had been a long time since I'd killed anything.

—Pull it in, said Barnacles.

—What?

—It's gan up and doon like the lum taps of hell, he said.

I reeled and the fish came up one two three four. Barnacles handed me the priest and as he recast I gripped the girth of this fish and tried to hit it. But it wriggled up towards me and gasped. I swung and it wriggled away and gasped. I hit the gunwale.

—Hit the buckin thing, Barnacles said.

Bang! It shuddered. Bang! It died.

Once I'd killed one it was easy to kill more. By the end of the day we had thirty mackerel each. We filleted them and threw the guts to the gulls. When I got off with my bag heavy with fish Barnacles asked what was wrong. I told him I was sea sick and he said something about trying it out when the seas are high.

—Waves twice the size of the boat, he said, —Aye, three times.

When I got home Connie didn't want to know. I put them in a bag in the freezer. But I never ate any of them fish. Not a one. We ended up feeding them to the dogs.

A week later Bailey had a set of fits. I was in charge when he was post-ictal this day. It made me angry to sit as he tugged at the lead so I took him a walk. It was six in the morning and we were well beyond Cruggleton Bay when I heard movement in the trees. I stopped. It was coming towards us and it was big. Connor slunk off fifty feet. I lifted a stick. Bailey stood in a daze.

I held the stick in the air when this black head come out of the rhododendron. It was a cow. Its chest appeared and once it made a hole big enough, it was born out of the bushes. I lowered the stick.

—What ye doin in there? I said.

It was a Galloway Beltie. All black with a wide band of white round its middle. And hairy like a dog. It took no notice of me. It was interested in Bailey. It lowered its massive head and made a noise way in the back of its throat. Bailey responded with the same noise higher pitched. The cow kissed Bailey. I mean actually kissed him on the lips, its breath enveloping Bailey's head. And they nuzzled each other. This whole affair went on for three minutes. Then the cow looked me in the eyes and disappeared backwards into the bush. I heard it retreating through cracking branches and mud. Then there was nothing. Bailey barked once.

—Oof.

And he was back to normal. The session was over. I expected Connie not to believe me but she told me it happened to her before.

—On the same path?

—Mm mm.

—Was it a big black and white cow?

—A Beltie, aye.

—What did you not tell me for?

—You wouldn't have believed me.

—Connie... see the thing you see when you look into the dogs' eyes?

—Aye?

—I seen the same thing in that cow's eyes.

—I know, she said.

—Know what Connie – I'm not eating cow-meat again.

She came over and hugged me. We took all the red meat from the freezer and fed it to the dogs that week.

A few days after that I had this really vivid dream. I was back on Barnacles' boat. Out we went, turned off the engines, set up the rods and Barnacles started hauling in fish. My rod went and the bend was immense.

—She's a big bastard, said Barnacles and I started reeling.

It was a big one. A mackerel five feet long. I heaved that fish onto the gunwales. Its mouth was opening and shutting. I could've got my whole head inside the mouth. I grabbed the priest and started whacking it. It let out a strange noise and I whacked it again before I realised it was the same noise the cow and Bailey had made. Blood spurted from its mouth.

But it wouldn't die.

No matter how many times I struck, it would not die.

—Kill it. Buckin hit it! Hit the buckin thing, Barnacles was shouting and he lifted an iron bar.

We dragged it on deck and set about it. But the more we hit it the more it slithered about. It made that noise again. Then I noticed something about the head. It was changing. As I was hammering it with this bar it turned into Bailey's head. He was yelping.

—Kill it, Barnacles was shouting, —Kill the fuckin thing. There was blood spattered on Barnacles' face.

—Stop! Stop! I screamed.

But Barnacles kept hitting him.

—It's Bailey, stop it Barnacles, it's Bailey!

But I couldn't pull him away. He had killing eyes.

I woke upright in the bed with sweat pouring off me.

—What's up? said Connie.

—I'm going to see if Bailey's all right, I said.

I brought the dogs into bed. Held onto Bailey all night. Next morning I told Connie about the dream and she said it was sign never to go fishing again. I phoned Paddy. He's not into all that dream shite but he listened and agreed with Connie.

—Don't kill things Manny, he said, —There's no need for it in this day and age.

And for a while I believed that's what the dream was about. But there was a much bigger meaning. A meaning I was to realise lying one day on the ham hok with Bailey. A meaning that would change my life forever.

Bailey

Bailey say womble womble when the Mummydaddy come rirr in street wiv car. Bailey like Daddy say c'mere to I fix your nye. c'mere till I fix your nyes. Cause the Blongo got the bad eye on the urra side. Stuff in it. Likey likey no no. Bailey like nurra wan? The Daddy sometime say.

Mmm carrots.

No like bushes. Come on Bailey say the Daddy but likey like bushes no no. Stik in the nye. Aw he does not like the bushes say the Daddy. The bushes is lubbbish. Lubbish bushes. But one day cow comes out. Cow talky Blongo. Say the thing.

The thing.

All Ye Faithful

The next set of fits was a week before Christmas. Connie was in Glasgow shopping and I was dog sitting. I put Bailey on the couch, got the computer downstairs and started on Peter's latest notes. I sat back and looked at the project. There was nothing left of what we'd agreed on all that time ago in Soho. The time when Bailey had his first fit.

I looked at Blongo and imagined how it must've been for Connie that day. Jees it felt bad. Me swanning about bigging it up and her up here thinking Bailey's dying. I tried to write. But I couldn't. There was no juice. I didn't have anything for these characters. The characters were Peter, his life, his pals, London cafes and Gyms. I closed the computer and thought seriously about what I was doing. I phoned Peter and told him I wanted out. He asked why and I told him.

—It started off as a black comedy called Daddy Doom, Peter, and now it's based in the gym where you train and based on your pals.

—No no no.

—Aye aye aye.

—We're just trying to make it more contemporary.

—Contemporary?

—Yes, living where you do you know, not in touch and all that.

—Wait a minute, I said, Barnacles going out for his lobsters every day, that's contemporary, the things we do here on a daily basis that's contemporary. It's contemporary cause it's happening now. You can't get more contemporary than what's happening today.

—Barnacles? he said.

—Exactly, I said.

There was a pause then he said, —It has to be contemporary to sell.

—What you mean is trendy, Peter. And trendy doesn't last shit.

—If that's how you feel, he said, —I have to respect your decision.

I thought he gave in too easy. I thought he'd have at least tried to persuade me to stay. But you can never tell what telly people are up to. You couldn't follow these bastards in the snow.

We left the conversation with a sense of finality. There was nowhere for me to go cause the BBC demands you waive your moral rights. They could sack me any time they wanted and bring in another writer. That's what they do when you don't write exactly what they tell you to write. It made me angry thinking about it; the people professing to be the most moral of all, who positioned themselves as our moral guardians, were the most immoral. Amoral even. Anger was building. Connor curled up on the couch and Bailey was on his cushion, his eyebrows raised in two tan triangles, looking at me.

It was late afternoon and pretty dark. There was an atmosphere of gloom. Then a band was coming up the street playing O Come All Ye Faithful. No... it wasn't a band, it was a PA of some kind. And then lights. All sorts of blue and red flashing lights. And someone shouting through a loudhailer.

—Ho ho ho, he was shouting, —Ho ho ho.

Sounded like a big electronic Santa.

It was a magnificent sleigh with a big papier mâché reindeer. All towed by a tractor and these elves rattling red buckets and chapping doors for money. I don't know what charity it was and I never found out. Cause the sudden noise and lights set Bailey vibrating. And just as I got to him the door went.

Bang bang bang.

This green and yellow elf could see me.

—It's okay Bailey, Daddy's here.

Bang bang bang.

—Ho ho ho. Merry Christmas.

♫ Oh come all ye faithful.

The sleigh stopped and Santa looked in. Loads of elves watched too as I held onto this big dog and the couch moved in little scrapes across the room.

Bang bang bang.

—Fuck off! Fuck off! Fuck off! I was shouting.

Bang bang bang.

—Ho ho ho.

♫ Joyful and triumphant.

His legs started going. I held the harness and as he ran up against the wall I could see these forty-something farmer's wives, dressed as elves, commenting. I gave them the thumb.

—Get to fuck, I said.

They tutted and left. Singing.

♫ O come ye o co-ome ye to be eth lee hem.

Hours later, when Bailey was calm I sat drinking tea in the dark. That was one depressing afternoon. The money to come from Daddy Doom aka The Gym had evaporated. My writing career with it. And then them nutters setting Bailey off. That's when it came to me. Maybe they hadn't set him off. Maybe it was me. My anger. Him and Connor were on the couch terrified the same way I used to be when my father was on the rampage. I saw myself from their point of view.

Five minutes later off he went again. And even though I'd had that insight I couldn't stop the anger. About half past eight Connie drew up. She came in smiling with bags of Christmas shopping. But when she seen my face her smile fell off. I swear I could hear it hitting that stone floor.

—Is he away again?

—Aye. Fuckin Santy set him off.

—Santy?

—Aye – that cunt Clause. A big float and all these fat elves begging for money. Lights and music, I said, —He just went off.

She got down beside him.

—Oh Blongo did that Daddy not look after you?

Even though I knew she was joking it got to me. My anger rose and Bailey went off again. He fitted all night and into the next day. My guilt made me stay up with Connie. We struggled through the next day taking turns at holding Bailey or making tea. I walked Connor and it was bliss to be out. I sat on Cruggleton Bay and looked at my life. It was one dark place. The house was a prison. It was all anger and a crazy dog. It was getting too much. Going far beyond where a normal person could go.

—Daddy can't take much more of this Roo-Roo, I said, —Maybe he'll have to go away?

Connor nudged me. Gave me a stone. I flung it. But instead of chasing the stone he gave me another one. I flung that and he ran. I wondered if that was dog-ese for Bailey and him. A stone for Bailey and a stone for him. Or maybe just co-incidence. When I got back it was dark and Bailey was fitting. Connie had him by the harness.

—Going to hold that till I get to the loo, she said with this accusatory melody. I grabbed the harness and Bailey was all over the place. Every tug jangled my nerves.

—Stop it!

He jerked and twisted and vibrated.

—Fuckin stop it Bailey!

Up he went over the back of the couch, catching me a gouge on the leg with his claws. I punched him. He didn't feel it. Kept paddling the legs. I punched him three times hard saying, —Fuckin stop it now.

Connie charged downstairs and pushed me away.

—Leave him. Leave him ya cruel bastard. He's sick!

She wrapped herself round him and hushed him. I was crying quiet tears of rage. Then I said, —Look at the fuckin state of us Connie.

She said nothing.

—We can't go on like this.

She said nothing.

—We're like an insane family here.

She said nothing.

I walked up and down the room as if I might find the answer tucked away somewhere.

—Look, I said, —Let's go out a drive. Do something. Get out of this, this fuckin dungeon.

—What did you hit him for?

—I lost my temper.

—You lost – your – temper.

—Aye. I lost my fuckin temper, I said, — Like this, I said and started smashing things shouting *like this*. —And this. And this. Plates. Cups, table mats. CDs.

—What the fuck's wrong with you!? she screamed.

—Temper, I said and sat down shaking.

—That's your war cry, temper.

It was probably the best answer I ever gave in my life;

—Aye Connie, that's cause I'm sick too. Like him.

She looked away a second and when she turned back her face was different. Not quite forgiveness but somewhere away from hate. And me? I realised the truth of what I'd just said. I was sick.

—Right we'll go a drive, she said.

We put Bailey in the hatch and Connor in the front. He curled in the footwell like when we first got him. I remembered the yellow spot. We drove about them country roads with rain battering down. Now and then a car passed and I'd see Bailey's grinning face in the rear view. But the hum of the wheels calmed him and he finally lay down.

We pulled onto the harbour. The waves lashing in. It was a wild night where you couldn't separate the storm from the sea. Now and then you could see the tiny white frill of a wave, then the whooshing ink. Connie spoke. Her voice muffled in the car.

—What do you want to do? she asked.

—I don't know.

We sat listening to Blongo's legs paddling in the back. Running on his side.

—I know we'll have to do something, I said.

—What?

I paused then said, —Maybe we'll have to get rid of him.

—What?

—Well, I can't see any other way out. Can you?

She said nothing.

—He's getting worse and worse Connie.

It was the only time Connie ever hit me. A punch right on the lips. My lip bled.

—Ya fuckin bastard what did ye do that for?

—Maybe *I'm* sick, she said.

I started the engine and drove away with her ranting.

Ranting about how that dog has changed our lives. How he's brought us down to this beautiful place. How we've got a house beside the sea cause of that dog. How we'd took up windsurfing, and walking. How we were totally different people cause of that dog.

When we got home Connie took the dogs to bed and closed the door. I could hear her cooing to Bailey and wondered what the fuck I was doing on this remote peninsula with a crazy dog and a wife who loves animals more than me.

That's when I heard the purring. It was Fluffy guy.

—Fluffy ch ch ch.

When he jumped on my chest he felt light. And when I started clapping him he was only bones.

—Aw Fluffy, —I said, —Poor Fluffy guy.

He purred.

Bailey

Howwwwwwwwwwwwwwwwwwwwil I says. When the Daddy plays the vlin. He make lot noises on the vlin but one noise Blongo no like. Likey likey no no. It go eeeeeeeee in Blongo's ear and Blongo go Howwwwwwwwwl. And the Mummy tell the Daddy stop the vlin but the Daddy stopy stopy no no and the Blongo hide in kitchen.

Near the food.

Retreat to solitude

The next morning I was playing the blues on the vlin when Connie came down. She'd had enough. She wanted me out. When Bailey was sick all I did was give her grief. She could cope with it but it was clear I couldn't. My anger was killing her. When I pointed to Bailey being the problem she let rip.

—You want to murder him.

—No – you're choosing a dog over me!

—That's not the way it is. Why've you always got to see everything in black and white?

—You're choosing a dog over me. What other way can it be?

—You promised you'd deal with your anger.

—I am dealing with it; I'm never off the phone to Paddy.

—But none of it is working Manny, is it?

I couldn't answer.

—D'you want to know why you're angry? You're angry cause of these bastards in telly. Every time you do anything for them you're raging. And you take it out on us. Give it up Manny. Give that up and you'll be okay.

—Oh! So not only is she choosing a dog over me she wants me to give up my dreams.

She was genuinely shocked I'd used the word dreams.

—Dreams? You know what my dreams are?

I didn't with a cheeky shrug.

—Us Manny. All us. We're my dreams. All us and peace.

It got through to me that.

—It works okay when everything's going all right, but when something happens you're out of control. You unleash your anger on us. You don't need AA, I can tell you what's wrong!

—I bet you can.

She came over.

—Manny, think about it. Go away and think about it. It's them. You want to be famous but there's nothing in it. It's all in here, she swept over the animals with her hand, —It's in here, she slapped her chest, —And here, she slapped mine.

—You only need three things to be happy Manny, she said, —Things to do, somebody to love, and stuff to look forward to.

Bailey slipped into another fit. She looked up from down there on the floor beside him.

—You need to sort your head out Manny, or it really is over between us.

—And you need to realise that I'm worth more than a daft dog.

—No, you're not Manny. Nobody is. Nobody's worth more than any animal. They're worth more than us. We're the only species that if you wiped us out the planet would get better. We're a fuckin curse.

There was no talking to her. I packed a rucksack. Sleeping bag, wee cooker, bags of noodles and a few tins of this and that. I walked along the hall expecting her to call me back. She didn't. And as I left that village I didn't really have a clue where I was going.

I just walked.

And walked.

It started snowing. And by the time I was halfway to Glentrool the road was blocked. A log lorry had skidded in the snow and its wheels were spinning as cops and mechanics tried to get it moving. Blue and orange lights swept the fields. The wheels were making this whining noise. It was going right through me. The cop expected me to say something. He stood upright and made a friendly face. But I just said *hi* and walked on.

It must've been minus five when I reached Glentrool but I had to open my jacket cause I was generating heat from a core of anger. I turned down into the forest and the snow was a foot deep. The road untouched. No tracks. No footprints. When I passed over the bridge the waterfall was frozen like a photograph. A massive curl of ice with water sluicing over the top. Icicles the thickness of your arm. I stood for half an hour letting the sound of water block everything out. When it wouldn't work any more I moved on. The single track road looked like a wide white clearance through the trees.

Half an hour later I was at the foot of the Merrick. I knew I had to find shelter. I had a bivvi bag but in this weather you need more. I remembered the bothy where Bailey was a wolf. Three hundred yards into that hill it felt like the Himalayas. The blizzard whipped round me like blankets. Everything was white. My feet were the only certainty. That's how I knew which way was up. On we go. As I struggled upwards the dream of the fish kept pushing in.

And I kept pushing it out.

The wind slapped into me. The clips of my jacket stung me in the face.

—Bastard! I screamed into the wind. Bits of ice were spinning into my lips. —Bastard, I shouted and punched at the wind like it was alive. I punched and screamed till I had to crouch down to get my breath back.

It was a relief to come to the trees. The branches hanging

heavy with snow. The interior dark and the wind deadened so that the temperature rose. I got the stove out and turned a few wads of snow into tea. As I sipped on a rock I felt like a photo of a Buddhist monk Paddy once showed me. It was a monk sitting on a rock drinking tea with sandals, cold snow, clean air and a clarity of mind. But my mind was turmoil. The tea was falling into my heart. Roasting it.

It didn't feel like the same bothy. In my mind it was filled with the glow of fire and Connie in awe at Bailey being a wolf. But now it was a disappointing shell. The dark windows sucking in snow. An empty place, halfway up, or halfway down a mountain.

Once I'd unpacked, laid out a foam mat, sleeping bag and bivvi I set about gathering wood. Dry wood's still easy to find even in the winter. Find a dead standing tree and break some branches off. The place felt better when I got the fire going. Night was coming in and I blocked the window spaces with a lattice of green pine branches. Only the odd eddy got in; the flames rising and falling.

When my anger subsided I understood the difference between solitude and loneliness. I wondered what Connie was doing. I had two packets of noodles and another cup of tea, had a pee out the door and got into my bag. I was warm and fell asleep.

I think it was a dream.

I'm sure it was a dream.

It must've been a dream.

I heard scratching and woke up. I expected rats but wasn't sure if you got them this high up. In this weather. There was light slicing through the lattice. That was crazy cause if there was a moon the lattice was too tight to let it through. Then I saw it. In the opposite corner. It looked like a wolf. Grey,

almost white. I knew I should've been scared but I wasn't.
I was in wonder at this thing and when it turned it was Bailey.
I tried to say his name but silence came out. He was showing
me something on the floor. It was the wee pyramid of food
he'd made last time. It had meaning words can't explain.
It had presence.

I tried to say his name again. My mouth opened but no
sound. He came and stood by me. I looked into his eyes and
saw love. I mean I saw what love is. Love. This love lifted me up,
still in the bag, then placed me down. This ghostly Bailey, he
lay beside me and he was warm. As I fell into a deep sleep with
my nose buried in his neck I could feel my anger bleed out.

When I woke I felt around and when he wasn't there I
opened my eyes. And another thing. This immense feeling of
cleanliness was in me. A clarity and a serenity I'd never felt
before.

It didn't last long.

As I made tea I filled with dread. Maybe I'd seen Bailey's
ghost? That Connie had got him put down. She'd chosen me
over the dog. I felt a stone fall into my gut and stretch it like
elastic. I fell back so that I had to hold the wall. I was sick, splat,
on the floor. Then I started crying.

—Bailey, I screamed, —Oh fuck Bailey! I'm sorry I'm sorry,
I'm fuckin sorry.

As I beat my fists on the floor my whole life stripped away
from me. Bit by bit it fell like snow thawing on a mountain;
avalanching until all that's left is bare, undeniable rock. I was
left with selfishness. It was there like an edifice for me to stare
at. I tried to pray but all I could do was repeat Bailey's name.

I don't know how long I stayed like that but I woke in a
crumpled heap. I was terrified to leave the bothy. I looked at
the food. I could stay a week, maybe more. But Connie would

257

be on her own. What the fuck was I doing to her? I thought of the first time I'd seen her in the casino. Everything we'd been through passed through my mind. I'd taken something beautiful and destroyed it. That was the true nature of it.

The wind had died completely. There wasn't a sound outside. When I took the lattice off I was blasted by white. The snow was three feet up the building. I slung the rucksack on and started down, sometimes on the crust, sometimes sinking in. I was sobbing and hoped I wouldn't bump into anybody. When I came out the other end of the forest they were coming up the hill; Connie, and Connor circling, and Bailey striding by her side. The true meaning of happiness.

—Bailey, I shouted and he ran at me.

I let him flatten me in the snow licking and gowlering. Connor arrived. The sky was blue and into it came Connie's face.

—I love you, she said.

—I love you.

There was a lump in my throat and she could hear it.

—And I love my doggies my Blongo and Roo-Roo, I said.

Connie sat in the snow. We made a fuss of the dogs and started back down.

—I knew this is where you'd be, she said.

—I had this amazing dream, I said and told her all about it.

She told me in the middle of the night Bailey stood up and stared at the wall. He stayed like that for an hour. Nothing could budge him. When he came out he fell sound asleep. I felt a chill.

—See from this day on Connie, I said, —I'm going to be in control of my anger. I promise.

—Just try, she said, —That's all.

—I will, I said, —That dream's changed something in me.

She put her arm round me and Connor attacked us.

Connor

Catchy burdies. Wheee. Up in sky an me runny through catchy catchy oof the Colin shouts. Mummydaddy clapping on sand. But sometime the Daddy go in the water. Me no likey the water. Water water no no. Save the Daddy. Water keepy noe up. Keepy noe up. Jumpy save the Daddy life. Daddy laf.

Burdies is laffin at me.

The Snow Road

Paddy was trying to get me into Buddhism. I knocked him back but the picture he painted of the temple in the Cairngorms stuck in my mind. I told Connie I fancied going for a few days. To chill out. Connie fancied it too. Even though Connie is a Buddha she's not a Buddhist. But she knew they love animals. Revered them even. Treated animals as equals. Connie was never religious but she thought they had it right. Paddy said you only had to turn up and book in. Try some meditation and yoga and Tai Chi.

It was a long drive but there was togetherness between me and Connie and the dogs. We took our time. Serenity began to flow when I seen the distant mountains. I wanted to go up there and stay forever. Build a wee igloo in the snow. In the white. In the peace and silence of some high rocky place. It was afternoon before we got to the Cairngorms. We seen the sign for the temple halfway up the Snow Road. I was really looking forward to it. This might be a turning point in my life. As big as when I first went to AA.

It was an amazing sight when we seen it. Even the dogs stood up and said wow in dogese. It was like the middle of the Himalayas – prayer flags and snow and monks wandering with yellow and saffron robes. I felt a rush of serenity. This was the right place for me.

—Stop, said Connie.

—What?

She pointed to a sign.

No Dogs.

—No Dogs, I said.

—No Dogs, she said.

—No Dogs?

I couldn't believe it. At first I thought it was some kind of joke. Or that somebody had put it there. Or maybe you had to Zen riddle it. I scanned the temple and the grounds. People going everywhere but no animals. Not a one.

—Can't believe it, no dogs, I said.

—Maybe they're scared in case they dig up the Karma, said Connie.

And we fell about laughing. A monk passed and joined his hands nodding at us.

—Oh, he's really holy, said Connie and we reversed out of that place. It was dark so we booked into a bed and breakfast that said Dogs Welcome. The woman made us an evening meal and we told her our story about the no dogs Buddhists. She laughed and by the end of the meal she'd convinced us that a young couple like us shouldn't be going to a monastery, we should be up that mountain skiing.

—Life is first, she said.

We decided to give it a go. Next morning we took the dogs a walk in Glenmore forest. They were biting the snow and tumbling round. Me and Connie threw snowblobs for them to catch.

—Snowblobs! she shouted.

Connor tugged a wee branch and whoosh – a rush of snow smothered him. We had to dig him out with Bailey's help. When his big hairy head poked out, he barked a *What's your game*? bark. Connor skidded through the trees rounding up the things in his mind and when they were tired we headed up the mountain.

We hired all the gear and the Funicular was full of shiny happy people. Wide white smiles cutting across red faces. Ice melting below their nostrils. The conditions at the top were perfect they were all saying. New snow on an old base. Powder. Just as the doors were closing I heard a couple of voices.

—Haud on!

—Haud the doors ya bam!

I couldn't believe it. Two neds got on. Followed by one fat bearded social worker trying to calm them. The atmosphere changed. People stopped talking. Withdrew. They shrunk visibly. And the space left; the neds filled. All about how he said this and I goes like that and he comes like that and he pulled out a blade and I took it off him and shoved it up his arse.

One of them noticed the driver behind a plate glass panel and thumped it.

—Hey you ya bam! What's your game trying to dub they doors up before we could get on?

The driver tried to reason but the ned started kicking the glass. It was only the social worker shoving his folk-singer belly in that saved the glass.

On the mountain I forgot about every ned that ever lived. It was gusting to fifty and approaching whiteout. But me and Connie went sliding and falling about laughing and picking each other up. Considering we'd no lessons we soon got our ski-feet. Connie was quickly fed up with the beginners slope and went looking for a better run. I followed. We found one marked easy. But they must've meant easy if you can actually ski. Visibility was ten yards. Down we went. Together. It wasn't too fast. Until we hit a ramp that was. Then another. Then

263

another. Then we were going too fast to stop. The fuzzy outlines of humans would appear and we'd shift to the left. Another hazy outline and we'd shift to the right. I prayed,

—If I hit anybody at this speed God, let it be the ned.

We gathered and gathered speed until it was scary. Schuss! We'd got ourselves into a situation where one wrong move and we'd crash. Schuss! I didn't dare even twitch. Schuss! The fear was exhilarating. Schuss! If I was going to crash I wanted Connie beside me. And she was. Right on my shoulder. We breathed out in union when the mountain levelled off and we slowed. We let out a cheer and laughed. Going up the Poma was all grey shadows coming and going. A hiss of snow as they passed and then silence as they disappeared into white. We went down again with our fear traded in for exhilaration.

The third time we went down flecks of snow and ice were biting so hard we decided to get goggles. We couldn't really afford them but we'd no choice.

In the shop the Funicular neds were prowling about. No intention of skiing and every intention of stealing. The women had contacted security cause when we got to the goggles the doors burst open. Two big guys careered in and grabbed the neds.

—What you doing ya bam!

—That's assault that so it is!

—I'll get you done ya big fanny!

But these guys weren't Guardian readers. More like middle class ex SAS. One of them slapped the big skinny ned, sending his baseball cap spinning to the floor. He started shouting he wanted the cops called. He wanted this guy done with assault.

—He assaulted me there. Did you see that? he said to the woman behind the counter.

—No.

He turned to me.

—Hey big man, did you see that? He thundered me there.

—Funny, I said, —I thought you punched him.

—What?

—You punched him. And your pal threatened to stab him.

—What?

—That's what I saw.

—Ya wank, he shouted, —Ya fuckin wank. You're getting stabbed!

I laughed and just then their social worker arrived.

—Get them done Frank. Get them done. They assaulted me. I want a sorry by the way. I'm not leaving here till I get a sorry.

But the two big guys dragged the neds off through the social worker's protests. All I could hear was, *I want a sorry. I demand a sorry.*

Connie looked at me.

—And you're not angry.

—Eh?

—Neds giving you abuse, and you laughed.

—So I did! Told you I was cured, I said, —How did I ever end up doing time over one of them useless bastards?

Connie squeezed my hand.

—Shh, she said, cause the woman was coming over.

—That's the state of the nation! said the woman.

Back outside our goggles turned the snow pink. The dogs growled when we looked in the car. But wagged when we took the goggles off. We took them for another snowblob fight, ate lunch in fogs of breath, kissed Bailey and Connor icy kisses and went back up the mountain.

We spent the rest of the day going up and down that scary slope. Near the end of the afternoon we took on a blue run. I was skiing down quite the thing. Getting faster and faster.

Schuss! I'd never gone so fast. The hiss of the snow and the wind. Schuss! I was glad to be alive. All of a sudden the cloud cleared and the whole world was blue sky and white mountains.

Maybe I looked at the scenery too long cause next thing I was upside down, in the air and still moving. Falling down the slope of the mountain. But slow. Everything was oh so slow. I was upside down, dependent on nothing. And on everything. I could hear my breathing. I looked up and there's my skis. And there's the blue sky above them. And the silence. It was actually beautiful. The peace of it all. In that one eternal moment I caught a glimpse of infinite peace. It was a gift. Everything was a gift. Everything life flings at me is a gift. Even grief's a gift. Sadness – a gift. Laughter –a gift. Pain – a gift. Not so you can learn from it and become a better, stronger person. It's just a gift cause it's all life.

All these thoughts before *boof* I had to cover my head and plunge into a gigantic drift of snow. When I looked up Connie was laughing.

—Spectacular, she said, —Your best yet.

When I got out there was a me shaped cartoon hole in the snow. There wasn't a mark on my body.

Bailey

Me go to work wif the Daddy. Lie on the cushy get the carrot.
Daddy clicky at the fing. Talk to him own self. Laugh the
Daddy sometimes looky at the Blongo. Daddy said writey book
bout Blongo. Blongo epilectric.

Blongo glad Daddy no talk to him Peter I bitey balls no more.
Him I bitey balls me no like. Bailey bitey balls peeps Blongo no
like. Peeps peeps bad bad. Make the Daddy angry. Daddy
angry no good. Me like the Daddy.

The Clairvoyant

By the end of winter we'd been skiing five times. I'd not been
angry once. We were so up we managed to look at Bailey's fits
with a different eye. We had a small room upstairs and I lined
the walls with old judo mats. Floored it with cushions and
quilts. When Bailey went into fits we put him in there and
that freed us. I know it sounds cruel but he bounces about and
when he's finished he falls asleep. He's not had an epilepsy
injury since. When there's visitors and he's having a fit it's like
a scene from *Jane Eyre*.

I found out Chinese herbalists treat epilepsy as a digestive
disorder. Connie drove up to a shop in Glasgow. She explained
all the symptoms and the wee Chinese man listened and
nodded. But when she told him it was for the dog he looked
at her.

—Dog. Faw the Dog?

And he chased her, shouting in Cantonese. When she
skipped into the Savoy centre she noticed a clairvoyant's
cubicle. Let Mystic Rose guide your future. There was one
teenage girl in white sitting in a cloud of worry. Connie sat
down and read the old magazines. But this worried nineteen
year old she started talking to Connie. About her boyfriend
running off with her pal the wee cow that she is. Last she
heard he was in London. She wants to know if he's coming
back. If he's coming back to her. Before the baby's born.

—Oh the baby, did I mention the baby?

Connie nodded no.

—The baby, she said lifting her top up, —I don't look it but I'm three months.

There wasn't a bump or a bulge or a hint of a curve. That was one flat belly and Connie got the feeling this girl wasn't right. That she might not have a boyfriend. That she might not be pregnant.

A woman come out crying what looked like tears of relief and the teenager went in. After fifteen minutes she came back out and punched the air.

—Excellent, she said, —I've to get him back. He's coming back! And she walked off through that mall; the embodiment of hope.

Connie sat there. Nobody called. She listened. Maybe she'd missed the signal? Or are you supposed to go in when the other person comes out? Like Confession. She listened again. There was movement but nobody called. Eventually she put her head in.

—Come in dear, said this voice.

Connie slipped her wedding ring off and went in. The room was square with heavy curtains down every wall. Dark except for ribbons of light at the base of these curtains, making Mystic Rose look at once terrifying and omniscient.

—Close the door please.

When she did she was cocooned from the city. No noise could come in. When Connie was seated Rose whipped a black velvet cloth away revealing a crystal ball dead centre of the table.

Rose dropped her head, taking deep breaths like asthma. Breathing, in fact, exactly like Floyd had been doing. When Rose's head shot up Connie got a fright.

—Fifteen pounds, said Rose.

—Oh sorry, said Connie and fumbled for the money. Once Rose had stuffed that somewhere she got down to business. Stared at Connie, stared into the crystal ball.

—You're not married.

—No, I am.

Rose took Connie's hand and looked for a wedding ring.

—I don't wear a ring.

So Rose leaned back and closed her eyes. Opened them. Trying to be scary but she was so comical Connie had to stifle her laugh by sneezing.

—You've got relationship problems.

—No.

—No?

—We're getting on great the now, me and Manny.

—Rose leaned forward and stared into the crystal ball.

—Ah! I see... I see...

By this time Connie was leaning in so that their heads were almost touching.

—I see... money troubles.

Connie didn't respond. She was going to ask about cures for Bailey but not now.

—Yes, that's it; financial worries, Rose said and looked up. It was more a plea for confirmation.

—You've got money troubles?

—No, said Connie.

—No?

—None. We're doing all right the now.

This time she leaned forward and got both hands on the crystal ball. This time she was going for it. Pulling out all the secret stops. She got her face up close and stared. Tried to see something.

Anything.

And all the time muttering a random selection of words. Love. Death. Sickness. Worry. Travel. Fear. Family. Sister. Far off lands. Cousin. Brother. Mother. Father. Guilt.

But Connie only reacted when she had to stifle another laugh with a fit of coughing. Rose pounced.

—Health! she shouted, —You're worried about your health.

—No. I'm fine. Never been better.

—Your husband's health then?

—He's doing great too.

But by now Connie *wanted* to have a problem. It had started as a bit of laugh but now it was embarrassing. Like being locked in a room with a stand up comic who isn't funny.

—Right! said Rose and grabbed Connie's hands with surprising strength. Clamped them onto the crystal ball and put her own hands on top. Stared into the ball with all her mystic might. Connie could see her own distorted face and she supposed that was all Rose could see too. Finally, Rose sat back exasperated. And although she still held Connie's hands tight to the ball she dropped the long clairvoyant vowels.

—You must have some problems, she said.

—No. Can't think of any.

Connie could feel Rose's hands slackening when she thought of something.

—Floyd, said Connie.

—Floyd? said Rose, clamping her hands on again, —Your son?

—Cat.

—An animal. I can see animals. Yes, I see a cat. Black?

—Red.

—Ginger, that's right. A ginger cat. He's lost.

—Dying.

—Very ill, that's right. He's very ill. Floyd. I see a ginger cat. He's ill. He's old.

—Young.

—He *feels* old due to sickness. But I see him pulling through. Yes. There he is. Oh my, he's up a tree. Smiling.

—Smiling? said Connie.

—Cats smile, she said.

—He's incurable.

—No. No. I see him smiling up a tree. But I can't see the disease, the disease is... is...

But it was obvious Rose wasn't upon her cat diseases.

—FIV, said Connie.

—FIV?

—Feline immunodeficiency virus.

—I've never heard of that.

—It's the cat equivalent of AIDS.

Rose's hands shot out from underneath Connie's. She snapped back into her chair. Stared at Connie and said,

—AIDS?

—For cats.

—AIDS? said Rose.

—Humans can't catch it.

Mystic Rose threw the black velvet over the crystal ball and nodded at the door. Connie said thanks and left. When she was a few feet away she could see, in the giant mirrors, Mystic Rose making for the toilet. In her hands was the crystal ball wrapped in that black velvet cloth. Off to kill every last germ.

Connor

I like terment. Grr!

Virtuoso

Since I left AA I disciplined myself to go to the ham hok every Wednesday night and play the violin. Bailey liked to come and over time I realised he liked long slow notes. Deedily dee music made him jumpy. He loved the lower half of the G scale and if I played it with slurs his muscles released the bones and he became a big furry bag of relaxation. Once he was relaxed I'd lie with my head next to his.

This particular evening I'd fell out with Connie. I can't even remember what over but I was in the ham hok talking to Bailey. I woke up with stars through the trees. Bailey was snoring and night animals moved about. I felt this incredible sense of peace. Like something had been lifted away from me. Connie was right all along. Film and telly was killing me. It was affecting me and my relationships and maybe even Bailey.

Even though I'd packed it in with Peter I half expected him to call back. I was still holding the corner of the towel. But I knew I had to let it go. I looked at Bailey's prehistoric body and the bones under the fur. His face, its whiskers and his nose the size of a golf ball, but black, his nostrils opening and closing as he breathed, his eyelashes, and his long mouth. His ears folded back on his head. And his paws tucked up to his chest. He looked like he was dreaming something good. Somehow the space between me and him was nothing. We were the same.

Connected. Then it evaporated, the feeling, leaving me clean inside.

I picked up the vlin, played a quiet G and he opened one eye.

—Was you dreaming the Blongo?

He lifted his head from my chest and I scratched the soft fur under his chin.

Connie came out with tea. Me and Bailey watched her down through the garden. The windows shone broad through the garden. Connor was twisting in and out of the light.

—Rice cake Bonio biscuit, she said.

Bailey struggled out of the ham hok and went to her. Maybe the more love you generate for animals the more it affects you. It hit me that Connie's not beautiful just cause of her looks. Her beauty was coming from somewhere else. That's what all the animals see in her. That's what it was in the casino that first night.

—Where's the Daddy? she said and Connor sniffed me out.

They all came into the trees.

—I thought you'd got lost, she said, and gave me a wee kiss on the cheek. Held my hand and gave the ham hok a wee swing.

—Sorry, I said.

—I've made something to eat. Mon!

She ran up the garden with the dogs. I watched them go into the light and thought what life would be like without them. I was immersed in that when Connie shouted.

—Manny, come on up and see this. Hurry.

I grabbed the vlin and shot up the garden. When I got there Connie was staring at the telly. She pointed to the screen. An orchestra was playing.

—What?

—Wait, was all she said.

I waited but it was just an orchestra.

—Remember you were saying the arts makes you a more, what was it? – sympathetic all round human being?

—What?

—What Paddy said to you when you got the violin?

—Aye.

—Watch this.

It was a big symphony and there was a beautiful Chinese girl playing solo. The camera was all over her like a rash. It was more about how beautiful she was than the music. And the orchestra? The camera ignored them.

—How come ugly birds never get to be virtuosos?

—Look at her, Connie said.

—There must be, by chance, as many brilliant ugly virtuosos as beautiful ones. More even – mathematically, I said.

—You won't think she's beautiful in a minute, said Connie.

Connie wasn't the jealous type so I was puzzling as I watched this girl hold the instrument against her chin. Chin and cheek. I tried mine.

—This is more comfaraybil Bailey, I said, —Let's check the fingery dingeries.

But I only knew first finger position and she seemed to be in every position at the same time. She was mesmerising. We ate our toast and watched. This was the most interest Connie had ever shown in the violin. At the end of the concert this girl, she got interviewed.

—Recognise her? Connie said.

I didn't. The interviewer started talking about her sister and she looked behind her. Here was her sister appearing from the orchestra with a violin of her own. And as they espoused their love of music and expressivities of the violin Connie said,

—I bet they're floating on harmonies of high civilization. Fuckin, sailing on a sea of quiet etiquette.

—Who are they?

—Think beach, said Connie, —Think husky.

I remembered them. Their civility cracked like a veneer. I put my violin down.

—The cows that were going to set their huskies on Blongo!

As I looked at this girl on the telly her smooth voice faded and all I could hear was her repeating

—Our dogs will rip your dog to shreds.

Shouting.

—Our dogs will rip your dog to shreds.

Screaming.

—Our dogs will rip your dog to shreds.

Screeching.

—Our dogs will rip your dog to shreds.

Then her voice was lost in the high, high notes of anger. I switched the telly off and lifted the bow. Connor got on the couch and stuffed his head under a cushion. And as I played that B on the A string Bailey stared to howl.

—D'you like the vlin? I said, —More Vlin?

Eeee eee went the bee.

And as I tripped over them strings I knew I'd never be a virtuoso.

—Daddy never be an oso Blongo, I said.

Connie said, —Thank fuck. Don't want you becoming a more empathetic, well rounded human being.

—Haaawhooo, said Bailey, Haaawhooo.

I looked at the dogs lying on the couch. Bailey and Connor. And Connie laughing and although we didn't have a coin I realised how rich we'd become.

By the time spring came I was a completely different person. I hadn't lost my temper once. Bailey was getting better but Floyd was getting worse. I came in from walking

the dogs one morning to find Connie in the bedroom and
Floyd on the bed sucking his ribs in and out.

I took the dogs into the garden.

—What's up?

—Alright Kenny, I said.

He was the last person I wanted to speak to. The strain was
all over my face and I was bent over like a comma.

—Catching a blues vibe here, he said.

He'd catch these right obvious vibes invisible to the rest of
the planet.

—Cat's dying, I said.

—What's wrong?

I told him about FIV being the cat equivalent of HIV and
how Floyd was like a son to Connie. She was in the room with
him and I was hoping he'd die soon. Get it over with. Kenny
looked up at the room and closed his eyes gently. Tilted his
head to the tree-shagging gods.

—He's not dead, he said.

—I know he's not dead Kenny, cause if he was fuckin dead
Connie'd be screaming the house down.

—Stay cool, man, you need a calm vibe when there's illness.

I was about to tell him to get to fuck when he tells me he's
got this mate Jonathan. Not long moved up from London. He's
into alternative medicine.

—How alternative?

—Radionics.

I'd never heard of it. Kenny said what he does is takes a
hair from the patient and puts in this wee glass tube. He
inserts that into a machine with knobs and dials. It analyses
the hair and then Jonathan decides on the treatment. I had
been reading about Chinese medicine on the net. They took a
hair and analysed it. Depending on the structures of proteins

they got a picture of your health over time. My anger started to subside. Here was hope.

—Where does he live?

—Near Whithorn.

—He takes a hair and puts it in a machine?

—Aye.

—And analyses the hair?

—Then decides on what treatment he's gan to give.

—Does he do animals?

—I could ask him.

—Go'n phone him Kenny. Eh?

When I burst into the bedroom and pulled a bunch of hairs out of Floyd's arse Connie thought I was losing my mind. I told her quickly,

—Kenny Crusty's got this mate who's got a Chinese machine that analyses hair and tells what's up and prescribes medicine.

Her face lit up. Kenny was at the front door shouting up.

—Have to gan.

I kissed Connie and she was smiling as I left.

The cottage was an ongoing project. Jonathan was over six feet but gentle and slow moving. He thought about every sentence before he spoke but you didn't feel he was calculating. His out-to-here pregnant wife made the coffee. Kenny had to go, he was showing somebody how to contact their spirit guide.

Jonathan was from London but not as arrogant as the film and telly people I'd met. He'd been a big shot in finance. Had a nervous breakdown and got out. Done the whole mind body spirit thing when he hit upon Radionics.

By the time he'd finished telling me this we'd walked the length of the cottage. Here was this room. Sure enough there was a machine with rows of knobs and dials and wee glass tubes. Some had human hair in them and were lit up. One lime green, one yellow and another deep blue. It was kind of pretty. There was a state of the art computer; massive flat screen with all sorts happening on it. It was obvious the machines analysed the hair and the computer sorted out the data. It was well set up. The machines looked like old bakelite radios only instead of Stuttgart Oslo Paris Moscow and London there was these symbols I'd never seen before. Chinese probably. Jonathan sat without speaking, touching the dials and now and then clicking at his computer.

He was getting a lot of emails and when I was telling him about Floyd the phone went. It was a woman from Ireland who'd heard about Radionics and wanted to come and see him. She must've asked how much it would cost cause he said two hundred pounds for the first consultation. I took a breath. We only had three hundred and I was trying to find work. But if he could cure Floyd or even have him on the mend a while it would give Connie time to get used the fact.

He nodded and mm mm'd like a doctor as I spoke. He took the clump of hair and loaded it into a glass tube. Put the tube in the machine and turned a knob. The tube glowed pink and lit Floyd's hair up. There was this buzzing and although it was coming from the machine I felt like it was coming from me. I really thought this was going to work. Jonathan adjusted a dial and flicked his computer keys. His wife brought some coffee. We drank and chatted about everything except Floyd. There was a bleep and the pink light turned red. Jonathan leaned across and moved a knob and a dial.

A long time after I'd finished the coffee I got the feeling they wanted me to go but he'd still not gave me any medicine. I was too shy to ask. Maybe he forgot about the pills? His wife said they had to go before the shops closed. I left thinking maybe it took a few hours to analyse the hairs and he'd phone to come for the medicine later.

When I got home Connie was upbeat. Floyd was getting worse and you could see he was in constant pain. As I told her what happened I could tell she was waiting for pills.

—He never gave me any pills. I think the machine takes a while to analyse the data and then he'll phone us.

She sat with her head down stroking Floyd.

—Will you sit with him till I go to the toilet?

I clapped him as easy as I could. I felt good I'd been able to do something. I was not being fuckin useless.

—Daddy's getting you a magic cure, I said and he looked up at me. He opened his mouth to meow but couldn't. Instead of being red the whole inside of his mouth was white. I don't know where it came from cause I'm not one for crying. But the tears cascaded out. I felt terrible for the wee fucker. He'd had the bad luck of nine cats and here he was dying on a towel on top of the bed in agony. Connie had came back in and when she seen me crying she cuddled me. Those tears meant more to her than all my running about looking for a cure. Our relationship went deeper that day. I said I'd go down and make us some tea.

When we'd finished that, it was starting to get dark and still Jonathan hadn't phoned.

—Did you give him our number?

I realised I didn't. And he forgot to ask for it.

—He could get it off Kenny Crusty easy enough.

But it was starting to bother me. And when Floyd sicked up the latest batch of internet concoction I decided to drive over. The anger was rising but I seen where it was coming from and kept it under control.

It was a surprised Jonathan who opened the door. I could feel puzzlement as we walked to the room of dials. Floyd's hair was still lit up red in the machine and I presumed the analysis was still going on. We had a strange and uneasy conversation. He asked how the cat was.

—He's getting worse.

—Worse? He seemed surprised and turned the knob a bit.

—He's in pain every breath, I said, —Connie's breaking her heart.

He leaned in and looked at the dial.

—She's had that cat since he was a kitten, I said, —He lost half his skin once when he fell into a hot bath. Went missing when he was a kitten in the roughest part of Glasgow. Kids tortured him. When he came back he was wild.

I don't know why I was telling him Floyd's life story. I suppose my thinking was the more he knew the easier he could make the medicine. He listened and then said something that surprised me.

—He should be improving, I've been treating him for four hours.

—Eh?

—I've been treating him for four hours. Since you came here earlier.

I didn't know what to say. He tapped the big bakelite machine with the middle knuckle of his index finger. Did he give me the pills? Nope, I'd have remembered that. I was focussed on pills. I was fuckin obsessive with pills. Nope – he never gave me no pills. If he did I would've remembered.

—When will it be finished analysing the hair? I asked.

—Pardon?

I pointed at the little part of Floyd lying in its glass house in the red glow. The buzz seemed louder.

—The hair. Does it usually take this long to analyse?

He looked at me then said, —Ah! It's not that kind of machine.

He went on to explain Radionics. The whole universe is vibration. Using Floyd's hair, the machine picked up his particular vibrations. It analysed these for anomalies. Once it found them a specific coloured light came on. That was the machine sending new vibrations through the cosmos to Floyd. These new vibrations would kick him into the correct frequency. That's when I noticed the machine wasn't connected to the computer. My face was falling. He could see that I needed more. This was the most animated I'd seen him.

Right, he said, and he got out a wee card like a Ouija board. It said *yes* on one side and *no* on the other. There was an arch of numbers from one to nine and some of the same crazy symbols on the knobs and dials machine. He opened a small wooden box and took out a pointed crystal on a chain. He was pulling out all the stops. I didn't say anything. What could I say? He started the pendulum swinging.

—Is Floyd going to be well?

He swung the pendulum to yes.

—Is Floyd going to be with us for a while?

He swung the pendulum to yes.

—How long is Floyd going to with us?

He drifted the pendulum to four.

—Is that four weeks?

The pendulum swayed back and fro.

—Four months?

It stayed where it was.

—Four years?

The pendulum swung with force over to yes. He turned to me.

—The crystal is never wrong. The crystal says Floyd will be

with you for four years. Nothing to worry about. Just let things take their course.

He stood up, indicating softly but firmly he wanted me to leave. When I said it, I said it like a wee boy.

—I thought you'd give me pills.

—Do you want pills? He was totally sincere when he said that.

—I thought you'd give me pills.

—I can give you some pills.

He opened a drawer. There were hundreds of small bottles. All the exact same. And in these bottles were hundreds of white pills the size of pinheads. He scattered some onto a sheet of dark card.

He swung the pendulum over the pills.

—Just taking them up to the right frequency, he said.

Something made me want to laugh. But I didn't. He gave me the pills and adjusted the knob.

—To account for the pills, he said.

Connie could see my disappointment. But when I told her all about it we laughed. We did laugh. Despite everything we laughed. And we decided we'd be as well using the pills. You never know.

Floyd struggled on for three days. Connie never slept. She stood vigil by his side and I admired her all the more. On the third day, at four in the morning, he was in so much pain we phoned Eileen. She knew why we were coming and got out her bed to meet us. She'd said not to leave it too late. Not to let him suffer. It's sometimes hard to let things go but, as Connie said; life is falling off a cliff sometimes.

It was horrible and I never want to see it again. Floyd curled in pain on Connie's lap on the way up. He made a noise that made me and Connie burst with a cry of real despair.

—Aw fuck, look at him, I said.

She leaned over, her hair hanging round him like a curtain.

—Floyd son, Floyd – it's Mummy!

He died.

I stopped the car. We sat at the side of that road in the early morning light and cried.

—Poor Floyd. Poor fuckin Floyd, I kept saying.

—There my wee darling. You're alright now, Connie was saying, —You're alright now.

We looked at each other. There was no hiding the tears this time. I leaned across and hugged her.

Eileen confirmed he was dead. She never said anything but we knew she thought we'd let him go too far. And we did. We put him through pain he shouldn't have went through. On the way home I started ranting about Jonathan and his Radionics.

—If it wasn't for that we'd have made the decision earlier. Put Floyd to sleep.

But Connie could see through that.

—Don't blame that big guy. He was only trying to help. He never even charged us. If it wasn't Radionics it would've been something else. It was us. It was our fault.

She was right. We let Floyd suffer cause we didn't want to. We passed our pain onto him. We'd learned a lesson.

We didn't say it but both of were thinking about the dogs dying. Mostly our children will outlive us. But with an animal you're almost certain they won't. And cause of their unconditional love you're in for big pain.

—Goodnight, sleep tight, I said to Floyd and chinny chinned him one last time. —Chinny chin, I said and turned away.

We buried him beside the cherry trees. We got a statue of a forest baby cheap in a garden centre and put it down as a gravestone. It's got a peaceful smile on its face. Sometimes I sit there with Bailey and remember nights I'd lie on the couch with Floyd purring on my chest.

It makes me smile.

Bailey

Blongo luv the Daddy now.

Langoustines

Things were changing in me and were about to change again. One scorching day in summer I got a letter from Peter cc'd to everybody in the BBC. Thanking me for my sterling work and my agreement that Peter, who was after all a writer himself, should have a go at writing The Gym. Making it more contemporary. I laughed. Connie took the letter and she laughed.

—Remember when I agreed to that? I said.

—Oh yes I do, you said Peter, you are such a wonderful big Irish poof, and so much better than me at writing, why don't you make this work for me. I'm talentless.

—That's right, I said, —I remember it now.

She was staring at me.

—What? What is it?

—You're laughing.

—No wonder. He just steals my project from under my nose and tells his bosses I agreed to it!

—No, she said, —A year ago you'd be mental. You'd have took it out on us.

As she hugged me I heard the drill of a diesel engine outside. The door went and the dogs barked. It was Barnacles and he was in a hurry. His driver's door was flung open. Had to go up to Troon. Deliver the lobsters, pick up his bait. I wondered why he was handing me this bright red bucket. It was half filled with water and all these wee orange fellahs. I thought they were baby lobsters. I took the bucket, said cheers and he shouted chilli sauce as he was driving up the street.

Connie puzzled when she seen the bucket.

—Barnacles brung us these, I said and sat the bucket on the floor. She bent down looking in. So did I.

—Langoustines? she said.

They were a bright orange that's hard to explain. Maybe it was the red of the bucket reflecting but they looked like cartoons. There was at least fifty going every way possible in that confined space. You could see they weren't used to moving about in hardly any water. Some swam frantically crashing into the sides. Others sat on the bottom looking up. Others were still and might've been dead.

—He said they're good with chilli sauce.

—They're alive.

—Some of them.

—Most of them, she said, and swirled the water. The agitation caused the still ones to move their limbs. We watched them in silence with water slipping off her hand back into the bucket. She'd been spending a lot of time in the garden since we buried Floyd and the tan on her face was burnished by the red glow from the bucket.

—I think you just drop them in boiling water like lobsters.

As soon as I said it I knew it was the wrong thing. Still crouched down, she put one hand on her thigh and looked up.

—You can't drop them in boiling water – have you ever heard the noise a lobster makes?

She stood up.

—They scream when you kill them, she said.

—No they don't, I said.

She pointed to the dogs.

—How would you like it if somebody dropped one of them into a pot of boiling water?

—That's different.

—Is it?

—Okay then, I said, —Let them die. They'll die naturally. Then we'll cook them.

She looked at me and went out into the garden. I heard her walk across the grass and I knew where she was going. I sat for a while in the quiet cool of the kitchen watching the langoustines. I don't know how long it was but they moved less and less until they were still. When they were all dead I crept closer. They exploded, their claws and feet rattling on the sides. They weren't going to die easy. I made a pot of tea. The sun was coming in sheets through the half shut blinds. I knew Connie was staying in the garden out of the way so I took her tea out. She was sitting beneath the cherry trees beside Floyd's grave. Connor was watching her every move. She looked up and I could tell even from halfway down the path that she'd been crying again.

—Well?

—Not yet, is all I said, and put the tea on a stone.

When I got back to the kitchen Bailey had his head in the bucket like a giraffe. Fishing.

—Bailey!

His hairy head popped out, water pouring off. A langoustine struggled in his front teeth. He was holding it delicately and staring at me.

—Leave it!

No way, was the look on his face. He slunk down and his tail curled under. He let out a gowler.

—Leave it Bailey!

I moved to get the langoustine and *crunch*. It fell on the

floor in two halves. The head part was running away on these long spindly legs. For a moment I could see it all from the langoustine's point of view and it was horrific. Bailey warned me away with a snarl, scooped the tail up and ate it. Then, as he grabbed the head, I noticed Connie in the doorway. Bailey pushed past her gowlering and into the garden to nibble away at his catch.

—Did you give him one of them?

—No.

—You fed him one didn't you?

—I came in and he had his head in the bucket. I couldn't get it off him.

She shook her head.

—He was like that (snarl) going to fuckin bite me. You know what he's like – he's a thieving bastard.

Connor came to me then Connie, nuzzling and kissing and asking us please be pals. Please be good. Please stop arguing. And he won't stop until you truly are calmed down. Once we were calm he took to wagging his tail, fascinated by the things in the bucket. Connie hadn't looked in since she came in from the garden.

—Are they dead yet?

I swirled the bucket and they weren't. The water was getting warm. She wasn't for waiting out in the garden while I let a bunch of wee animals die in the house. I suggested to put them in the freezer, see if that would kill them quicker but that's not where she wanted the conversation to go. She stared at me. I knew what she was going to say and was searching for answers before she said it.

—We'll have to put them back.

—He catches them way out at sea. What d'you want me to do – swim out with the fuckin bucket in my teeth?

296

—The sea's the sea. Put them in on the beach. I'm not letting them die.

And she looked in for the first time since she came in. So did I and guilt flooded me. I'd try to tell myself it was okay. I wasn't killing them. They were dying themselves. As if that's what they were choosing to do. But she was spot on. It just felt wrong us letting them die right there on the kitchen floor.

So, we put Bailey and Connor in the padded room. Threw two trays of ice into the bucket. Covered it with a black bin liner. Connie went out to open the boot of the car and check for people. The signal was three knocks and out I came holding the bucket to my chest. The langoustines were sloshing about. I placed it carefully in the boot and clicked it shut. The sun was blazing.

—Barnacles better never find out about this, I said.

We drove ultra slow down South Street, so slow that a caravan driver was agitated behind us. I made some kind of joke about the irony of that but Connie was focussed on releasing these wee fellahs. We wound our windows down but the heat was still unbearable. We drove past the harbour onto the shingle beach that faced south to England. It was almost impossible to be seen from there. Almost. Just as I opened the boot Kenny Crusty came out of nowhere with his dog.

—Aye! he said, —sun energy. I know how to absorb it.

I snapped the boot shut.

—Some day, Kenny, I said, —Hot.

He sensed my agitation and nodded at the boot.

—What's in there – a body?

—No, just wasn't shut right.

Connie started throwing stones into the sea for his dog. Kenny watched it swimming for ages then walked away doing Tai Chi. His dog followed shaking rainbows off its fur. But by then four holidaymakers had arrived with a picnic basket. We got back into the car and reversed off the beach.

—Go round the other end, Connie said.

We stopped where the long line of yellow sand comes to a point at the trees. We couldn't see anybody. We opened the boot but I started to get paranoid. The whole village with its painted houses stood across the bay looking at us. It *was* like trying to get rid of a body. The bucket sat there ominous and none of us could lift it. Connie felt the water.

—It's getting warmer. I don't want them to die!

—Fuck it, I said and lifted the bucket. But she heard something and pushed it back in. We scanned the bay. The noise had come from the trees. It could be cattle or there might be somebody in there watching. Truth was there was nowhere secluded on that whole bay. No matter where you went someone spotted you. The only secrets were the ones you kept inside your head.

We were beat. The langoustines were dying and the tide was on the ebb. I tried to think of other points where you could get down to the sea with a car but I couldn't. The only ones I could suggest were so far away that they would all be dead before we got there. Then I noticed Connie was crying.

—You shouldn't've took them.

—He asked me months ago. I forgot!

—You shouldn't've fuckin took them.

—Oh aye blame me cause a guy does us a favour.

—You should've said no.

—How the fuck could I say no? I didn't even know what they were at the time.

—So you told him to bring things and you never even knew what they were?

—No – I didn't tell him anything. He asked me and rather than offend him I say aye.

—What if they were big fuckin things like alligators?

I thought of a bucket of alligator heads snapping at me and burst out laughing. So did she. We gave each other a hug and I suppose from across the bay we looked like a couple making up after an argument. Then I had an idea.

—The stream, I said.

—What?

—The stream. Drive along the stream and when we're far enough out of the village dump them in there. They'll make their way back to the sea no problem.

She thought it was a great idea. We rushed off at ten miles an hour. Both our windows down with the heat. The stream runs for two miles alongside the road into the village. We waved to a few passing villagers who were probably talking about the argument we'd just had at the end of the bay.

When we got far enough out I stopped. A car went past and flashed its lights. I waved. Then it was all clear. Connie got out, opened the boot, grabbed the bucket, disappeared through the trees and down the slope. I heard her mashing about in the mud then a pour and a splash – like somebody being sick. There was nothing for a few moments and I was beginning to think she'd fell in when up she came through the bushes with a big smile. There was mud halfway up her shins with a perfect line at the top. She got in and put the bucket at her feet.

—Lost my shoes. Stuck in the muck.

She was breathing hard with elation and relief. The bad feeling was gone. I leaned across and kissed her. Told her she was a lifesaver.

—Did they swim away? I asked.

—Some of them were dead. I think. They washed away with their arms hanging down like this. But the rest of them turned and faced the sea and swam. You should've seen them. They were like wee orange compasses. And they say animals are daft.

—At least we've saved most of them, I said.

She kissed me and said, —Next time just say no.

I nodded and we drove off down that long straight road passing the langoustines. Then a thought came to me. An urge to go to the bridge and see them coming under it. I know it's daft but I wanted to see if there was any change in their expressions when they tasted salt water. It had been some day for the wee guys. From the lobster creels to a bucket – the big Lurcher monster fishing for them, the journey in the boot of the car and the slosh into a freshwater stream. A trace of saltwater in their nostrils – if they've got nostrils. It would be magic to see their faces when they surged into that ocean and freedom. Connie thought I was mad.

When we got to the bridge, I was about to swing the door open and jump out when a van came round. It was Barnacles.

—Shit, said Connie and tried to hide the bucket under her legs.

—Awright, he said.

—That was quick – Troon.

—Roads were empty, he said, —Did you eat the langoustines?

—Aye! we both said at the same time. Barnacles was a bit taken aback by the ferocity of our answer. The langoustines were probably passing underneath at that point. Then I let fly.

—Had them with chilli sauce right enough. Aw they were great. A wee bit of lemon an all they were great weren't they Connie? Weren't they great eh?

—Aye. Brilliant.

—Right, Barnacles said.

I think he could see the bucket. But he never said anything. He just said he'd bring us some more next week. That was the day me and Connie made a pact never to eat another living thing.

Contents

Connor

Colin luv the Daddy too.

Connected

It came on in the autumn. The Gym. It was my stories alright, my ideas. But they'd all been re-set in London. All my characters transformed into gay media types. Talking about London. Doing London things. It was one big ego trip for black polo necks. I was glad it was shite.

Till I read the reviews next day. The Gym was groundbreaking. The Gym was profound. Best thing this year. A writer of wit and imagination. It's about time television allowed its writers to write. I didn't read anything after I seen the word genius. It should've been the worst day of my life. Yet it turned out to be the best. Connie suggested I take Bailey down to the ham hok.

—That always chills you out, she said.

But the longer I lay there the more disgusted with myself I became. Disgusted that I'd let them telly cunts run rings round me. Made me jump through hoops. Disgusted I'd changed my ideas for them. I fell into a spiral of disgust. Disgusted that I'd shattered my integrity. Disgusted at the hair of my head, disgusted at the hair of my body, my nails, teeth, and skin. I was disgusted at my flesh, disgusted at my sinews, bone, and marrow. I hated my kidneys, my heart and liver. All my fuckin membranes. I detested my spleen, my lungs and bowels. My fuckin intestines and all their gorge, dung, and bile. I was disgusted at my brain, disgusted at my phlegm, pus and blood. My sweat stank. And I hated my fat and grease and snot.

and

tears.

There they were running down my cheeks. Tears. Bailey nuzzled me. I spoke to him.

—Daddy sad Blongo. Daddy gisdusted with himself. Daddy let the bad peeps jump him through big hoops.

Bailey licked my tear. I don't know if it was salt or something else. I ran my fingers through his coarse hair and he closed his eyes. I realised he was the same. Made of the same things. But I wasn't repulsed by him. I thought of the sculpture he'd made in the Gardiniums Sardiniums that morning. Green jelly – like ploppies from outer space. Jellied things. Translucent lime. And still I wasn't repulsed. I was attracted to everything about him

I loved the hair of his head, adored the hair of his body, his nails, teeth, and skin. I loved his flesh, loved his sinews, bones, and marrow. His kidneys, heart and liver. All his beautiful membranes. I treasured his spleen, his lungs and bowels. Them warm intestines and all their gorge, dung, and bile. I cherished his electric brain, his phlegm, pus and blood. His sweet sweat. His fat and grease and snot. I loved his spittle and piss

and

his tears were silver angels.

But as I held onto him and swung that ham hok in the autumn air I came to understand that he, Bailey, existed within or above or beside these parts. He wasn't them any more than they were him. He was luminous within them. I kissed his noe.

—Gowler, he said, but didn't move one millimetre.

I realised I too existed within or above or beside all my revolting parts. And that's when this immense joy appeared. It didn't burn up slowly. I was instantly incandescent with it.

Every form of fragmentation had ceased. The true nature of things was pouring in on me from everywhere. Time, thought and apparent reality stopped and I understood the universe. I was the universe and it was me. We were all the universe and all were me. Everything was one thing.

Everything was one. I grabbed Bailey.

—Daddy loves you, I said, —Daddy loves your hair and your bones and your epilectric fits.

He pushed his noe into my neck as if he understood. Took a suck of my smell. There we were, both of us, having transcended matter, on that ham hok with birds whizzing above the trees. The sky and clouds above. Air on my face and people walking the streets of this village. People everywhere, animals everywhere, everything everywhere, all things counter, original, spare, and strange – everywhere were one.

I felt immeasurable connectedness. We're not disparate entities. Not me, not Bailey, not the trees, not the birds. We all occupy the same space. We all extend throughout the universe. If only we didn't believe our petty little saving lie that we have form. Nothing exists except in how we choose to see it. We are everything and nothing at all. These bodies, mine and Bailey's – we've formed them pick and mix from the universe. If we take the long way round we arrive at each other. At everything. The same is true of the short way.

When Bailey and me had reconstituted I had changed. Profoundly. I sat still and thought of the dream I had on Snowy's boat when the fish was Bailey. I realised exactly what it meant now, that dream and drew in a breath of revelation. And in that breath was the whole world. The very truth of the universe. That is where he has taken me. My Epileptic Lurcher.

Goodnight sleep tight

Connie thinks we should make a film about the dogs. Bailey should be played by Forrest Gump and Connor by Die Hard. Bailey he goes two weeks fit free, falls into three days severe fits and out again. Regular as clockwork. It's fit management with us now.

One thing is routine. Routine is good. He likes routines.

Here's what happens every night no matter if we're here or away:

At ten past ten Connor tells Connie it's time for tab a let drinky link. He does this even when the clocks change. He nudges her arm up with that stone head of his.

—Anybody in the hou want a drinky link? says Connie. When Bailey stands up Connor's already in the kitchen, his paws drumming on the floor. I watch the news as they drink and Connor is first back. He jumps on the cou, gives me a nudge, jumps down and goes to the door. He'll repeat this till I get up. I never see the end of the news.

—Gardinium Sardinium?

And he runs around wild looking for Bailey.

—Bailey we want him! I shout and in Blongo strides with big horse dressage legs.

—Gardinium Sardinium?

Connor asserts his position first at the door with gowlers. When I open it he has a chew at Bailey.

—No fighting no biting, Connie says.

Then into the garden. Bailey can pee for Scotland.

—I pee long, I say as he squats like a lady dog and the pee runs out. He squints at me as he pees.

—You pee like a lady dog Blongo.

Connor is out, leg up, pee, leg down and over to the kitchen door. Connie talks to him through the glass.

—What is it? she says bending down, —What wanting?

—Oof.

—What kind of oof?

If it's a clear night, while Bailey I pee longs I look at the stars. At least once a week I get to make a wish on a shooting star.

—I wish Bailey would stop taking fits.

He's coming up for ten years old now and I know there's no chance of that. But other wishes have come true. Wishes I hadn't wished. My epileptic Lurcher has got us into skiing, camping, hill walking, kayaking, rock climbing, windsurfing and scuba diving. He's turned me into a different man. Shown me the meaning of life.

Bailey comes bounding up the garden.

—Good blongers! I say.

I clap his head and he veers for the living room door. Always the wrong door.

—Blongo – wrong door, over this way quick.

He bounds to the kitchen and Connie says, —What wanting?

—Womble womble, he says.

They press their furry faces to the glass. I've got this thing where I've got to touch every panel on the door and when I get to the bottom I say, —Clappy door.

Sometimes I've got to lift Bailey's paw and scrape it down the door.

—Clappy door, I say and he does it.

—What wanting? says Connie.

—Oof oof womble womble, they say, scrape scrape and a wee howl.

When Connor digs with his titanium tipped claws Connie opens the door. He could go right through it in seconds. Although Connor always gets into the Gardinium first, Bailey's first into the kitchen. He tries to scoff Connor's grub so Connie's on her guard.

—That's not yours Bailey, that's Connor's, and she pushes him away snarling and chomping whatever he's managed to grab.

Once they eat their food Connor leaves the kitchen, through the living room, up the spiral staircase, bumps the padded room door open with his nut and slumps into his bed. Bailey follows Connie in case there's food.

—How do you want the something? she says to him, —I gave you the hundreds and now you want the something. I've got the nothing so you can't have the something.

She cuts a carrot and gets a biscuit for Connor.

—Up to bed wiff a biscuit, she says and Bailey bites her hand. She says wiff a biscuit ran together as all one word. Wiffabiscuit.

—No, don't bite the Mummy, she says, —It's up to bed wiff a biscuit.

I put out the lights, switch off the telly, turn the wood burner down and lock the doors. I meet them at the bottom of the staircase.

—Up to bed wiff a biscuit, I say.

But he won't move until I say, —Get him by the handool Mummy.

—Sorry Daddy, what a silly Mummy, mon Bailey, get you by the handool, and she grips his collar and he pick his nervous way up.

311

When we get to the room Connor gives us a where-have-you-been look. Bailey stands in his bed so Connie's got to sit him down.

—In your bed Bailey. In y'bed.

He gowlers and chews her arms as she sits him down. I'm in the doorway at this point. She leans into Connor's bed and says,

—See you morning night night. Kisses him and moves to Bailey.

—See you morning night night. Yoo turn Daddy, and she leaves the room.

I dive onto Connor and give him a hug making this deep whooaaah noise. He answers that back copying.

—Mmmmwhao, he replies, sinking into the comfort of his bed. Then I put my mouth in his ear and sing the goodnight song.

♫ Goodnight sleep tight, don't let the bed bugs bite, if they do squeeze em tight and they won't come back the morra night – alright!

—Mmmmwhao, he says.

—Kissy lips.

He does.

—Cover em ups, I say and wrap his duvet round him tight. He likes that.

—Fix your lovelies, I say and I take the blears out of his eyes.

(I'm stopping right here cause Bailey just went into a fit. I lay beside him and kept his head from banging on the floor. Connie came up and said she'd take him downstairs once he's calmed. He's nearly the size of her and we laughed, both of us, at her carrying him down out of this attic – his giant legs trailing off the floor. I can hear him right now flailing about the padded room like a giant fish. And do you know what? We're not stressed, not me nor Connie and Connor is on the cushion licking his paws.)

But back to a typical night.

—Pully ears, I say to Connor and pull his ears up straight so he can hear.

I give him the Collie kiss; stick my noe into his ear and sniff in and out three times. I give him my ear he copies; in and out three times. Then I kiss his big black noe.

Bailey gowlers soon as I approach.

—Aw don't gowlers the Daddy.

—Gowlers.

—No no don't gowlers the Daddy.

I sing him the song,

♫ Goodnight sleep tight, don't let the bed bugs bite, if they do squeeze em tight and they won't come back the morra night – alright!

The more I sing the more he gowlers, lifting his lips up and snarling. Right up close he looks like a wild wild wolf. I take the piss and I think he knows it.

—Pleeeeeeeeez I say, as if he's about to rip my throat, —Pleeeeeeeeez, in a cry for some clemency, —No killit the Daddy.

—Gowlers.

—Kissy, I say.

—Gowlers.

—Kissy lips.

Out through the savagery of his teeth comes his tongue and kisses me. Soon as he's kissed me he reverts to gowlers. I wrap my hand tight round his top muzzle and kiss all over the face as he tries in vain to bite me.

—Cover em ups, I say and cover him.

—Fix your lovelies, I say and fix his eyes. Once he's covered up I go to the door.

—See yous morra night night. I look in their eyes one boy at a time and click the light out. Close the door hoping Bailey doesn't have a fit. If he does Connor gives it one oof and a clap at the door.

We wake up and listen in the silence of the middle of the night.

—Oof, clappy door.

When I go in Connor shoots straight onto Mummydaddy bed. Bailey's about to fall into a fit. I wrap blankets and cushions round him. It was the best idea we ever had that padded room. When I get back I have to shove that ten ton Collie over. He gowlers but once I'm cuddling into him he says,

—Mmmmwhao.

And I say it back. Me and Connie fall asleep scratching his belly and listening to Bailey bump about that room in the middle of the night. I think nobody could be happier than we are.

And right here, right now as I write the last lines of this book I can hear him below me bumping about. My epileptic Lurcher.

When it was all over I lay there with my head on his chest. He was panting and I could feel his heart beating ding ding ding ding ding. I started stroking him on the leg as I lay. As I did that his heart began to slow down. Then, after a while, I realised it wasn't his heart, it was mine.

I know now that when I shout on Bailey his name echoes throughout the whole universe – coming back to us – through us – in us – with us.

Some other books published by **LUATH** PRESS

Monks

Des Dillon
ISBN 1 905222 75 0 PBK £7.99

Ye must've searched out solitude in your life. At least once.

Three men are off from Coatbridge to an idyllic Italian monastic retreat in search of inner peace and sanctuary.

... like hell they are. Italian food, sunshine and women – it's the perfect holiday in exchange for some east construction work at the monastery.

Some holiday it turns out to be, what with optional Mass at five in the morning, a mad monk with a ball and chain, and the salami fiasco – to say nothing of the language barrier.

But even on this remote and tranquil mountain, they can't hide from the chilling story of Jimmy Brogan. Suddenly the past explodes into the present, and they find more redemption than they ever bargained for.

... better than Irvine Welsh.
THE SUNDAY HERALD

Singin I'm No a Billy He's a Tim

Des Dillon
ISBN 1 906307 46 6 PBK £6.99

A Rangers and Celtic fan are locked in a cell together.

What happens when you lock up a Celtic fan? What happens when you lock up a Celtic fan with a Rangers fan? What happens when you lock up a Celtic fan with a Rangers fan on the day of the Old Firm match? Des Dillon creates the situation and watches the sparks fly as Billy and Tim clash in a rage of sectarianism and deep-seated hatred. When children have been steeped in bigotry since birth, is it possible for them to change their views?

Contains strong language.

A humorous and insightful look at the bigotry that exists between Glasgow's famous football giants Celtic and Rangers.
RICHARD PURDEN

The Glasgow Dragon

Des Dillon
ISBN 1 84282 056 7 PBK £9.99

What do I want? Let me see now. I want to destroy you spiritually, emotionally and mentally before I destroy you physically.

When Christie Devlin goes into business with a triad to take control of the Glasgow drug market little does he know that his downfall and the destruction of his family is being plotted. As Devlin struggles with his own demons the real fight is just beginning.

There are some things you should never forgive yourself for.

Will he unlock the memories of the past in time to understand what is happening?

Will he be able to save his daughter from the danger he has put her in?

Nothing is as simple as good and evil. Des Dillon is a master storyteller and this is a world he knows well.

The authenticity, brutality, humour and most of all the humanity of the characters and the reality of the world they inhabit in Des Dillon's stories are never in question.
LESLEY BENZIE

It has been known for years that Des Dillon writes some of Scotland's most vibrant prose.
ALAN BISSETT

Me and Ma Gal

[B format edition]
Des Dillon
ISBN 1 84282 054 0 PBK £5.99

If you never had to get married an that I really think that me an Gal'd be pals for ever. That's not to say that we never fought. Man we had some great fights so we did.

A story of boyhood friendship and irrepressible vitality told with the speed of trains and the understanding of the awkwardness, significance and fragility of that time. This is a day in the life of two boys as told by one of them, 'Derruck Danyul Riley'.

Dillon captures the essence of childhood and evokes memories of long summers with your best friend. He explores the themes of lost innocence, fear and death; writing with subtlety and empathy through the character of Derruck.

Winner of the 2003 World Book Day 'We Are What We Read' poll for the novel that best describes Scotland today.

Dillon's book is arguably one of the most frenetic and kinetic, living and breathing of all Scottish novels.... The whole novel crackles with this verbal energy.
THE LIST 100 Best Scottish Books of All Time

Six Black Candles

[B format edition]
Des Dillon
ISBN 1 906307 49 0 PBK £8.99

'Where's Stacie Gracie's head?'

... sharing space with the sweetcorn and two-for-one lemon meringue pies ... in the freezer.

Caroline's husband abandons her (bad move) for Stacie Gracie, his assistant at the meat counter, and incurs more wrath than he anticipated. Caroline, her five sisters, mother and granny, all with a penchant for witchery, invoke the lethal spell of the Six Black Candles. A natural reaction to the break up of a marriage?

The spell does kill. You only have to look at the evidence. Mess with these sisters, or Maw or Oul Mary and they might do the Six Black Candles on you. But will Caroline's home ever be at peace for long enough to do the spell and will Caroline really let them do it?

Set in present day Irish Catholic Coatbridge, *Six Black Candles* is bound together by the ropes of traditional storytelling and the strength of female familial relationships. Bubbling under the cauldron of superstition, witchcraft and religion is the heat of revenge; and the love and venom of sisterhood.

They Scream When You Kill Them

Des Dillon
ISBN 1 905222 35 1 PBK £7.99

From pimps to Shakespeare, langoustines to lurchers Dillon's short stories bite . . . hard. Welcome to Dillon's world; a world where murderous poultry and evolutionary elephants make their mark. Des takes you from the darkness of *The Illustrated Man* and *Jif Lemons* to the laugh out loud *Bunch of C*****.

These stories are instantly accessible and always personal. Relationships and places and language are set precisely with few words and no flinching. If you're an alcoholic, recovering alcoholic, insane, a policeman, prisoner, gold digger, farmer, animal lover, Scots Irish or Irish Scots you may well recognise yourself somewhere in this book.

A brilliant storyteller of his own people, of all people.
LESLEY RIDDOCH

... raw, exciting Dillon with his taut use of language and a racy approach to literature and ideas, sometimes verging on the bizarre... as irresistible as ever.
DGB LIFE

...collecting it all together enhances the reputation he's established with novels like Me and Ma Gal *and* Six Black Candles, *and highlights what an asset we have in Des Dillon.*
THE GUIDE

Picking Brambles

Des Dillon

ISBN 1 84282 021 4 PBK £6.99

The first pick from over 1,000 poems written by Des Dillon

I always considered myself to be first and foremost, a poet. Unfortunately nobody else did. The further away from poetry I moved the more successful I became as a writer.

This collection for me is the pinnacle of my writing career. Simply because is my belief that poetry is at the cutting edge of language. Out there breaking new ground in the creation of meaning.
DES DILLON

Selected and introduced by Brian Whittingham.

...to spend an hour in Dillon's company and listen to his quick-fire verbal delivery is to sample the undiluted language of the man that is the raw-material used in the crafting of his writing. The computer terminology Dillon is a WYSIWYG person (What You See Is What You Get.) No airs and graces and no fancy lah-de-dahs, though in Dillon's case it's worth remembering, moving waters run deep.
BRIAN WHITTINGHAM

But n Ben

(b format edition)
Matthew Fitt
ISBN 1 905222 04 1 PBK £7.99

The year is 2090AD. Global Flooding has left most of the Scotland under water. The descendants of those who survived God's Flood live in a community of floating island parishes, known collectively as Port.

Port's citizens live in mortal fear of Senga, a supervirus whose victims are kept in a giant warehouse in sealed capsules called Kists.

Paolo Broon is a low-ranking cyberjanny. His life-partner, Nadia, lies forgotten and alone in Omega Kist 624 in the Rigo Imbeki Medical Center. When he receives an unexpected message from his criminal father to meet him at But n Ben A-Go-Go, Paolo's life is changed forever.

He must traverse VINE, Port and the Drylands and deal with rebel American tourists and crabbit Dundonian microchips to discover the truth about his family's past in order to free Nadia from the sair grip of the merciless Senga.

Set in a distinctly unbonnie future-Scotland, the novel's dangerous atmosphere and psychologically-malkied characters weave a tale that both chills and intrigues. In *But n Ben A-Go-Go*, Matthew Fitt takes the allegedly dead language of Scots and energises it with a narrative that cracks and fizzles with life.

Help Me Rhonda

Alan Kelly

ISBN 1 905222 83 1 PBK £9.99

Rhonda. The answer's Rhonda. I hate Rhonda. Hate her with a passion. A desire. I love to hate her.

Sonny Jim McConaughy is no stranger to trouble. He blackmails his lawyer, scams the insurance company, drinks, takes drugs and sleeps around.

However, Sonny Jim has stumbled into more trouble than even he can handle, waking up to find himself accused of attempted murder with no memory of the previous drunken night. So his girlfriend Rhonda, determined to stop him destroying them both, pits herself against him in a desperate battle of attrition.

A book to make you laugh and cringe throughout, filled with grit, realism, dark humour and a hilarious cast of misfits.

...shares a flair for the colourful language and violent scenarios of the Trainspotting scribe.

THE EVENING TIMES

Writing in the Sand

Angus Dunn

ISBN 1 905222 91 2 PBK £8.99

At the farthest end of the Dark Island lies the village of Cromness, where the normal round of domino matches, meetings of the Ladies' Guild and twice-daily netting of salmon continues as it always has done. But all is not well. Soon the characters are involved in a battle to either save or destroy the Dark Isle. But are they truly aware of the scale of events? And who will prevail?

It is a latter day baggy monster of a novel... a hallucinogenic soap... the humour at first has shades of Last of the Summer Wine, alternating with the Goons before going all out for the Monty Python meets James Bond, and don't-scrimp-on-the-turbo-charger method... You'll have gathered by now that this book is a grand read. It's an entertainment. It alternates between compassionate and skilful observations, elegantly expressed and rollercoaster abandonment to a mad narrative.

NORTHWORDS NOW

A gold, confident debut, packed to the gunnels with memorable characters and wry humour.

THE LIST

Details of these and all other books published by Luath Press can be found at

www.luath.co.uk

Luath Press Limited

committed to publishing well written books worth reading

LUATH PRESS takes its name from Robert Burns, whose little collie Luath (*Gael.*, swift or nimble) tripped up Jean Armour at a wedding and gave him the chance to speak to the woman who was to be his wife and the abiding love of his life. Burns called one of 'The Twa Dogs' Luath after Cuchullin's hunting dog in Ossian's *Fingal*. Luath Press was established in 1981 in the heart of Burns country, and is now based a few steps up the road from Burns' first lodgings on Edinburgh's Royal Mile.

Luath offers you distinctive writing with a hint of unexpected pleasures.

Most bookshops in the UK, the US, Canada, Australia, New Zealand and parts of Europe either carry our books in stock or can order them for you. To order direct from us, please send a £sterling cheque, postal order, international money order or your credit card details (number, address of cardholder and expiry date) to us at the address below. Please add post and packing as follows: UK – £1.00 per delivery address; overseas surface mail – £2.50 per delivery address; overseas airmail – £3.50 for the first book to each delivery address, plus £1.00 for each additional book by airmail to the same address. If your order is a gift, we will happily enclose your card or message at no extra charge.

Luath Press Limited
543/2 Castlehill
The Royal Mile
Edinburgh EH1 2ND
Scotland
Telephone: 0131 225 4326 (24 hours)
Fax: 0131 225 4324
email: sales@luath.co.uk
Website: www.luath.co.uk